Butterfly

Warmest regards

NENITA DAQUIPA

To order additional copies of this book, contact:
Xlibris
1-888-795-4274
www.Xlibris.com
Orders@Xlibris.com
704368

CONTENTS

I thank my parents who planted my seed, nurtured my growth, and allowed me to fly from their nest. Most grateful appreciation goes to my husband who gave me space and time to blossom. And most endearingly my heartfelt gratitude to my children who questioned my existence thereby allowing me to develop the person I am today.

I want to fly like a butterfly, though I may soar away from home, I know I will never be lost!

PROLOGUE

No you can not go to the dances.

*No you can not go with your friend to
visit his family in Minnesota.*

No you can not play baseball. Only bums play baseball.

*No you can not go to public high school. You will
go to Jesuit high school, otherwise I will buy you a
one way ticket to Timbuktoo. Then I will pick you
up when you finish high school in four years.*

My parents named me Nadia, and I spoke these words to my children.

My mother Aure married late in her life when she was already a professional. She would run from their farmhouse hideaway to the air raid cave shelter in the back hidden by the banyan trees on hearing the sirens announcing the advancing Japanese marauders, several times a day. I was developing in her womb. There was nothing my father Tibo could do but hold her by the arms and around her chest for balance. The path was gravelly with many larger rocks. Medical care was not immediately available. There was no medic such as those found in mash units.

They were teachers. But war imposes many restrictions on life and places everything on hold till peacetime.

Years later I was diagnosed with severe distortions of my spine and spinal cord, however this did not prevent me from living a normal life, unaware of my body's distortions.

No monument in any park or building will show my name, Nadia. There will be files that eventually end in the trash or recycling bin. It was just an ordinary life. For all kinds of issues or reasons, mine is not an important story to tell. There are gaps, uncertainties, and questions that can not be answered, still I think it is a story worth telling.

Although Nadia delivered such words not in a melodramatic tone, nevertheless the messages must have been loud and clear. Lightly whispered to each child during certain phases of their lives. Delivered especially at times when they had the satisfaction of being useful and were having fun. While cutting vegetables for meals; while measuring flour and sugar to bake their favorite kuchen, cookies, or cakes; while doing the laundry, helping fold the clothes; while vacuuming their rooms weekly; and sharing meals at the dining table.

Also whispered outdoors while constructing a Japanese style bridge across the creek, digging holes, and moving earth to place pillars and wrap thick rope to create a pier like atmosphere. Then pumping air into a raft so they could ride and paddle along the creek. Or just pushing bulb trowels to plant flowers and vegetables.

Fr Mike would usually drop by to compare the sizes of their tomatoes, harvest zucchinis and eggplants. "How deep do we dig to reach hell?" asked 3-year-old Maurice. He usually asked questions. Always the inquisitive one.

Nadia also loved the clusters of crocuses peeking through the still snow-covered edges of the viburnum tomentosum hedges. Tiny leaflets were sprouting from tree branches, a signal of new life beginning. Soon the purple-to-black yellow-lipped irises will come together with the African jasmine flowers, bringing along the sweet scent of spring.

Most children just listen to adults or pretend to. Store the information somewhere in their head space to be digested, retrieved, and acted on later.

Parenting is a difficult task. It is a learned skill, an art. To be responsible for the mental development and culture that chisels fineness and delicacy to the unformed features of the child is a task many do not want to undertake. Skills are compiled from personal experiences in childhood, observations of contemporaries, books read, history, as well as the environmental culture.

How did she manage to do all of this? Did she?

All parents want what they believe is best for their children. Cultures and experiences dictate what it is that is best. Philippine culture and tradition believe and respect age, wisdom, and authority. As well as the fact education is salvation and power. These values are absorbed from the environment like sponges devour water and amazingly are wrung out at strangely unexpected times when needed. Part of the territory one gets from observation or heard from ancestors. Parents wish the children to absorb them, become their habit, and get resurrected at times when they have to make decisions.

Children are the parents' most valuable treasure, they are lovingly held close to their hearts. It is exciting to be within the mind of a child, to see with their eyes, full of wonder and innocence. How awesome it is to be a parent. A gift given for another chance to make right, omissions and commissions. Oh to be a child and have no worries, content in their parents' loving arms, to watch the smiles on their faces, hear the sound of their voices, relish the food they are served, enjoy the toys they are provided, the stories they are read, the places they are taken to.

One by one the children followed the "rules". One of Nadia's rules was: do your homework. I will not help with your homework, your homework better be completed by the time I come home from work so we can play together. However I will provide for you. I will take you to places you want to go and to places you never even dreamed of and more. We will listen to all kinds of music, see movies, go to the theater, taste authentic ethnic food wherever we find it on our journeys. You can be whoever you want to be or do whatever you want to do within reasonable boundaries. It is a choice, your choice. Your Dad and I will always support you.

Was Nadia authoritative? Authoritarian? She knew she was trying not to be distant. Definitely she was not inattentive.

There were rewards and consequences explained.

Did those messages have any significance? What were the impact of those messages? Was any damage accumulated as a result?

Was she too harsh with her children? Why? How did she become such a personality?

Were independent, decisive self reliant individuals raised? Since one had only one life, she felt it her responsibility to help her children make it a success. Nadia believed the lessons learned in childhood define one's future. Knowledge of good and evil is disseminated from parent to child.

For all the things parents tell their children for their own welfare, does any good come out of it?

If you want to see the valleys go to the mountaintop

Eileen Caddy

BEGINNINGS

Nadia had emigrated to the United States in her youth.

The immigration experience is complicated. Every country has its own morality, distinct climate, peculiar flaws, and special traditions.

Why would someone leave the comfort of home for some distant shores?

The young lawyer was so unhappy with local politics, for activities his sister was also engaged in. The anti-Marcos activists. He decided to stop fighting within and left the country as a tourist. Many years passed before they heard from him. He sought asylum in the United States, studied, and successfully passed the bar exams. Now they hear he is working for some twenty lawyer firm in Los Angeles, California.

His sacrifice paid off. Now his sister is joining him. Also seeking asylum in the United States.

Mr. Dominguez had joined the Bolo Battalion during World War II. When he and his compatriots enlisted in the US Military, they were promised full benefits, after all they were protecting "American interests" in the Pacific Rim. They marched from Bataan, were bombed in Manila, and were chased through the Visayan jungles so that the American flag could continue to wave proudly in the Pacific. They were the eyes and ears of the United States searching for the Japanese who were pillaging the country, raping women, and killing everyone in their path. Andy's maternal aunt was one of their victims. So was Nadia's uncle who was dragged into the Death march.

Yet he survived.

Years later, too late for most of them, gratefully, the US decided those soldiers should be provided veteran's benefits. The caveat was that they had to come to America to collect. Their families worked and saved to afford passage. Soon almost eighty year old Mr. Dominguez and his wife arrived in America. War continued its cruel claws for him. To live in an unknown place, to acclimate his body to the changing temperate weather, alone, separated from his friends and families, he made the ultimate sacrifice for his children. Later he was able to apply residence status for them. Eight children, five boys and three girls.

One by one they were able to obtain their passports. At the US embassy in Manila, where there was a long line of applicants, these young men were proudly showing them off to the young ladies in line, offering marriage!

No takers.

Nadia's cousin Tommy was an architect. He loved Frank Lloyd Wright and wanted to pursue postgraduate studies or personally visit the many Wright buildings. He later married a fellow architect, an American, to the dismay of his parents.

"She is from a different culture. Does she understand our values: respect for age, wisdom, and authority?"

They were concerned for how their grandchildren, if and when they were lucky to have some, would be raised. There won't be any "elders" to show how Filipinos live their lives.

So many professionals: nurses and doctors left the country. So called "brain drain". The US was recruiting them. Filipinos speak English which was the language of instruction in the past. No fear of not being able to assimilate. They did not have any reservations leaving home knowing they would be advancing their professional skills and knowledge. Like raindrops that alight on a leaf, they might sparkle with the sunshine. Of course secondarily earn a modest living to financially help the family back home. Leaving home by choice, partly by necessity.

There were US Army, Navy, and Air Force military installations in the Philippines. There was no obligatory military service anymore. The US had volunteer military forces hence applying to be a soldier, a sailor, or an airman was easy to do. And after a few years of service, they would become US citizens.

Many decades earlier, coming to the United States as a laborer to work in the farms was done as *sakadas,* stowaways. The month long sea voyage did not dampen their spirits. They volunteered. Working in the bowels of the ships, whatever it would take for them to have a chance for a better life. They knew America was a land of many opportunities. The pains of alienation were alleviated by meeting on weekends to share experiences and later on to gather advice in nurturing their children and reliving their traditions. For they understood, role modeling by the elders was the best way to teach the young.

As much as they tried to assimilate to their new environment, they retain their regionalistic values. Like the cows who graze in their delineated parcel of grassland, Filipinos stake their claim to leadership in their particular ghetto. They come from a country composed of over seven thousand islands divided into three distinct regions: Luzon in the north, the Visayan Islands in the middle, and Mindanao in the south. Many areas in these regions have their own dialect, rituals, and traditions. They have forgotten that their national hero, Jose Rizal, once exhorted them to unite for the common good of one nation instead of for their individual provinces.

Imagine what could happen if Filipinos spoke with one language?

Moreover, they were colored, varying shades of brown. They were not allowed to mingle with the Caucasians. They understood this hierarchy because Filipinos also had an ingrained hint of class hierarchy, a tendency to pull their own bench, rich or poor, light skinned or dark, which region they come from, their accent. Though they know they are just like turtles, they believe they have different shells. These regional traditions are inbred in their bones like rebar that reinforces the concrete of buildings however, they provide a hindrance to their unification to have one voice in the adopted country.

Vicky, the daughter of their neighbor was engaged to an engineer who had gone to the United States. He came back to marry her and after the required wait for their marriage visa, she joined him.

Filipinos being compassionate and patient, she found her calling starting an elder care facility. It was completely natural for her since Filipinos cling to family which not only include the parents and children, but also grandparents, aunts, uncles, various cousins. And all friends become an aunt or uncle, lovingly called *Tita* and *Tito,* known as the extended family.

Even in other cultures, particularly in the Jewish world of old, caring for the family's sick and the elderly was a woman's customary role. It was just a matter of transferring skills acquired at home to a larger situation. She was a success. Her clients and their families loved her facility for the joy their loved ones were provided since Filipinos by nature are fun-loving. Celebrations with singing, dancing, and of course eating follows just about any excuse to gather: a new job, a promotion, a visiting friend, not to mention the usual birthday, anniversary, or holidays.

The largest ethnic group in California is the Filipinos. In fact a recent study shows there are 3.5 million Filipinos in the United States and over 40% live in California. Yet the government tends to ignore them as a voting block, unlike the recent Vietnamese or Russian refugees. The latter have clung to their culture so well, however they understand "united we stand, divided we fall". They know they should follow one leader at a time. Hence they have successfully fulfilled their dream of creating a community of shared values including building churches and community centers where they can gather and nurture their young.

Though not true of Filipinos, a problem with some immigrants is that they pretend to be the adopted country's citizens, however underneath the surface they return to their barbaric and foreign customs and allegiances. Just like what one rotten egg does in a box, the behavior of a few spoil the rest.

In 2005, the United Nations reported there were nearly 191 million international migrants worldwide. In 2006, the International Organization for Migration estimated foreign migrants worldwide was 200 million: 70 million went to Europe, 45 million went to North America, and 25 million went to Asia.

However, not everyone who leave their country immigrates.

Christopher Columbus or Ferdinand Magellan were assigned to explore the unknown by their superiors. To enrich their kingdoms.

Or Roald Amundsen navigating to find a possible trade route connecting the Pacific and Atlantic Oceans.

Or Marco Polo in search of various trade routes for silk or exotic spices.

In those situations, although the world was not as globally known and connected like the present, they had the financial, material guidance, and moral support of an entire country cheering them on to succeed!

Here we talk about individuals with the courage to break away for adventure, or to fulfill the challenge to further knowledge and share what has been gained to help fellow human beings prepare for the battle of life.

This is the story of one such individual, Nadia, who ventured to go beyond her safety net.

She made sure every millimeter of her imagination and memories were safely stacked in her brain: all visions of the seas and the lands that she would miss, all textures, sounds, tastes, and smells she had grounded herself in and loved for so long. She was fearful that these might be lost to her forever. Though filled with excitement of her journey, she was heavy hearted as she carried them with her across the Pacific ocean.

Happiness is a butterfly which when pursued is always just beyond your grasp, but which if you will sit down quietly may alight upon you

Nathaniel Hawthorne

AWAKENING

Twenty-four years passed.

The Great Wall of China is spectacular. Known to the Chinese as the "Long Wall of Ten Thousand Li", it is a series of concrete fortifications built east to west meandering across the northern historical border. Its purpose was not only to protect the Chinese Empire from all outside aggression especially the neighboring Japanese who were bent on expansionism, but also to preserve the integrity of their culture from those of foreign barbarians. Hence it was to provide border control. Various means to delay or detract the enemies were in place. Watch towers, troop barracks, garrison stations are located every several hundred meters.

What good are these if there is no means of communication of the impending attack? Smoke or fire were used as signaling enhancements to the defensive mechanisms.

The photographs in various magazine and book advertisements do not capture the immensity of man's engineering prowess, the superb military strategic thinking, architecture, technology, and art of ancient China. It was built continuously from 3rd century BC to the 17th century AD. The long grey wall is strikingly awesome amidst the backdrop of beautiful forests of various shades of green, blue, and brown trees in the hills, mountain ranges, and valleys.

An archaeological survey found that the entire wall with all its branches measure out to be 21,196 km (13,171 mi). The air is light and fresh. One sees endless silhouettes as far as the eye wanders into the horizon. In some areas the wall even looks like it is soaring to meet the ocean of clear blue clouds. A tower in one of the vantage points extends to about 1,000 meters above sea level, an excellent place to view the world.

The steps vary both in height and width. Extra care is needed to watch the steps as one navigates the wall. In the searing summer heat, dressed in her favorite wardrobe to travel: white blouse and black skirt, she emerged from the tour bus into the blinding July sun. The harsh hot humid air sped into her nose, deep into her sinuses, throat scraped, parched dry, allowing her to question the validity of this trip for her.

Nevertheless Nadia proceeded in her red beribboned floppy hat and an opened umbrella over her though these did not prevent the biting sun from pricking her skin as though it had fangs. She could only reach one tower. She did not want to risk a fall. She did not have to prove she could climb. It was enough she was there.

Her son Michael ran the first few steps and reached five watch towers. What an achievement. On his return, he was sweating profusely, his University of San Diego (USD) gray tee soaking wet, but with a wide grin, satisfied with his accomplishment. A performance one could be proud of. No sign of weariness, no breathing distress, just a picture of pure joy and elation. Exuding an air of healthy youthfulness.

The tour guide led their group to the tourist spot for souvenir pictures. The shortest of seven American couples and her 6.3-foot-tall son, she was relegated to the left front end. Like the curious cat, thinking she knew about composition, she went near the photographer to peek at how the photo would finish. No one bothered to look as she did. Everyone was more interested locating the best prominent spot in the placement. Make sure they would be seen clearly in the photo. The three taller women in front center were dressed in colors purple, purple, yellow in that order. Not thinking that it would be offensive, she talked to the purple and yellow ladies.

"Is it okay if you two exchange places so the photo color palette would probably look better as in purple, yellow, purple."

One of the purple ladies proclaimed "No, I am the tallest so I should be here". Said with an attitude. Head held high with a slight tilt, shoulders stretched wide, chest stuck out, body extended taller than she already was, her huge Gucci bag on one shoulder, tan short pants, shocking pink tees with matching pink tennis shoes.

Delivered with the look How dare you! Order me around!

Ouch, is that what the curious cat heard before she was killed?

Nadia hated confrontations, but if the bringer takes it to her door, she will find her there. However, she decided there was no door yet.

Well. Beware of this purple woman, she thought to herself.

Nadia conveyed the incident to her son, admonished him to stay away from purple lady and remind his mom if she did otherwise.

Shortly thereafter they reached Xian.

The first emperor of China, Qin Shi Huang ordered the construction of the now famous Terracotta Army and his mausoleum just to the east of Xian, immediately after his ascension to the throne. He was only 13 years old.

He was also credited for starting the construction of the Great Wall.

Now, they were admiring the many soldiers lined up like a marching army deep in the underground. They were at the site of the uncovering of 8,000 life size clay figures. Each one had identifiable individual features, were arranged in various ranks, she assumed from their costumes, with weapons, and chariots drawn by horses. It was said that no two figures have the same features.

By this time they had already settled into their individual routines. Being a tourist means following lines. They were lining up to have professional photographs to use as Christmas cards. Or just plain souvenirs of the trip. Amazing how all these Caucasians, with the magic of eye pencils and eyeshadows, looked like exotic Asians dressed in Chinese outfits, on makeshift stages, sitting on one of the horses, in a chariot, or just standing up holding a fan like a coquette.

A hug from behind startled her. Purple woman had embraced her. An action feeling like a thunderbolt. Sent shivers down Nadia's spine.

What have I done now, she wondered.

"You are such a bundle of light and sunshine." Said purple lady.

Nadia was pleasantly surprised at that moment, shocked. Compliments knocked her off balance, feeling woozy, almost seeing a cliff she was about to fall.

There was a slowly expanding silence like the universe, which she had seen in her patients as a sign of aging. Was she in the stage where the insidious incremental signs of aging were attacking her body and mind already?

There had been many times when she was disappointed that she could not find the right retort when needed. To some this comes swiftly, but not to her. And later on she would regret why she could not provide an intelligent reply sooner than later. She had not been a master of herself still.

Shortly she was set in her orbit saying, "My goodness, you just made my day".

She did not understand why she quoted Clint Eastwood. She had enjoyed watching his movies. From playing cheap Italian western movies to what she believed were profound meaningful life stories in films he has produced and directed, he has earned her respect. Besides he has aged gracefully, still tall and lean with a lined face that reflects a beautiful character he has earned through the many years.

Regretfully Nadia wished she had come up with a better response. With much pride in her heart she shared this joyous feeling that purple woman delivered with her son.

Michael, Prima Donna said I am such a bundle of light and sunshine! "Are you proud of your mom?"

"NO. YOU ARE NOT!" He responded with a sneer.

Why is it that children's voices break hearts?
What a shock! What a mind boggling revelation.
Does a person change character in a few days?
How does that happen?
Is it really possible?

She backed a few paces away for she became breathless. As well as to position and steady herself well, try to imagine and see the bigger picture. Stand upright balanced to prepare for a discussion.

But her son had already moved on.

She was devastated.

Internally she wept for past and future lost shared joyful moments. Consoling herself, she reasoned, after all this journey was just beginning. A door just opened for her to make time for that discussion eventually, try to discern her son's opinion of his mother.

And discuss the same issues with Maya and Maurice.

What wrongs were she guilty of?
She does not remember offenses formally charged.
She felt the shaky gaze of what could have been.

Is it too late now for this meeting of minds?
Will it just lead to regrets?

She will not think about that today. After all, tomorrow is another day as she remembered Scarlett.

Even if one dislikes their parents, knowing them helps to understand where they come from. Persons' characters are molded and inspired by what their parents have done. We measure ourselves against our parents, and each generation tries to do a little better.

Nadia knew she must be brave and do the difficult thing, after all an examined life is fodder for making adjustments before it is too late. She believed people profit more by the mistakes made by one's own living than by doing the right thing through someone's advice. She joyfully looked forward to this journey.

However she considered this incident a mere tick bite as opposed to an injustice hence there was no need for a sense of history at the moment.

*Action may not always bring happiness, but
there is no happiness without action*

Benjamin Disraeli

DECISION

When Nadia emigrated to the United States in her youth, she was faced with a dilemma? Though she knew her visa was for five years only, she meant her American experience to be all encompassing.

To assimilate into a new culture or not?
What to retain and what to adopt?
How about the language issue.
Will the Americans understand her?
Do the Americans speak like the British?
Do they enunciate each syllable?

Gradually she dug deep into her forgotten past, both actions and inactions. She hoped to reassemble long buried memories, replaced by this activity called living. By schooling. By new experiences. By new friends. By colleagues. By wifehood. By motherhood. By grandmotherhood.

Life is difficult and all of these callings have problems attached to them.

She was looking back fifty years but could still see the same movies and activities of her childhood. The voices of the unknown future for the girl of ten and the distancing silence of the past forty years. She could see that energetic girl of ten and feel the aching body of the fifty year old she was.

She contemplated the enormity of this undertaking. She understood the new culture, this great country called the USA she had assimilated into had some effect on her. That could not be prevented.

How do you stave off the sea from coming to shore, or block the rising waves from brushing against the cliffs?

Philippine immigrants tend to assimilate to the new culture. There is no language difficulty. English was the primary means of communication in schools in the past hence everyone is able to speak English well enough to engage in conversation although the accent might be a deterrent to complete understanding. The national language, Tagalog, was just one of the subjects taught in school, therefore not all Philippine citizens speak Tagalog. Taglish is slang for a mix of Tagalog and English, a lot of Philippine citizens use it.

Trying to empty her heart and brain of "junk" so the information retrieval would be made easier was a grand task she had to accomplish.

After all, memories are not irretrievable.

Was this going to be a pandora's box of horrors? Or would it be full of pleasant surprises worth sharing, memories of happy times for everyone to remember?

Or possibly this process could open and enlighten her to issues she should have dealt with in a different manner?

Will this be an exercise in futility or make her a better person?

Nadia proceeded with an optimistic attitude. After all, although life by itself is difficult she thought it was her responsibility to be content and cheerful anyway.

During this phase of her life, she had been reconnecting to the spiritual journey she had embarked in her childhood which had been temporarily diminished or had taken a detour during her process of "living". She realized the pleasure of the possibility for knowledge of a reexamined life, which though difficult, she believed was a possibility she had to endure.

With much joy, she imagined the journey. She had lived her life not with a rigid, programmed certainty like an engineer, an accountant, a robot, or a computer. It was more a life that was pleasurable with anticipation of whatever the result would be. She understood life's hills and valleys.

She had already been keeping a journal for the past 15 years. Words crawled on the blank sheets of her Pages document. She had allowed her hand to take her pen and did not intimidate her heart and mind to hold it back. Courage is a trait common to the young. Nothing in her life could be so terrible or dreadful as to protect others from it or shield her from everyone.

Photographs since her childhood had been carefully kept in various albums which she had captioned, hence both written and visual sources were readily available. She did not have a camera but everyone took photographs and she kept those where she was in. A soft whisper in the back of her consciousness was saying this will all pass, will be gone, and the past matters more than we realize. If we don't know and understand the soil of the ground we are on, we will be lost. It is important to have something to remember what had gone before.

She had discovered several years earlier that the pictures she had carefully kept in photo albums had turned amber, were in varying stages of decay. The photo albums did not have non-acid, non-lignin paper she was advised was the reason. So called archival papers. This was not in her vocabulary then. She had used glued corner reinforcements which when wet would stick to the pages. The photo itself would not stick, yet damage was evident.

She even had the album covers imprinted in gold:
CHILDHOOD.

COLLEGE MEMORIES.

Later she used larger albums with clear see through plastic inserts and different colored paper pages. Scrapbooking. As long as she kept them, she will remember and will never be lost from her family.

To prevent further decay, one option was to replace them in albums with the appropriate paper. Better yet, why not use the computer? She had learned Microsoft Office, Word, Word Perfect, Excel. Enough to get by in the business world.

But graphics! That was a different kettle of fish.

Hence with the help of her now adult children, she embraced the high-tech Apple age. One by one she scanned the photos into her IMAC computer that her son Maurice had been insisting she should purchase. That computer was the best for graphics apparently. Though the photographs were no longer their virginal best, faces, and backgrounds were still identifiable.

Her days and nights were kept busy. Photos scattered all over her home where there was counter space.

"There's Aunt Denny and Uncle Augie posing with all of us as we went down the mountain after visiting Aunt Felisa. I could still taste and smell the freshly baked cinnamon flavored broas Aunt Felisa was famous for."

Sometimes Andy would help. Sharing the past is easier and more memorable than reliving it alone. He was introduced to the members of Nadia's clan who he had not met.

"That is Mama Mattie and Papa Teo, the parents of my handsome cousin Romy."

It was a joint journey down memory lane.

Trying to merge the past with the present, working the past with one's head in the present. Nadia was in a good position to review her world and discern.

Look to this day! In its brief course lie all the realities and truths of your existence: the bliss of growth, the glory of action, the splendor of beauty.

Kalidasa

MEMORIES

"That's our neighbor's house. They had 12 children. We would hear the bell calling the children for mealtimes."

Memories keep one grounded. Nadia was going to embark on a similar journey she took in her youth which was the beginning of an adventure that she had to succeed. Must succeed!

Many moons ago, she and her mother were taking the 3 day boat ride to the metropolitan city, Manila, the capital of the Philippines. She was to enroll at the university for pre-medical studies and if things worked out, she would become a physician.

She had lived a sheltered life. Nothing much happened in her island hometown. But her house was in the center of the business area where people chose their own little corner to gather, happy because they could discuss and hope for something tolerable in the future. She could hear them talking about everything under the sun, dreaming of what could be possible, discussing hopes and aspirations for themselves and their children.

Or just plain gossip. The latest rumor on the mayor and his secretary, followed by guffaws. Or the lovers engaging in sexual intimacy behind the shrubs in the back of the school building. There is magic made of sighs and grunts in intimacy, bonded tightly that nothing can come between. Not the fear of discovery or being assigned to damnation in hell.

Waiting for an invitation to lunch or dinner. A baptism, wedding, anniversary, birthday or a funeral. Any of these happenings was always cause for a celebration which included food, singing, and dancing. Everyone present was invited to share a meal. People would save or take a loan for these occasions. It would take them a whole year to recover financially.

A source of discussions and arguments between Nadia and her mother.

"Why would they celebrate if they can't afford it?

Isn't that hypocrisy?

Trying to live beyond their means?

Why does it have to be "*bonga*", excessive?"

"You can't prevent anyone from celebrating." Her mother would say. "It is a decision they have to make for themselves. People always have a choice, whether they make the right choice is another matter."

"Besides, you should stop talking nonsense. You should realize words have meaning and should be uttered after careful deliberation." Her mom admonished.

Years later, Nadia met some of these men who wait for a meal at the street corner. They told her they were thankful for her family's unselfishness. They mentioned something about "crabs".

On days when no celebration was on the agenda, they could come to Nadia's backyard kitchen and their cook would certainly give them a meal. The cook had taken these instructions from her parents to heart. On her parents death, her brother Rolando's kitchen became their refuge. Her parents lived the life they wanted their children to see, and learn, to show something that was right. These men, upon their future success, learned the charity lesson too. They would call a particular businessman, give instructions to donate a sack or two of rice to a grieving family.

"So what's the story about crabs?" She finally asked

"Well, we Filipinos are labeled as competitive, only among ourselves. We try to pull down successful *kababayans* (compatriots). Just like crabs pulling down other crabs who try to climb to get out of the baskets they are kept in." True.

There was a shop across the street from their home owned by a lady seamstress, Bessie. Her Singer sewing machine was in one corner. A large table was in the center of the room where she would do the cutting and where her customers would show their designs. Nadia remembers sitting in a rocking chair in one corner of this lady seamstress' shop. Bessie allowed her to stay reading in her shop while she worked on her customers' orders.

Her place was the hub of activity for the women of her hometown. Nadia could eavesdrop on their conversations, rather, their orders. This sleeve should be done a certain way: the length mid arm, to the elbow, or long sleeved. The length of the hem should be such and such in relation to the knee, the hemline stitched this way and that or with embroidery, the decorations, buttons, flowers, beads placed in distinctive locations to accentuate or highlight a good feature of the body. Or hide something not so endearing.

Or they would show her a photo of the dress they wanted made for them, taken from some magazine or newspaper. So many embellishments Nadia was hearing and too confusing. However Bessie did not have to write all these information. Amazing lady with encyclopedic memory.

Bessie was exceptional not just with her memory. She could make a dress, pant, or shirt for anyone. Big or small, tall or short, young or old. Without any pattern. Everyone dressed with custom made clothes.

None of the "Off the rack" clothes people wear in America. One need not fear meeting someone at a party wearing the same outfit. Givenchy, Yves St Laurent, Coco Chanel, all in this lady. Very creative.

And while they discussed their orders, those waiting would belch out the latest rumors. They did not need the National Enquirer. The wireless network was just as powerful and all encompassing. And Nadia kept all this information in various files in her brain, just like how a computer works. After all, the brain is just that, a computer.

Those who whispered were annoying. Those that she could not hear or understand, she wove up little stories or various scenarios with those names or places she heard.

How fertile the imagination of childhood is! This was a place where she could make her mind soar, dream.

Bessie also had a wonderful voice. Nadia could hear her singing in the chapel by her house during their nightly rosary. On Friday evenings, she would lead a prayer procession around the neighborhood in what was called "block rosary".

During Christmas season, Bessie would lead a group of carolers and Nadia was allowed to tag along.

Christmas caroling in their island involved singing holiday songs and performing a short skit in various homes, already prearranged. The homeowner would make a monetary donation. This was her big fundraiser for various causes. None of the books she read talked about caroling as a fundraiser although she knew from reading her favorite British classics how royalty or the rich would sit down in their mansions entertained by various professional artists.

Nadia would wonder how golden hair and blue eyes really looked. These books made her think she wasn't going to amount to anything because she only had black hair and brown eyes. And she was not fair skinned.

However it was reassuring that some smart sisters were described as plain, with dark hair. Hence she imagined there was hope for her.

Some say we don't get to choose the people we are. We don't get to choose our own hearts. Yes, she could have been born somewhere in another part of the globe, to some other mother, or a single woman. And her life experiences would have been different. But she heard the oft repeated refrain from her parents, that she did have a choice in what her future could be.

We believe what we want to.

Besides her mom would say "never judge a book by its cover".

After all, it is not only about outward appearance. What counts most is inner worth, innate dignity, the latter reenforced by John Paul II later on when he proclaimed: Everyone: Catholics, Jews, and non Christians are all God's children.

All these refrains planted seeds of hopeful, future joyful journeys.

You gain strength, courage, and confidence by every experience in which you must stop and look fear in the face. You must do the thing you think you cannot do.

Eleanor Roosevelt

DANGER

"Cousin Connie and Lis are looking out from the second floor windows watching the kids play jump rope on the streets."

Still early morning but the day was already heating up. Just another usual hot humid island day. Good for the skin but not for comfort. There were not enough hand fans to go around. Moreover they did not last long. Made of paper or coconut leaves. Though all their clothes were made of cotton because it "breathed". Nonetheless it did not allow enough air circulation. Windows made of glass with wood casings were kept open for the breeze to enter.

However, the dense air just hung static in the atmosphere. Maybe they should just have made netting for clothes. There was no comfortable place. Outside, the day was stiflingly hot, the sun beating down with its full force. Nadia decided to go to her Grandma Ida's house where it was always cooler from the many grand old trees with spreading branches. Walk through the shortcut under the branches of the coconut trees where it was cooler. But she had to be careful, some of those large mature fruits fall, and many a child had been hit in their head, resulting in brain damage.

A pond with taro plants and their large spreading leaves swayed with the occasional breeze. Seeing the wind move and the sight of the water made her feel cooler. Amazing what the mind can do. There were turtles and frogs croaking reminding her of happy childhood days playing with them.

Despite having already taken two short showers, she needed another in the late afternoon before tucking in for the evening. Nobody complained about the waste of water from showering. The wells had plenty of water. And it was just a few steps away from their house, beyond the banana trees. Nardo would lug bucket loads of water from there to fill the tanks that would drain into the bathroom and kitchen. As he worked, naked above the waist, his bulging shoulder muscles would glisten like moisture on the windows as he sweat. He was the handyman, the go-to-person for every detail that went wrong or needed maintenance in the household.

She picked a loose spaghetti strap salmon colored cotton nightgown. She could not do any reading in bed. The kerosene lamp might cause a fire should she fall asleep without turning it off. Instead she tried to figure out what she could have said to persuade her parents. Maybe she could bribe Nardo to take her to the ceremonies, peak through the windows.

But no, Nardo would not do that. Too righteous.

Tonight was a huge celebration. It was a beautiful night, suddenly with a cool breeze. Weather in the island was variable. Dry heat was bearable. One just had to go beneath the trees. It was the humidity that was irritating. By nighttime, without the sun's piercing hot rays, the cool evening breezes from the ocean brought great comfort.

The tenth anniversary of the town judge's tenure was cause for the social. The powerful men and women of the municipality would be there. People purchased tickets to be part of the celebration. To watch, to see, and be seen, with whom, and to be amused. Music and lanterns added to the festivities.

Judge Joe roomed in their house during the week. His family lived in the capital city. He had a car, however he preferred the peace and solitude the island evenings provided.

Nadia's parents' home was like the hotel in town. One enters the front door passing by several potted flowering plants on layers of pedestals into a tiled living area. Comfortable wooden chairs were in the living room, some with woven rattan seats. The house was roomy, immaculately clean, with indoor plumbing, however there was no hot water. They boiled water, poured it into a bucket. This is how they had lukewarm water as they bathed.

There was no electricity and no gas stove at the time so Nadia and her friends would go out to pick firewood in the open spaces, under the trees, bushes, and in the jungles. Nardo would tag along with them, carry the huge bundles and cords of kindling back home. This was not a difficult job, especially when done with friends, and everything else that friends do.

Her mother walked the hardwood floors of their home not with house slippers but with a rag under her feet so the floor was dusted as she moved around. She would touch some of the furniture with her fingers checking for dust. The maid would be counseled not to miss that spot again.

All out-of-town relatives and friends would stay in their home, provided with towels and sleepwear. Aure did more than what hotels did!

The previous lady judge, Judge Gertie, had stayed with them so long that her mother insisted she bring her own maid. The lady judge was prim, proper, and very rich. She was kind, gentle, loving, and exuded no airs. Nadia hated milk and refused to drink it. But her mother insisted she should. Good for her growing bones, Nadia was told. Judge Gertie counseled Aure to just add coca cola to the milk and to everyone's delight Nadia drank the delightful concoction from a glass.

Judge Gertie also gave Nadia many books. One of those was "You can change the world". Really? Little Miss island girl can do that? A promise of things to come.

Nadia imagined the ballroom decorated with various fresh island vines. Green plants were situated by the doors that were framed with garlands of flowers. No plastic decorations here. She could smell the sweetish aroma of the white with yellow centered *kalachuchi* (frangipani) that were currently blooming profusely, like foam on the tree tops perfuming the night air. And the fire red blossoms of the acacia tree finishing off the color scheme. Red and white lanterns hung from the ceiling like the planets in the sky.

Off the center of the room would be the huge banquet table where people would gather to engage in whatever banter they could, show off their intellectual prowess. Or where the hangers-on would try to whisper into some politician's ear a particular cause close to the heart to help the poor or their constituents. Or start off conversation with the upper hierarchy of politics seemingly to show old friendships buttering up smoothly, hoping to collect a favor. Thereby delaying their enjoyment of the delicious satisfying palate, sacrificing, and soothing their growling stomachs for over an hour of conversation that was of no special interest. Hors d'oeuvres was not a tradition.

Of course the centerpiece of the dinner table would be profusely and elaborately decorated with the special, just the right age young roasted suckling pig biting an orange. Roasted just right so the skin would be yummy crispy and the underlying fat completely dissolved at the fire pit. No occasion worth celebrating proceeds without the roast pig. *Lechon.* And there would be the obligatory noodle dish, *pancit,* signifying wishes for long life, never mind that the noodles were cut short. Vegetable dishes such as beans and squash with shrimp cooked in coconut cream, some small leafy greens called *malunggay* and *pechay.* Abundant local fruits include the jackfruit, mango, banana, avocado, star apple. And of course the baked desserts such as *leche flan* or creme brulee, except the former is not torched to create a crusty caramel on top. *Empanadas, ensaymadas, torta* and various other *kakanins* (sweet carbohydrate-rich dishes).

Just thinking about these treats she couldn't eat made her salivate with hunger.

The cousins were downstairs busy with their school work. Later they would crochet and tat. Crochet is making fabric from yarn or any thread using a needle with a hook. They made curtains and bedspreads which her mother used on special occasions. Tatting is making lacy patterns to use as lace collars, or doilies that her Auntie Denny would use as embellishments with her sewing. Holding a length of thread in one hand while using a shuttle with the other makes it easier to go through loops to make knots. These they did while discussing the latest rumor.

Tonight Nadia would miss this nightly routine.

She wanted to go with her parents to the dinner dance. Observe what other people dressed for such occasion and listen to what the elders were saying. See the ladies whose dresses were made by Bessie, how they would look on them.

Above all watch them dance. There was a handsome *mestizo* couple who danced well. The tango was their specialty. They beautifully executed this dance with much facial and body emotion, so romantic, and consequently the dance became erotic, she heard. Oh, to be able to see them. She begged her parents, promised to do so many extra errands just to be allowed to join them.

Without success.

Her parents said NO. Not appropriate for children.

The kerosene lamplight would last only so long, so soon enough the house was enveloped in darkness. She remembered hearing the grandfather clock tick nine times.

Hers was the right front corner bedroom on the second floor of their house, windows on both sides. There was a large fruit-bearing *caimito* tree (star apple) close by. Outwardly the fruit looks like an apple, but not firm. The inside is cream colored, looking like and tasting like fuyu persimmon. She could just open her window and grab one of these fruits for snack. Under the spreading branches of this tree were her mother's orchid collection. Several dozens of them. The many colors, shapes of the blossoms were a feast for the eyes. The leaves had varied patterns. How can one deny the existence of a Supreme Being that allows these unique works of art, a spectacular display of colors, and designs, when one only had to provide soil and occasional water? And to think they grew wild in the jungles.

She did not close her windows so their delicious aroma would perfume the night air, soaring up especially into her room.

Nadia heard her father's blood curdling scream, waking her from her slumber.

Or was she just dreaming?

It sounded so primeval. It had to be just a dream. A very loud pop is what awakened her and though still groggy, she was able to recognize what she heard as definitely her father's strong voice. She struggled to remember where her father was.

Why would he yell like that? Who was he yelling at? She had never heard her father yell before, yet she knew his voice.

Then she remembered.

Her mind dreaded what she was thinking. She had never heard a gunshot before, however her father's so very loud yell alerted her to that possibility. Reflexively, she ran down the steps, opened the front door, stood in the street center and yelled "HELP".

Without commercial lights, evenings in her town were dark, one would see thousands of brilliant stars. The night sky would show them clearly, looking like fireflies. They seemed so close enough to think one could reach out to touch them. More likely the stars sparkled like diamonds in the sky. The constellations. Big Dipper, the Little Dipper, she could locate them as a child. There was no coal emitting industrial factory to pollute the sky and obscure their radiance. From her bedroom window, the stars and the moon peeked through the branches of the trees.

Nights were also especially peaceful with deafening quiet. The many soft melodious sounds of nocturnal creatures were a soothing, never-ending symphony that became part of the nightly background music like muzak in the US that one forgets their presence, simply dismissed as part of the environment. She could easily hear their neighbor half a kilometer away playing his violin. This was his nightly routine and she would sleep to his music. Pachelbel's Canon, Gounod's Ave Maria.

So her very loud scream was easily heard.

Shortly, people awakened from their slumber came out to the street too. Theirs was a very small community and everyone knew everybody by name, very neighborly. Not just knowing each other, but looking out for each other, concerned for each one's needs.

They recognized her voice. For Nadia was all over town, on the streets playing with everyone. Sort of tomboyish. Always wearing her white blouse, later turning beige, and colorful flowery short skirts, long dark hair tousled and shiny from the coconut oils they used. No tennis shoes, just thongs everywhere she went. Riding her father's Columbia bicycle, fresh air brushing her face, feeling freedom. Looking back, she realized she had very good control. No other girl could do what she was doing on that mountain bike.

A few men walked towards the direction where she told them she heard her father's voice. The wait seemed an eternity. Nadia busied herself pacing from the street to her house and back, full of dread, yet hopeful for the best for everyone. The men, women and children engaged in discussions and theories. She did not want to hear any of these for they just added to her anguish.

Why? What? Who were involved?

Did a stranger come to town unnoticed?

Filipinos are usually peace loving. They respect age, wisdom and authority. They try to understand and follow the law. They do not start a fight even if bullied, they try to reason the issue in their minds. Though if needed they will not run from a fight. That is what she learned from those evening sessions with her families.

Shortly, the men came back. She was overwhelmed when she saw her father walking, unharmed. Hugged him, cried, tears of joy. Her neighbor's passenger bus took the judge and others to the hospital eighteen kilometers away.

Through the darkness, she saw her future change. An incident like that made her realize there was danger out there. Her life of fun and innocence ended that night. It could have been her father.

But childhood memories can change. Happy times would still come.

Long bicycle rides to her uncle's orchard to pick *sineguelas, mangos, iba*. She would stop when she saw other children play and join them. Jump rope, tic tac toe, hide and go seek.

What if?

She loved her parents. There was no teenage rebellion in her bones. She just followed the unspoken rules, learned from observation. No television distractions.

There were two movie theaters in the capital city, seventeen kilometers away. Who would want or why would someone pay to stay in a dark room while she had the run of the whole town, the sea, the beaches, the many fruit trees she could climb, the many streets she could play tag in?

Traffic was unknown. There were just a few buses on a specific schedule for people on business or shopping trips to the capital. So the streets were a large playground for her and her friends.

Her family had a car. Nadia never learned how to drive. It was not automatic so the car would lunge every time she shifted gears and the engine would die. Besides, driving was dangerous. Drivers would weave, no lanes to follow. Cars converging, merging, overtaking.

There was no need for her to drive, what would the driver do then?
Years later, Nadia's father refused to believe she could drive.
He would not believe the concept that people drove within lanes.
That there were traffic lights and signs everywhere.
That people signaled to turn or change lanes.
That all drivers actually observed the rules, well, almost all drivers.
Unlike the chaotic streets in the Philippines where everyone honked their horns, dared each other with a stare for a chance to get ahead.
Everyone ignored the traffic lights or signs.

The stories and words she told him of her experiences driving just vanished speedily unheard, into space like Mercury.

Eventually they learned the bullet was for a judgment made against the shooter's brother by the judge. This incident was the subject of so many discussions for so long as people gathered in their usual street corners, while drinking the local coconut wine, *tuba.* Everybody had competing theories on what happened.

Civilization brings knowledge, however a little knowledge can be dangerous. And old superstitions and beliefs do not die, are not easily dismissed. Justice is blind. The objective judge followed the law.

This episode in this peaceful town was an anomaly.

Years later, the Judge walked with a limp. Thankfully the bullet had hit only his hip. Though errors arising from ignorance that lead to violence are rarely unforgivable, they leave an indelible imprint of a constant wave of darkness that threatens to suffocate.

If you desire to see the mountain top, rise into the cloud.
But if you seek to understand the cloud,
close your eyes and think.

Khalil Gibran

ISLAND HOME

"That's me and my cousins visiting our national hero Jose Rizal's house in Calamba during one summer."

Towns are like people. Old ones have character. New ones are just like another. Panglao is one of the smallest of over 7,000 inhabited islands known as the Philippines. One of the many smaller islands in the province of Bohol, located about 630 kilometers southeast of Manila, the capital of the Philippines.

Her teacher mom said the name may have come from Panglawod, meaning "to the open sea" or may refer to a fishing implement, "panggaw", used by local fishermen. And there were three other smaller island satellites: Balicasag, the scuba diving paradise as well as the home of the sweetest oranges, Gac-ang, and Taporoc. It has educational institutions—a high school named San Agustin Academy, Lourdes High school, Cristal-e College, and elementary schools.

There are no lakes or rivers. Drinking water is gotten from wells and underground springs. Her family drank rain water drained from their roof gutters into a large concrete water tank. There was an implement connected to the spout that would allow the early rainfall to drain first into the ground, wash off the dust and leaves that had accumulated, before the spout is diverted for water to flow into the tank for drinking. This water was sweet and cool. Water for other purposes as in cooking, bathing, washing clothes, were drawn from wells.

All of these jobs were done by Nardo. No one else dared climb the ladder to the rooftop during the rains.

There were two kinds of wells. One was a concrete platform with a pump to bring the water from underground springs. The other was just a large hole with a four feet high cemented wall around the rim to prevent someone from falling. Water is gotten by lowering a bucket. Washing clothes by the wells was another way to socialize with the neighbors. The cloth is soaped and tamped by hand, or with a paddle, then bleached, rinsed, and finally hung on clotheslines. A place for the young children to play hide and seek. Air dried clothes had a very sweet smell. The ironing would follow. Every work opportunity like this was grist for social interaction.

The 2010 census showed a population of 29,603 people, roughly about 5,000 families, mostly related by blood or marriage. Everyone knew everybody's business. Nadia was born, raised, and underwent her primary and elementary school education there, a native island girl.

It was an idyllic life taking no notice of the sun or time. It was a childhood not filled with suffering or boredom but of wild freedom, a closeness to family, to the earth, and to the sea. There was not a forbidden place to go. Everywhere was safe, no evil lurking behind bushes or trees. Beautiful long stretches of white beaches lined with leaning palm trees, framing the blue waters in the distance just like an infinity pool, clear cloudless blue skies, cool ocean breezes.

As a young girl while walking along the beaches, she could hear the waves as they lapped against the shore. Blue to gray waves then white bubbly foam. The endless coastal sands trembled with life. There were plenty of sea shells, and tiny critters sharing the sandy beaches, creating their little holes to lie underneath. The many exotic shells were multicolored, different sizes. They had been washed ashore. Her favorite was the chambered nautilus considering the complicated shape, color, and the different musical tones they emitted. And there were small ones which she picked and kept in her pockets.

It was interesting to observe the many prints of animals or people who had passed by that the sands revealed. A veritable history of its own. Various shapes and sizes of shoes, sandals, different sized or shaped feet or tracks. As the tides rose and fell, the sands would get washed, reoriented, water would fill the holes, and a new face would appear, starting a new chapter.

Mangroves abound, trapped the seaweeds along the beaches. They would cut branches from these mangroves for their Christmas trees, wrap the bare branches with green crepe paper. Even after her mother talked about purchasing artificial green, silver, or gold Christmas trees, Nadia preferred the mangrove branches.

Each person takes a roll of green crepe paper and patiently wraps the tree limbs. The decorations varied with whatever were available. Popcorns tied in a line. Popcorns glued to create balls. Paint sprayed on different shaped wood or cut coconut shells. There were no electric lights; tinsels provided the glitter.

And the children did not expect presents under the tree. After all, Christmas season was a celebration of the journey to Christ's birthday. None of the many constant reminders of how many shopping days left before Christmas.

One tradition carried a week before Christmas was when a couple would knock on people's homes to reenact Mary and Joseph's search for a room. The homeowner would say "no room for tonight". Called *rico rico*. And eventually someone would allow them inside where there would be an early breakfast shared.

Children looked forward to the Christmas Eve midnight mass. Church would be standing room only. Candlelit paper stars would be let loose from the church back balcony and pulled towards the altar. This was truly amazing, the church being dark. Called the parade of stars, "*padagan sa bituon*".

Music for these masses was awesome. She grew up praying in Latin, masses were done in Latin. But music was in English. Away in a Manger, O Little Town of Bethlehem, Silent Night, Joy to the World, etc., played to the accompaniment of guitars, banjos, trumpets, mandolins, and drums.

Though already groggy and sleepy, one had to stay awake. After all there was still another celebration. The midnight breakfast of specially made carbohydrate-rich sweets after mass that one did not want to miss. The *lechon* would follow in the daytime.

Whatever the celebration, she always managed to take time to escape to the beaches. To look out as far as the horizon would allow and wonder what was out there. If she came early, she would see the pink to orangey sky hovering over the blue waters. The flat endless sea was a good place to scan her limited small world and to imagine the larger world beyond. She knew there were other islands with irregular silhouettes, hilly, and mountainous. Panglao was flatland so there was not a mountain from where to view the horizon beyond. She saw her first hill when her family visited an aunt 60 kilometers away, located in the mainland. It was exciting to climb that hill with her cousins and admire the scenery.

The surrounding beaches where she lived were bland white, sugar-like powder, and she took them for granted as being the norm. She thought the whole world had beaches that looked like her hometown until she traveled later.

First experience that shattered that impression was in chemistry class, when they were told to get sand for one of their experiments. It was a huge dilemma for her. The classroom was on the rooftop. She had to find sand NOW! There was not an atom of sand anywhere, the white sand she knew. The whole world was not blessed with white beaches like her hometown, she realized. Any dirt was sand.

Then another revelation later on: there are other places with white sand too. She visited Tanzania and in Bagamoya, she saw they had beautiful white beaches.

Bagamoya was the original capital of German East Africa.
"Is there a special meaning to the name?" She asked the tour guide.

"The slave trade brought slaves from the African interior on their way to Zanzibar passing through this port. It could mean 'lay down your heart', or 'give up all hope', as in there is no more hope for escape. Or the porters carrying 35 pounds of loads on their shoulders from the interior of Africa would 'take the load off and rest'.

The view was spectacular, white beaches, blue waters, endless views of the horizon reminding her of home. And closer to home, Panama City in the gulf of Mexico near Florida evoke the same memories.

The fauna of the island was typical tropicals. Monkeys, varieties of birds, non-poisonous snakes, flies, mosquitoes although the island breezes would drive them away. They did not have to use mosquito nets.

The world's smallest monkey, the tarsier, is a species indigenous to another town in her home province of Bohol. A province is like a state in the United States.

The tarsier was highlighted in 1999 when Prince Charles, one of the world's well known naturalists, visited Hongkong for the turnover of the principality from Britain to China. He had been informed of the existence of the tarsier earlier and was curious and eager enough to want to see one.

Each measures three to six point five inches in height, the average adult is about the size of a man's fist. A foreign exchange student once played with one. Placed it on the edge of his eyeglass, yes, they are that tiny. Looks like a tiny teddy bear with huge eyes, in fact the eyes dominate the face. Their eyes are fixed in its skull, can not turn in their sockets. They are nocturnal and their diet consists of insects. The fingers and toes are long, the name comes from the long tarsal (ankle) bone.

Thus tourism to Bohol to see the tarsier started and awareness of their conservation became prevalent. Since 1986, the Philippine tarsier has been assessed as endangered.

Island flora is tropical likewise. Tourists to Hawaii would have seen some of them as in the frangipanis, bougainvilleas, various orchids, oleanders, lantanas, bananas, pineapples, guavas, mangoes, although roses, thrive too. Special natives are the fragrant sampaguita, a variant of the jasmine, and the ilangilang. And of course the tall and bending coconut trees as well as the very flexible bamboos. She can still remember the beautiful, colorful orchids her mother cultivated. Aure and her friends with their gardeners would go to the jungle and point to special orchids to pick and carry home.

There were lots of aunties, uncles, and cousins providing her with companionship. Plenty of conversations on any topic and stories. Heard narratives of their childhood, their escapades. How her maternal grandmother was the "Miss Manners" in town. Most of the families in town sent their young daughters to her grandma Ida, sort of a finishing school, teaching them ladylike accomplishments like singing, dancing, needlework, setting tables, deportments in general.

Grandma Ida had eleven children. Six girls and five boys. Naturally her children must have been good role models for everyone, hence the request. Her mother was number seven of the brood. She had the smallest family, everyone else had over five children. All the women stayed in the island. All the men left to build their fortune and lived in Manila.

However, most of them would bring their families home to their island for summer vacations. During these times, everyone would stay at her maternal grandmother's house for as along as they were in town.

It was a large house with enough bedrooms where the eleven children were raised, but during these visits everyone stayed together. The huge living room hardwood floor was where they would sleep right next to each other, like sardines. Talking themselves to sleep.

Now, Nadia wonders how the aunts' and uncles' backs felt on waking up in the mornings. Later on she fondly remembered these evening routines when she watched the Waltons as they ended their show nightly.

Meals were the local potatoes, bananas, rice, corn, fresh fish, occasional pork and chicken and lots of vegetables. There was a particular banana that had to be cooked. Sometimes the peeled, cooked bananas were pounded with shaved coconut meat with brown sugar added. Yummy!

Her contact with the "city cousins" was during these times. It was wonderful that their parents brought them home to the island primarily so they would all know each other. Those were happy days. Because of these visits, her Tagalog vocabulary was enhanced. The Philippine national language, a subject she excelled in during high school. It is difficult to learn a language unless one is able to practice, talk with someone. This she did with her favorite cousin, Connie, as they would tag along the boy cousins as they went hunting primarily for birds. And those were not wasted. They would barbecue them.

Many times, they would get a small boat, go farther into the sea to swim and picnic. Fresh seaweed with a little vinegar, crushed ginger, minced green onions was delicious. The cousins were tall, sophisticated city boys. Attractive. Nadia and Connie witnessed how some of the island girls would flirt with them, later made fun of at their nightly sessions. Although there were so many local cousins, she does not remember why no one else joined them on these forays into the jungles and the sea.

She and Connie would just stay at shore. They would climb the trees to picnic on the branches. Bring vinegar and salt to eat the tart fruit *iba,* and pomelo. They saw with brightly colored lenses, things that were ordinary then laugh, giggle, and sing.

Early evenings were spent sitting in the veranda enjoying the wafting aroma of the sampaguita or ilangilang flowers. This veranda was a roofed opened porch enclosed by railing all around with an opening for the stairs. The adults, sitting on benches or rattan chairs, would discuss all topics, nothing was off the table. For the sake of the young ones. Discipline issues, responsibilities, consequences. They believed education was freedom. That there were laws and as adults, individuals have responsibilities to discern them.

"Stand up when an adult enters the room. Bow and offer your forehead for a blessing or kiss the elder's hands. Help the older person as they walk along, or up and down the stairs. Offer your own chair to an elder. Greet the arriving person. Pass the platter of food along. Don't put food on your plate unless you can finish. There are many starving children all over the world. For every grain of rice you leave, that is one day stay of atonement in purgatory. Study, study, study. Your parents are working hard to send you to school. And don't forget to thank God when you wake up in the morning and before you go to bed." Some of those admonitions were heard.

Of course, they knew the ten commandments by heart, the many "do not's" as well as the beatitudes, the models for how to live.

She and the younger generations found this boring after so many repetitions. They were more interested in hearing the examples of young men and women who had misbehaved. And longingly opened their ears listening for the strumming of distant guitars getting louder slowly as they were getting closer causing their hearts to go fluttering.

The guitarists were young men coming to serenade the young ladies, a local tradition.

"Come on up here, join us." Her uncles and aunties would call out for them to join in the veranda. Tito Tommy would shake their hands, pat them on the backs and with his booming voice say: "Aure, can't you see these young men are hungrry. Where are your *suman, guinataan,* cookies, and biko?" Snacks and drinks would be offered followed by an inquisition of the young men's lives and families. Made them feel important.

"So you are Mr. Flores' son, how is he?" "How is your brother who went to law school?" And so on and so forth.

The serenade would become a chorus or karaoke session although karaoke was an unknown entity then. Her uncles and aunties enjoyed singing along the many romantic, sentimental, soulful songs native to the island.

As well as songs from America.

The US had colonized the Philippines, so the citizens were exposed to Western thought and culture. Apparently the West was a bastion of freedom and opportunity, Tito Tommy noted as he had traveled in his business world. He loved America best.

First it was the Spaniards who came to the Philippines. In fact, Nadia spoke Spanish with Grandpa Castro while sitting on his lap. They despised, subjugated, and humiliated the Filipinos right before their eyes, called them *indios,* who they considered inferior to them. The Filipinos wanted to learn Spanish to facilitate communication. They wanted to learn the language in schools. They were refused. The indios rebelled. A national Filipino hero, Jose Rizal, a physician, wrote a best seller in Spanish, *Noli Me Tangere,* translated Touch me Not or The Social Cancer.

He was executed.

The Americans sent the Spaniards home.

Then came the Japanese who were brutal, killed, and raped women. No love given to the Japanese. Then the Americans liberated them again. Douglas MacArthur was a favorite name she heard mentioned. There was a very strong sentiment that the islands remain a U.S. colony.

However Spanish influence was deeply ingrained in the Filipinos, in their lifestyle. She continued to speak Spanish. A not so great influence they introduced was the *siesta* and the *mañana* habit.

Mañana is a very bad habit. It means, this job can wait until tomorrow. The dishes forgotten, piling up in the sink, the laundry undone, no clean shirts and pants to change into, the trips to the grocery postponed causing Maurice to ask: don't you guys eat anymore? *Manana* is an excuse for thinking "tomorrow" like Scarlett. What's the big hurry?

Siesta is mid afternoon rest. Something that got her in trouble later on. While an intern in Pennsylvania, she was late for a one o'clock clinic where she was supposed to see patients, her first day.

"Where have you been?" Patients had been waiting long, the nurses getting anxiety attacks.

Siesta, was her answer. Lesson learned. Americans do not do *siesta*.

During her preteen and teen years, there were several cousins living at home as working students. The word cousin was loosely used to represent a distant relative or a close family friend. Their families would ask Aure and Tibo to pay for their schooling while they lived in the home and help with the chores. Her parents treated them like their own children, to Nadia's dismay.

Holidays were especially difficult for her because they would also receive gifts. She had to learn to be sharing of what she had. Difficult many times. Three of these cousins lived at the same time until they graduate from high school or some vocational school. However since all of them shared their daily experiences with various positive or negative comments or encouragements from the others, she enjoyed their company. The many conversations and laughter all day long even into the evening were very entertaining. They kept her informed of what young adults were involved in.

By the light of kerosene lamps, the cousins studied in the dining room table. During breaks, they would crochet or do tatting without help of patterns. The fanciful designs of the completed doilies, tablecloths, bedspreads, and curtains reveal their artistry and creativity. Butterflies, peacocks, harlequin designs. These were ingrained in their imaginations, memory, and Nadia visualized their appearance at art shows that she'd visit later on in her life.

She realized artful designs are universal and would come out with a little bit of creative gene. And they did these while discussing the day's happenings, their school activities, their relationships accompanied by a lot of giggles. She listened sitting cross legged on the hardwood floor watching them with increasing delight and enthusiasm, sometimes attempting to do crochet or tatting, however deciding this was not for her. With much regret. She was not as creative and patient as them.

She had no life pattern to create and preserve into a permanent image yet.

Besides, she was more interested in just listening to their stories, observing them since she did not have experiences she could share. She was not a multitasker.

Meanwhile in the back kitchen they could hear this maid with a wonderful voice singing "I see the harbor lights" or Frank Sinatra's "All the Way" or Nat King Cole's "Smoke Gets In Your Eyes". And Nadia would sing along in her head. She is convinced the maid introduced her to Frank Sinatra and his ballads. His songs talked about adventures, romances, life in general.

How complicated life was, Nadia thought.

The maid sang while she was preparing dinner. Oh, the aroma of onions, garlic, or ginger that were the usual spices. Sometimes the dish was cooked with creamy coconut milk. Those sweet memories of food, connections to music, and the resulting conversations that occur around the dining table were like meandering tributaries of lakes and rivers, bringing them to her consciousness whenever she heard those songs later on, wherever she was.

Her parents owned the first radio in town. A transistor radio. They would place it on the second floor window after nightly prayers so the neighbors could listen to the nightly soap opera everyone was following. This would be the subject of the following day's conversations as they go about their daily chores, discussing possible future scenarios to be confirmed or revised with the next episode.

With this radio in their house, Nadia would wake up to Voice of America, listening carefully. To prepare for the dinner questions that would inevitably be asked that evening. During dessert. It was amazing how much well informed she was of world happenings as a little girl growing up in that small island. World geography, world capitals, US states and their capitals, world events. It was not useful information at the time, did not mean anything to her in her daily life, but she had to be prepared for their nightly civics lessons. Later on this was a valuable gauge for her of how American schools were deficient in that matter.

Panglao was not a tourist attraction in those days. It was just a farming and fishing island, people living off their produce from the land and the sea.

*Far away there in the sunshine are my highest aspirations.
I may not reach them but I can look up and see their
beauty, believe in them, and try to follow where they lead.*

Louisa May Alcott

FIESTAS

"The young girls and boys are dressed in colorful outfits. They show some far east or middle east influence. After all, we were originally Malayans"

Once a month, the town held celebrations in various locations. Bicycle races, boat races, parades, and cockfights during the day. There was a particular bicycle race wherein the rider had to push a pin he held thru a ribbon-held circle hanging from a line. This needed accuracy, skill maneuvering the bicycle, and focusing on a particular ring. One gets bragging rights. Bicycles were decorated with primary color ribbons, whirly birds, and whatever imagined fancy.

And a beauty contest fundraiser annually. Families willing to sell as many tickets to raise funds so their precious daughter would be the honored queen or princess for the day. She would preside at a royal court on a float at the parade while the trumpets, bandolins, guitars, drums, and banjos play. Men and women would dress up in gaily decorated, highly colorful outfits while dancing as they followed the float processing on the streets around town. The previous evening was her coronation at the unwalled but roofed marketplace.

Years later, Nadia was honored to crown the queen. She marched down the long red carpeted aisle accompanied by the young town mayor. He was good looking, with a wonderful physique. Everyone thought they would make a handsome couple!

One of those afternoons was a street parade of the men who dressed up as women. They looked like gorgeous ladies of the night, with layers and layers of makeup, glamorous eyes, well coifed hair backcombed looking like beehives. Drag queens, she later learned they were called. This was most popular and colored with loud laughter, whistles, and street dancing.

Meanwhile there was food, oh there was plenty. Animals raised throughout the years are prepared for these huge feasts. And new clothes and shoes, as though it was Christmas. Every house fed anyone who walked into their home. People saved through the year so they could make this celebration as grand an occasion they could make. Called *fiesta* time.

Evenings were for fireworks and dancing.

Their interpretation of dancing at the time was that it was an art, or a form of exercise that involves body movements that are rhythmic, done to music. The girl falls into the circle of the boys arms, his right hand goes snugly into the curve of her lower back, then they move to the rhythm of the music. Sometimes the boy would pull the girl closer to him and if he does not feel any resistance, he pulls her even closer. And whisper sweet nothings into her ears.

Giggles, giggles, giggles.

They did not know what went on during these dances so she and her cousins made up these stories. She did not understand why her older cousins did not go. Eventually the details were revealed. Seems the girls did not have any control over who they could dance with during those evenings!

Years later, her husband confirmed the details.

It goes this way. The men buy colored ribbons. The announcer then calls out which color ribbon can dance for a particular music.

"Those with red ribbons can dance now". The boys with such color would position themselves to have first chance on the girl of his choice. He could dance as many dances as the number of color ribbons he had purchased. It could become quite expensive particularly if he is smitten by a special girl.

Another dance maneuver is to pick a lady then auction her off. Men start outbidding each other. The lady has to dance with each bidder until no one outbids the previous person or rather until no one bids anymore. Of course, there was an unwritten rule. The next bidder should allow the previous man a few minutes dance with the lady. Boys, rather young men would drive to remote places to enjoy this ritual.

It was a chance for socializing in a crowd. Courtship, in some instances could result. All's well that ends well.

There weren't many opportunities for the genders to meet. School. Church. One could pretend to read at the library. Or she remembers their maid would insert love notes of potential suitors between the pages in some of her books. These would eventually end up in the trash bin usually. Nadia believed no one was good enough! And those who met her qualifications were her relatives. She wished she had saved them for historical or bragging purposes.

Families could hold dinners or any such functions when they would invite their friends with an available or appropriate partner for their child. Most of the time, these young people who had known each other from early childhood acted like siblings to the parents' consternation. Therefore, nothing much happened along those lines. Most of the residents of the island were related if one traces blood lines far enough.

Someone once said, this town is full of roots!

Another social activity during these fiestas was presentation of a play. Every barrio or district of the town celebrated their own fiesta at various times of the year such that fiestas were usually a year round event. Basically a celebration to honor a particular saint, their patron saint. People believed a huge celebration was in order to thank for the many blessings received. Like Broadway shows or simple plays, with minimum set decorations. She imagined these were how the Greeks of old would gather to highlight issues for discussion.

In her town, these were just basically for entertainment, to showcase a local talent. Or possibly raise awareness and consciousness of some issues the director wanted to sow in their minds. People would walk distances to watch these plays. One of the best social activities for everyone to enjoy. For free!

A sample of those activities are found in a souvenir program in her file:
Sinakit sa Palad (Hurt by Fate)
Wonderland
Ang Pilipinas Kagahapon ug Karon (The Philippines, Past and Present)
And Pyesta sa Bag-ong Katilingban (Feast in the New Town)
Jeu de Theatre "Blood Compact"
Husto ra, Igo ra (Enough already)
Musical Extravaganza
Ang Babaye sa Karaang Simbahan (The Lady in the Old Church)
Amateur Singing Contest (like American Idol)

Children and adults participated. Because an aunt was one of the directors, Nadia was a child star. She remembers she had to cry for a role she was cast in. But the tears would not flow. Her auntie Denny started screaming at Nadia saying some not so nice words that really made her cry. People mistakenly thought she was a good actress.

Love for the theater, music, and dance was part of their DNA. She continued these pursuits later on as she took her children and husband to various Shakespeare plays, concerts, and Broadway plays in Cleveland, San Francisco, New York, Ashland, wherever they went. Visits anywhere always included an evening at the theater. Though acting was in her parents genetic makeup, she did not have a smidgen of that gift.

Cousin Linda and Marina's children have successfully pursued the arts in music, theater, and the written word. One performed in Broadway, one is a screenwriter in Hollywood, another was the understudy for the male lead role in Miss Saigon when it played in London.

Food. Something everyone always enjoyed, including them. Later on, she exposed her children to various ethnic food where they traveled. The aroma and tastes of various spices woke up her taste buds which were just used to salt, pepper, garlic, onions. The children learned to enjoy Mediterranean, Italian, East Indian, South American cooking.

Their first taste of Ethiopian food was in Washington D.C. and it was very interesting to say the least. One evening at the theater in New York was followed by an unforgettable Middle Eastern meal in a hole-in-the-wall restaurant. The aroma of rosemary, thyme, oregano, special spices, and herbs which they were reluctant to divulge, a trade secret, still lingers in their memories. The lamb steaks and lamb shanks were melt-in-your-mouth smoothly delicious. To this day Andy keeps looking for that restaurant whenever they visit New York.

Years later, a classmate invited her to dinner, asked her to choose either Peruvian or Italian. Italian restaurants were ubiquitous so she chose Peruvian since she had not tasted Peruvian cooking. An upscale restaurant by the sea and so yummy delicious, her classmate jokingly commented later on he made a mistake when he offered those choices.

Of course these later theater and restaurant venues were a far cry from what she had in her childhood. The costumes, the setting, the staging, she wondered how they looked perfectly fitted and so crisp every night.

A very good friend who knew she grew up on an island that was not even in the map remained impressed with her various artistic pursuits.

Some of her patients, seeing photos of her hometown, postcards of white beaches, with coconut trees, and nipa huts, wondered how a little girl like her ended up in America. They wondered why she chose to leave what they thought was tropical paradise? Questions like these, though out of curiosity or appreciation of a great journey, Nadia decided, were an opportunity for educating them. Reminded her of what she thought was a chance she should not waste.

Childhood memories happy or otherwise although easily recalled can change. Despite the seeming lack of material possessions, her mind and heart were filled with love. This did not mean hearing "I love you" all the time. It was all about "feeling", knowing, and understanding I love you all the time. There were many happy times. Long bicycle rides to her uncle's orchard to pick *sineguelas, iba, mangos.* No one else was allowed first pick of the crop until she came. Snack times after school from another auntie who lived down the street who would cook her favorite *guinataan* knowing she would visit. And her instincts just like everybody else were always insisting. She could smell the ripe fruits or the delicious desserts.

Though not used to touching and caresses, these kindnesses, were her mental and emotional lessons of love. Because they anticipated what her needs and enjoyments were.

*Expect the most wonderful things to happen,
not in the future but right now.*

EARLY SCHOOLING

"Andy, remember this is the oldest church in Asia. The many religious irreplaceable valuable artifacts are carefully catalogued and safely guarded in a museum in one of the rooms. My uncle Tom pays for the maintenance of the museum. There's Nanay, Tatay, Auntie Bev, cousins Connie, Aunt Lyd posing outside. The building exterior shows black spots from dust hovering between the stone blocks, which become soiled so that birds could drop some seeds there and with the rains like a sprinkling can, green things sprout."

Memories of childhood come up once in a while. Mother Aure was a first grade teacher. She would take Nadia to class with her. Called "visitor". Sort of her preschooling. And she did well, concentrated on everything the teacher said, absorbed all she heard. Amazing that this three year old could maintain her attention to the lessons during the class.

Every child's brain is a blank canvas, soft as play doh. It is the parents' responsibility to choose which seeds of knowledge are sown and spread or molded. She was curious enough to allow all this information to be painted on her blank canvas. Halfway through that school year, Aure went on maternity leave. The substitute teacher, Lisa was given a dilemma. Lisa decided she had to promote Nadia to second grade at year end. Her reasoning being, if she was not promoted to second grade, then the rest of the class couldn't be promoted, either. To Nadia's mother's consternation.

So she moved on to the higher grades. Would her young age create problems?

A classmate remembers her being given lots of "time outs" for being talkative. Another added that she would lead others on wild adventures during recess and be late for the next session.

One school subject was gardening, where each student was allotted a plot to plant whatever one fancied. Some students had green thumbs, their plants flourished while hers did not. One recess time, she and her friends went there, to the productive plots, pulled the thriving plants destroying half of their garden.

On that occasion, they were late for class. The teacher was her father. And he had heard of the havoc in the gardens, knew that she was one of the culprits. He was going to make an example on discipline out of her. She was made to stand in front of the class. And confess what she had done. The others remained quiet, fearing they would be next. But her father disciplined her alone. For he knew that she was the leader. Besides, his wife, Nadia's mother, certainly would not complain?

She was the peer who was creating havoc, sounds like. She must have had a reputation. Bright, intelligent but naughty. Was that the image the teachers expected of her siblings?

But she was really just immature.

Her mother was the 7th of 11 children. Five boys and six girls. Everyone was educated. All the men left the island to make their fortune elsewhere, mostly in Manila. All the women stayed on the island. They moved within one to five kilometers of their birth home. Growing up, she had many role models for different relationship behaviors and parenting styles. Although she did not do any research while growing up, these observations were ingrained into her subconscious, what with so many cousins to keep company as her peers.

There was an older, blind man, Jesse, who she thought was one of the uncles. He lived in the maternal grandparents' home. Turns out, he was the oldest cousin. His mother died at childbirth when she developed a disease which causes blindness to the child being delivered. She spent a lot of time with him fascinated by how he lived so happily despite his obvious handicap. He had the gift of music. Could play any musical instrument. Owned a guitar, a harmonica, violin, ukelele, banjo, mandolin, trumpet. He also had a Victrola. He taught her how to sing and they would sing together.

Most importantly, he could read and write Braille and so Nadia learned to read and write Braille.

Every Friday, they would gather in one auntie's house for dinner. These would be easy walks in the dark or on moonlit nights. Lots of foolishness along the way as were the ways of the young cousins. Dark nights would create various silhouettes and shadows, some looking like tombstones. A tree with a convoluted trunk and branches was the subject of many stories. The locals perpetuated the myth that these trees were enchanted, hence everyone avoided passing there at night. Yelling and screaming as they proceeded trying to scare each other seemed hilarious at the time.

Topics on whatever issues were concerning during the week would be discussed and the adults decided on options to proceed, the solutions, so to speak. Children were expected to perform. Recite a poem, sing a song, dance, or do whatever one wanted, or was able to do. Praise and competition with rewards in the form of a gift of money were given for special performances. As a young girl, she felt awkward, skinny, and totally unattractive, but these evening sessions taught her that the mind is a beautiful thing. Intelligence matters. The gifts were just small coins but to a child, this meant a great journey down the corner candy store.

Her mother had very good instincts, was usually persistent and sometimes annoying. She remembers her mother leading the weekly discussions with the aunts though there were two older sisters. And they listened to her because Aure was the smartest among the siblings, she heard from relatives later on. Her wish was to be a lawyer, however she could not pursue that dream. Resources were allocated to the men first. The female's place was in the home. She became a teacher. And one of her brothers became a lawyer. This brother and sister had a very close relationship, understood their strengths and weaknesses. Relied and trusted each other and their instincts. She became his counsel in common sense. Like a press relations officer.

She married another teacher. And they taught in the local elementary school.

As young ladies, an incident regarding palmistry was a story handed down the older generations. Nadia learned later and it went this way.

Turbaned traveling merchants came to town, walking down the narrow unpaved lanes. One of them saw the five ladies and wanted to sell them some of their wares and trinkets. Or thought whatever ideas come to men when they see ladies. However there is always safety in numbers.

How to get the attention of these ladies?

The men tried to impress them by reading their palms. One of them told Nadia's mother she had money in her hands, that was the good news, she would amass some wealth. Everyone was thrilled. The bad news, she would witness her youngest brother die. Of course nobody believed any of these, just an episode for laughter and jokes, were easily dismissed as nonsense.

Their Catholic hearts told them so.

Nevertheless through the years, her parents were able to prosper. Through hard work, good financial common sense, patience, and persistence.

She remembers days spent harvesting coconuts. Someone is hired to climb the very tall trees, separate the fruits from the trunk, drop them to the ground. Then men on the ground gather the fallen fruits into a pile.

They are fruits of a species of palm trees, different in the sense that they contain a large quantity of water. The husk is fibrous, covering a hard shell within which is white meat. The mature coconut has solid meat and less water. Once the mature coconuts are harvested, the husks are removed. The shell is broken with its attached meat, then kiln dried.

The shell is sold for charcoal and years later, she saw her father cut them into various shapes. He would use them for his handicraft class as the students create purses, place mats, hats.

The dried meat is sold to be processed for oil and wax. Some of the coconut white meat was shredded for baking purposes. This was all done in the capital city, Tagbilaran. During these times, her mother would do her shopping at the huge market.

The immature coconut has meat that is jelly like and sweet which together with the contained water makes for a very refreshing cool summer drink. They enjoyed some of these young coconuts as cool refreshments in the summer heat, when they would shave the fresh juicy meats, add water, and ice. Many times they did not have to add sugar. They were really that sweet.

Many of the young men and women would picnic (*nilamaw*) in some of these coconut groves. An excuse to get together.

Farming was her first science experiment for they also had a plantation of seasonal crops including corn, sweet potatoes, cassava, and her hometown's famous purple yams, a delicacy. She would walk or ride her bicycle the three kilometer distance to their farm thru a dirt path in the forests. Vegetation was lush. She regrets not considering a keener observation of the various types of shrubs along the way. However she remembers stopping to harvest the abundant guava fruits, available to anyone.

The purpose of her visits to the farm was to watch the men plant and harvest the crops. It was her connection to mother earth.

Watch the oxen dragging plows. Or, as her son Maurice commented on one of their visits, "look at the cow pulling the man".

These workers did their job with much joy and despite the ever-present sweltering tropical sun, they would work, share jokes, loud laughter erupts. With the back of their hands, they would wipe the sweat off their foreheads. There was so much laughter and camaraderie unimaginable in the many stories she read later on among the unhappy and bitter Negro slaves, Mexican workers, and Asian slave railroad workers in America. What a difference living the simple life filled with faith, hope, and contentment makes.

She did not have a specific chore to do. She would spend time in the kitchen, made herself useful to the cook. Was allowed to cut simple round onions. Cut diagonally, horizontally, or minced for various dishes. What difference does it make? Would the dish really taste any differently? The pungent smell not just lingering in her hands, but a stimulus to her tear glands. Cut vegetables. Moving closer to the stove, for she loved the feel of the steam caressing her face. To the laundress, by helping her hang the clothes on the clothesline. Picking up kindling, watering the plants in their planters. Her parents were emphatic.

"Your job is to study!"

She also made herself useful by carrying drinking water in coconut shell bowls with long handles to the sweat-drenched farmers. To the parched throats of the farm workers, she must have been a vision of delight. A reciprocal gift of a homemade sweet dessert would suddenly arrive at her home from any of them. A show of appreciation. An inherent quality of goodness in them.

Maybe she was really meant to perform some sort of service to her fellow men.

To prepare for the next season's crops, the workers would cut the purple yams and sweet potatoes. She gleefully looked forward to these days and watched with much anticipation every process made as the women cut them. In her child's eye, she could not see how those little white and purple pieces could produce bags of produce. But she was not inquisitive enough yet to study agriculture and its nuances, her mind was just a blank page in that category. The irregular pieces that were left were made into yummy *dis dis* (pies) and, salivating, she impatiently waited for them to be fully cooked and ready to eat.

Of course there were bananas, avocados, and jackfruits which were sold at the market.

So as the years went by, with the income from their labors, her parents were able to send their four children to private high schools and private university. One foretold palm reading fulfilled.

How do you like to go up in a swing Up in the air so blue
"Oh, I do think it the pleasantest thing ever a child can do"

Robert Louis Stevenson

BERTO

"That's my Aunt Bev's commercial bus, painted with many colorful advertisements on the sides, the other side quoting Bible verses."

Aunt Denny was the artist in her mother's family. Besides the dramatic arts, she was a seamstress. Nadia would spend many lazy days hanging out in her aunt's house, observing her sewing, fascinated by her use of various color threads, and incorporated designs, called embroidery. She did not hesitate to ask for a new dress with fancy embroidery, believing in the precept, ask and it shall be given unto you. She was married, however, she and Uncle Augie did not have any children. All of the nieces and nephews were their children.

Her house was about a kilometer away. People came and went through her door, customers with their various clothing orders. Besides, aunt Denny was also the politician in her family hence they came to her with their proposals or complaints. She must have been very good at diplomacy. Everyone who came, left with smiles on their faces. Mission accomplished.

She remembers riding in her Aunt Bev's bus as she joined the campaigning from barrio to barrio. Speeches, cheers, singing, clapping, fun stuff. None of the confettis and balloons she saw at political campaigns in the USA. She was an advocate for children's education and the arts, she never lost an election. After all, the townspeople remembered and enjoyed her theatrical productions.

Across from Aunt Denny's house was a water pump. The place was always full of people with their buckets, pails, gallon containers. Nadia would sit under the pomegranate tree in her yard while eating the delicious seeds watching the many people gathered at the well. And wherever people gathered, there would be stories told, everyone engaged in deep conversations. Their never-ending babble sounded like ducks quacking. She tried to remember most of them, kept in her memory bank. Apparently Elsa had another of her "shows" last night. This teenager's body would do wild contortions some evenings. They had brought in many doctors, quack doctors, priests, massagers. They used various leaves to fan out whatever possessed her. Used different oils and salves to no avail. They prayed the rosary every evening to prevent the "show". To no avail. Nadia was so curious, she went with her cousins one evening to see what was happening.

A large crowd had already gathered, spilling out from the small house into the street. People were praying the rosary. However, farther from the crowd were groups of boys and girls laughing out loud, imitating Elsa's contortions. They did not mean to be cruel, just being silly. One of the passages of youth. Nadia climbed up a tree so she could witness, sitting on one of the branches, for a better view of the actions in the home. Everyone there were so much taller. What was happening inside was whispered to those outside, sharing the information. In retrospect, this was like the child described in the book she later read "When the Spirit Catches you and you fall down". Epilepsy!

Aunt Denny was also a midwife.

She helped Aure deliver Nadia's brother Berto at home.

Nadia remembers the day. She was sitting on the front stoop with Rolando and Sylvia, holding hands, consoling each other. The adults were busy upstairs and the children heard their footsteps, not pacing, but racing, as they moved around. They heard voices but were unable to understand what they were saying. All they knew was that their mother was being taken care of by Aunt Denny. They were not allowed inside the house, had no idea what was happening. Imagined several scenarios, all seemingly not ending well. She took her brother and sister to the chapel by their home. They should ask Mother Mary help for their mother.

One decade of the rosary was enough for Sylvia. She was getting irritable. Between their house and the chapel was a *chico* (sapodilla) tree. There were fruits. Sylvia wanted to pick some to eat, was told they were not ripe yet, however she was insistent. Strong minded girl even then. Picked one, she cut it, took a bite, then realized her mistake. Back to the stoop, they sat and watched four women washing by the well talking and laughing out loud creating a little diversion for them.

Upstairs, Nadia continued to hear all the women busily moving from one room to another as well as to the kitchen. She had no idea what was going on until she heard a baby screaming. Aunt Denny claimed, this baby came out into the world kicking so hard. A fighter. Had the loudest yell, must have great lungs. She did not have to tap his bottom. A preview of things to come.

She and her siblings were just relieved their mother was okay. However the stars might have been misaligned at his birth or on the day of his birth.

His name was Berto. He became the youngest child. Handsome, everybody's pet. Underwent all the physical, mental, and emotional development at the expected phases of his growth. He was a lovable, handsome little boy. Shortly her mother went back to teaching. The older children had been going to school too, leaving Berto alone with the nanny.

Every night before dinner the family would sit in their rattan rocking chairs in the front porch, her parents resting after their long day at school. People would pass by on their way to the night market, stop by for a polite conversation with them.

Once Berto learned to talk, he pointed to a man on the street he called his "daddy". Early in his talking phase, he was already a trouble maker. His parents realized this man passing by the house and his nanny were lovers and would come to the house while they were gone. A source of many jokes and laughters. When the cat is away, the mouse will play.

The house help were treated as members of the family. They lived with them day and night. They left when they married and had children of their own or until death.

There are no secrets with children around.

The world says "the more you take, the more you have,"
Christ says the more you give, the more you are.

Frederick Buechner

SYLVIA

"Intramuros is a walled city in Manila which was a Spanish fort in the past. Well maintained, now a favorite tourist spot. There's Michael, his wife and cousins getting a tour of the place. There's your aunt Connie's business building where we had fine dining in an adjacent restaurant."

Sylvia was everybody's darling. She was chubby, cherubic, always smiling, everyone thought she was an angel. People would inadvertently hurt her sister's feelings when they would look at her, pinch her cheeks, oohh and aahh, how cute.

Then look at sister Nadia, so skinny to the point of emaciation, with the look "what happened to her, maybe she has parasites or has tuberculosis". At least that is how she interpreted their looks. She thought of the ways they were compared. Chubby, cherubic is only good in youth. Fat is the right word for an adult. Never lost her baby fat. Very intelligent. Did not want to go to the same school Nadia went to. Did not like the comparison. She claimed their parents asked her to stay home for companionship.

Really? No one could confirm this.

She did not want to go to medical school because Nadia was in one. Chose engineering instead. But there are no letters after one's name as an engineer. So she proceeded to take her masters and PhD in business management to add those letters. She eventually retired from the National Electric Company of the Philippines. Married a dashing, sexy seaman (Rolando's words) and had her only child early in their marriage. He had the connections in the marine world, but she had the verbal skills.

Together they developed a flourishing ship manning enterprise. She was the President and CEO. Don't ask how that came about. Just like Berto, Nadia did not know her well enough. Was able to acquire properties but was not happy. Outwardly, she was a very successful person, according to relatives.

However, material wealth was not enough. Love and success were not enough. There was still a hunger in her soul.

At a casual conversation with a friend priest about the Marcoses during their prime, he claimed they were guilty of the worst sin "greed".

"Why is that so? Why is greed the worst?" Nadia asked Monsignor Ricardo.

Because unlike the other deadly sins, there is no outward consequence to greed. No prosecution unlike the external consequences of wrath, pride, lust, envy, sloth or gluttony. Violence and obesity can result. The only consequence of greed is emotional turmoil. Greed just gnaws on the emotional, mental state regardless how much wealth or "friends" they surround themselves with.

She eventually decided to move to the US with the help of her sister Nadia however Sylvia conveniently forgot the grace this was provided her.

Ungrateful!

Nadia had applied for a tourist visa for Sylvia to come to the US, her graduation gift. The petition was immediately denied. Reason was:

Sylvia was a professional, was unmarried. The US embassy believed she would compete with the local Americans for whatever jobs and young men were available. And marry an American. So Nadia filed an application for an immigrant status, the application was approved several years later with Sylvia already married with two children. Nadia thought Sylvia, already a successful business person in the Philippines would not pursue this route. After all, life in the Philippines for those financially well off was far better than living in America. However to Nadias' surprise Sylvia begged her to provide supporting documents, meaning, financial information on her and Andy. This was to proclaim to the US Immigration Office that the applicant will never be a financial burden to the country. That Sylvia had relatives who promised to support them!

How huge of a responsibility was this?

Opening up one's financial resources for everyone to see. To support a family of three. She was reluctant, however Sylvia was relentless in her pursuit and Andy, the kind, practicing Catholic, was more charitable. Nadia capitulated. My, how times have changed and a huge mistake Nadia made. She is now living with much regrets.

Still she was reluctant, engaged in many discussions with Andy. After all, the reason why she invited Sylvia to move to the USA no longer existed. She was married, retired chemical engineer, and they had a thriving business, earning dollars while expenses were paid in pesos. The exchange rate then was $1 for 50 pesos. Sylvia was unstoppable, and persistent in her pursuit of Nadia, her sister's financial documents, they finally obliged. They should share their blessings is one precept their parents raised them with.

Andy's upbringing was just as good if not better than hers. He had a brother priest, and an uncle priest. He was more charitable in helping Sylvia than her. He claimed having a relative, especially a sister near them would be a bonus to their children who had not been exposed for long expanses of time to relatives. This was just speculation on Andy's part. Nadia did not hear Sylvia talk about her plans for where they would reside in the US.

Nadia's children's exposure to living with relatives, were only on occasional month long vacations to the Philippines. Her children would finally witness how Filipino families lived, with their cultural and Catholic traditions. Witnessing is always better than plain talking about them. Like greeting an older relative, reaching for their hand to kiss with either the forehead or lips, a blessing. Akin to kissing or hugging in America. Respect for elders. Sylvia was always invited to join Nadia's family celebrations.

Was Nadia mistaken. Great expectations, that was.

She only knew Sylvia had been approved to immigrate to the US when she received a phone call one spring day. Apparently, they had been living in the USA for six months already. Did not even inform Nadia of their intention to live far away in New Jersey. Of course this was understandable, she wanted to live near her daughter, however, the intent should have been communicated.

Sylvia was in tears, begged Nadia to let her and her son live with them because the situation did not work out in New Jersey, her choice to live understandably. Her married daughter resided there. She could not get along with her son-in-law, a clue to her character.

Apparently, the plan was for Sylvia's son to attend college in the USA. Without taking the SATs! The brother in law was not cooperative to the plan. Dictated household orders to her son. Sylvia believed her son was verbally and emotionally abused by Brian. She did not trust her daughter's choice of a husband. Or was she overprotective of her son?

She believed that now that she had come to the U S. she did not need Nadia anymore so she just located to New Jersey. Nadia, throwing caution to the wind, ignored this character flaw of Sylvia. But now what else could she do but beg her sister again.

How is it that Sylvia never learned the same lessons that was part of the territory one gets from experience or heard from one's elders. A red signal Nadia failed to recognize. Naive? She was too trusting, the Catholic girl she was, thinking her sister would cling to the same values their parents raised them on. So, she allowed Sylvia and her son to stay with them.

Within one week, Nadia was able to enroll Sylvia's son at a local college. She noticed, the son was very dependent. Unable to make decisions. Sylvia made decisions for him. Even purchased school supplies for her college son! These issues they could not accomplish during their six month stay with her daughter and son-in-law in New Jersey.

She left, not divorced, her husband, to fend for himself in the Philippines. He managed to build his business but she continued to live in the US.

When asked why she lived in the US, she would say "so I can live the best of both worlds". Said with both hands up in the air, grinning as wide as the Atlantic ocean, body swaying like doing the jitterbug. Very social. She is very active in the Opus Dei movement, which seems ironic considering the life she is living.

But does one really know what is in the hearts of couples? Just like Berto, Nadia did not really know her sister. She just noticed Sylvia was "needy" and a bean counter, able to manipulate everyone else.

Her cousin and favorite relative Connie, once asked "how does she do that?" However, everyone had become enablers blindingly following their Catholic upbringing.

Teenagers and young adults know their ways.

Nadia remembers how heavenly it was for her and Andy to sit down after dinner or on lazy weekend afternoons listening to their children play the piano, the clarinet, and the saxophone. Sometimes Maya would play the violin, Michael play his guitar, and Maurice play the drums. But those happened when they were very young. Later as they grew older they could not be persuaded to "perform" together.

However Sylvia would just say one word and her college son would play the piano, not a great player, but passable. Not a passionate piano player who is really enjoying but giving in to an order. Now that Nadia had a chance to know her sister, the adjectives became: selfish, ungrateful, showoff, social climber. Although to non-family members, she seemed joyful.

How did she turn up that way?
Or were Nadia's expectations of her sister too great and unreasonable?
How could they be polar opposites, night vs day, south vs north.
After all they were raised by the same set of parents.
Sylvia must have heard the same conversations about values, responsibilities, discipline, consequences, respect, tradition, she heard ingrained into her consciousness.

When Sylvia and her son first lived with her, they had unrestricted use of Andy's computer. However, they lived as though they were house guests.

No offer to help with the housework!
No offer to do groceries.
No offer to cook.
Not even to wash the dishes.
Just stayed in their bedroom or in the library to use the computer.

She started "blogging" about everything in her life, every day? Week? Sending it through the internet to everyone she knew including all relatives. It became tiresome after a while. Nadia was not in her blog list. However, she heard from relatives. Everyone else were getting annoyed with her "bloviating". She thinks Sylvia was trying to prove something. What?

Maybe like the cigarette ads that touts her success "look at me now". Someone must have commented on this issue because she shortened her recipient list.

Then came Facebook.

A picture is really worth a thousand words. She really toots her own horn. Nadia was embarrassed for her. Sylvia was blogging about issues Nadia thought were hopelessly unimpressive and inconsequential. Besides, Nadia so much despises a person who blows her own horn.

For some reason Sylvia's viciousness did not surprise her, she had hints of the trait in her childhood. But when or where, or how something happened to her she has to figure that out yet.

Change comes without invitation and often brings loss and sorrow along. She should treat Sylvia with the calm that comes after the storm. She knows Sylvia is very generous when it comes to aiding priests and nuns. Like she is buying or paying off a debt.

If the end brings me out all right,
What is said against me will not amount to anything

Abraham Lincoln

ROLANDO

"Your Dad took some American doctor's to see a cockfight at your Uncle's arena one day. Harry was uncomfortable, saying, the roosters don't have a choice, one of them will die."

Her younger brother Rolando was tall, good looking, a gentleman, a good catch. All the young ladies in town were longing for his attention. The envy of the other young men. He spent his high school years at the Trade School in the capital city. Very intelligent.

Years later, Maurice commented on the fact, he did not see any ugly person in Panglao!

Rolando wanted to be a priest, however the local parish priest was not a good model for priesthood. He delivered long boring homilies, a thunderer of ferocious sermons, the fire and brimstone sort. Listening to the priest made Nadia think the saints in heaven must have been rolling their eyes.

And there was no positive energy. He did not have programs for the youth or the community. Of course there were cathechetical classes for a few hours at the church during summer. All about the do's and don'ts.

Life in the spirit was slacking, dull, slow like the occasional slow tide rise. Her brother thought this was not the kind of life he wanted.

He decided to be an engineer.

So he was sent to Manila, to the University of Santo Tomas for mechanical engineering, where Nadia was already enrolled at the College of Medicine. However life in the big city was luring him into the fun life, movies, hanging out with friends. The country mouse easily gets lost when brought to the city. So many places to go, movie houses to choose from, new friends to make. She was too busy with her own struggles to notice what was happening to Rolando until years later when Sylvia related this story which she believes happened.

Her father was a man of few words. Action speak louder then words. Nadia did not remember him being upset with Rolando, except that one particular evening with her yearbook. He had one vice, cockfighting on Sunday mornings after attending mass. Apparently, Tibo learned about Rolando's life in the city and would no longer allow him the kind of life he was leading. He sent him a letter.

The letter said "If I could pack my closed fist in this envelope, you would have been knocked out already".

Nadia discovered her father had a flair for drama.

"Why did Tatay (father) send Rolando that letter?" Nadia had never received a letter from her father.

"Did he really". She verified with her mother this circumstance.

"Tradition" was her answer. "The tradition in this family is that one goes to school to learn and complete the education."

Rolando realized he needed to pay more attention, transferred to maritime school.

He always loved the sea. The embryo of an idea to be a seaman started in his youth. Her parents arranged to have him live with a fisherman in his home. He did not mind this situation. In fact, he enjoyed the fisherman's meals and later insisted that their, mother, Aure should provide the same food at home. It consisted of bran. A healthier alternative that the poor ate, hence they had lean healthy bodies, because of all those antioxidants in their diet.

A fisherman is someone who captures fish for recreation or commercial purposes. No one in her island was a recreational fisherman.

The life of a fisherman is very challenging. They wake up very early in the morning, in the cold, in the dark, to go to sea and wait for the fishes to bite, or to check on the fishing nets they had laid the night before. Dealing with rain, which usually starts slow, then with unexpected ferocity, in the middle of the deep sea, was not unusual. If the catch was bountiful, the fisherman would go to the capital city market. There were two bridges connecting her island to the capital. A certain notorious family would exact a toll on these poor fishermen before they could cross. They had no choice. After a few days of this kind of life, her brother wanted to come home. He still loved the sea, was going to have life in the sea but not as a fisherman.

He was most like their father, silent waters run deep. He enjoyed and did his best in maritime school. Finally found his calling. And graduated with honors after two years. Was to receive several medals.

This was the time Nadia was doing her internship, a very busy and exhausting time. Although she wanted to and was excited for her brother to graduate with honors, she could not attend his graduation. So sad, she missed a great evening for her brother. One of their cousins, a journalist, gorgeous, and very attractive, volunteered to do the honors of pinning the many ribbons and awards he received. Rolando's physical prowess with ladies was enhanced that evening. Picture the many admiring and envious glances Rolando's classmates had for her and very impressed that Rolando had a gorgeous girlfriend. His glorious evening ended wonderfully after all.

Soon after graduation, he worked with various shipping companies with flags from many different nations. He commanded assorted freight ships loaded with diverse cargoes and docked in ports worldwide. Rolando was easily moving up the ladder of management eventually retiring as Captain of the merchant marine.

The movie Tom Clancy's "Hunt for Red October" is one of Nadia's favorites because of the visuals it provided about the pathways underneath the waters, enabling her to imagine her brother's adventures. She is not equating him to some great submarine navigator. All she is saying is she thought of boating and the seas as just one romantic endeavor. Not the danger of the many deep ridges one had to go around. Remembering the Titanic, many possible icebergs are additional hazards.

He would tell of his anxiety for piracy during travels in the Arabian seas. For there was a distinct possibility that the nature of the cargo might not necessarily be what was in the bill of lading. It could have been illegal and he would have to answer for it if the unauthorized cargo was discovered upon inspection. She learned it was not a glamorous life after all. They just look so dashing in their uniforms though.

He was earning dollars while she was a struggling young doctor without any salary.

Great spirits have always encountered violent opposition from mediocre minds!

Albert Einstein

BIRTH ORDER

"It was a rainy day. We could not go anywhere. My cousins bet as to who was brave enough to stand in the rain. I did. That photo is proof."

Nadia was the oldest, with three siblings.

There are many theories touting certain personality traits. Some of those are: birth order, whether the child continues to live in the home or not, the spacing, as well as the number of children. Psychological development is not static. The mind continually grows and soaks up information from every encounter. Fascinated by every new exposure.

Likewise personality development is continuous, influenced by the competing demands of the parents' socialization and work. Thus sibling relationships can also change.

True to some theories, she was conscientious, assertive, and maybe even obsessive.

She left home at age twelve for high school. To attend St Joseph academy, also called College of the Holy Spirit, in the capital city of Tagbilaran. Located seventeen kilometers, a mere 15 minute drive away. She never understood the reasoning her parents followed. There was a high school in her hometown, run by the Catholic church, tuition was much less expensive than where they sent her. In addition, there was an additional cost for board and lodging.

However one can surmise their thoughts. Being in the capital city meant exposing their daughter to many more cultural events, making different groups of friends. Living with the nuns might change their daughter's less than feminine attributes, make her demure. Then they sent her off to Manila for college and postgraduate education. Even though there was a medical school in the nearby island of Cebu.

Tagbilaran City is the gateway to Bohol, known as the City of Friendship. A hundred years before the Spaniards arrived in the Philippines, this settlement was already trading with Chinese and Malaysians. Initial contact with Spain came in 1565 when Spanish conquistador Miguel Lopez de Legaspi signed a peace treaty with local chief Datu Sikatuna.

Known as the Blood Compact, this Philippine ritual signifies a seal of the bond of friendship. Each participant slices part of their skin, allowing a few drops of blood into a cup of water and wine. Swirled to make sure the contents are completely mingled. The resulting mix is divided into two cups, each party drinking till the last drop.

A Filipino painter depicted the event, El Pacto de Sangre, which won first prize in Paris in 1885 as well as at the Louisiana Purchase Exposition of St. Louis in 1904. A huge bronze sculpture created by a local artist from funds donated by Spain, stands on a beach about 8 kilometers from Tagbilaran at the supposed site of the original blood compact. A monument to the first ever peace treaty between Spain and the natives.

General Miguel Lopez de Legaspi had been sent to trace the route that an earlier explorer Ferdinand Magellan followed. Magellan discovered the Philippines in 1521 but encountered difficulties with a local leader, hence his trip ended in the neighboring island, Cebu.

All these years, away from home, she did not watch her youngest brother Berto and young sister Sylvia grow. He had been an enigma to everyone especially to her. They had no opportunity for one on one conversation. She did not even know what they did in their spare time.

Did not know what they liked to do, did not know what their favorite food was.

Did not really know them.

No sibling interaction with them or sibling relationship with them that usually lasts a lifetime. Berto was seven years her junior, while Sylvia was five years younger than her. Being a teenager, she also had her issues. She missed a lot of everyday kindnesses relatives gave perhaps due to her own teen self absorption. She was also concentrating on what teenagers occupy their time with, rushing off to be with her friends.

We never know how high we are till we are called to rise
And then, if we are true to plan, our statures touch the skies.

Emily Dickinson

HIGH SCHOOL

"That is mom?" The children exclaimed looking at Nadia's high school photo.

At graduation, just like other schools, the College of the Holy Spirit, where Nadia spent her four high school years, printed, and gave each graduate a yearbook. The high school yearbook that she thought she could brag about forever was tucked safely in her backpack. Through years of hard work, her parents would finally see some good results, a written document, proof of what she did during the four years in the girls-only Catholic school they chose for her high school years. The words "Honor Student" were written beneath photos of five students. She was one of the five. "Honor student" meant the top five "brainy" students. The nuns made sure every honor student was just that. No one knew who number one or number five were.

She did not remember really trying to be one of those. She was just plain living life.

She was more interested in life in the city, life away from family, exploring, having fun. There was an outdoor market where one could buy farm fresh fruits. The heavenly aroma of the golden yellow fresh mangoes, the firm green mangoes that made her salivate for the tart flavor she imagined especially when eaten with *bagoong*, the delicious yummy ripe yellow jackfruits, the many different species of bananas. All very pleasing to the senses. There were many green vegetables, but those had to be cooked first, so she ignored them.

The delightful smells of the many cooked foods all within her budget. She could buy a cup of *bachoy, dinuguan* with *puto* or a saucerful of *pancit*, and those would be enough for snack or even lunch.

She noticed many merchants, some with turbans around their head in the open market or bazaar. They talked in a different language completely alien to her ears. A vast array of colorful fabrics with unusual designs, unique patterns, alien to her eyes, hung in their stalls, some thicker than the usual fabrics. Their beauty caused her head to spin in amazement. Like she was Alice in wonderland. The unusual wares which included elaborately designed brass, silver, copper items of various sizes and shapes. Additionally there were various other knick knacks. She loved the shiny brass urns and jars. And knives, swords, machetes, scimitars of various shapes and sizes. It was a good place to entertain herself and dream about all these places where they came from.

Back home, she would look at the globe that was in their library, the room in their house where her father and mother would prepare their lesson plans.

She was also fascinated by the waterfall of their language, something she had never heard before. French? German? Russian? She was familiar with Chinese and Japanese. They were ubiquitous merchants owning many sectors of the town's commercial district.

"So where in the world are they from?" She finally asked her parents.

"Maybe somewhere called India or the Middle East." Her father replied. Her description of the turbans were the giveaway.

"They have traveled so far away from home?
Just to go to market?

After all there were so many oceans, seas, and lands they had to cross."
She commented as she traced those places in the globe.

She was glad they did, otherwise she would not have appreciated those
beautiful pieces of art.

Other lines in the yearbook were for activities the students were involved
in. She was involved in drama (the merchant in the Merchant of Venice
is an example), dance (dance in the moonlight, another example), sports
(was the spiker in volleyball and was very good at the balance beam).

The last line which changed her life forever asked for "ambition".
Whereas everyone wrote "to be a lawyer, to be a nurse, to be a banker,
to be a teacher, to be an engineer, to be a homemaker, (did she just want
to marry and have children?). All the usual career types, she wrote: "to
visit the holy land".

"What?" Her parents were not amused.

"Do you understand the meaning of ambition? Go to the dictionary."
Nadia could sense anger in their voices.

"Where else are you going to visit? Why not the whole world? Why
limit yourself to the holy land?"

How are you going to finance your world travels?"

"No! No, No."

Both her parents were pacing the second floor rooms, at times rubbing
their throbbing temples with the heels of their palms. Thinking, how
on earth does their daughter come up with these ideas. There was no
reasonable discourse, nor any yelling or screaming or hitting. This was
what was worse. The silence, just murmuring, and their body language.
They did not want the neighbors to hear the terror they were giving
their daughter.

"What have we done?" They must have been thinking.

"What sort of fantasy is she engaging in?" Wanting to take her by the ears, take her to a side and tell her a few words of advice.

Her parents spent the whole night discussing this topic, giving Nadia no rest. She never understood what she did wrong. If pouring out her real feelings and wishes were wrong, what was all that talk about honesty, being true to oneself about?

She did not remember thinking the answer to the ambition question through obviously. Did not believe those were her real feelings, she admitted to herself but not to her parents. After all, they taught her to tell the truth not because she would be punished or go to hell, but because it was good by itself.

Don't the young talk off the cuff?

Nadia recalled the piano lessons years earlier were stopped when they heard her talking about being a concert pianist. She thought it would be so much fun traveling from concert hall to concert hall in Europe, the USA, any other country. She really had no idea what kind of life that involved. It just sounded so glamorous. The performers in their formal suits, the ladies in their elegant dresses. One should not distract the audience with such colorful or the most fashionable outfit or with a lot of bling. After all they come to listen to how this particular artist interprets the classic arrangement.

At the very least, her parents who were educators were consistent. They believed in the usual career types. Be professionals like them. Be independent. Not raised to be married off to someone who would support her.

What they heard from her were what they thought were categorized as hobbies, or something fanciful that people with money did for leisure. Like going to the country for the summer. Like what ladies who go to lunch do. More of a cultural endeavor. Not one of service.

Though she had been forced to give up her piano lessons, music was always her recourse in times of anguish or fears.

The lecture lasted the whole night. She was raised not with much touching or caressing and was told not to waste her mind and time on trivial matters.

Wasn't this just tilting at windmills? Was this line that important really?

Usually, Nadia would tell her mother she had itchy scalp so that she would massage her head or brush her hair until she fell asleep. But not tonight. She was too embarrassed to ask. It was not appropriate. Although it might have stemmed the flow of disappointment they were in that night. They did not even notice the category "honor student". She did not hear a single praise for being an "honor student". She remained quiet throughout this whole drama, as though she was in some deep important thought.

Confused and disappointed, she concentrated on options for her plan of action for the morning. She decided to visit the Catholic high school to talk to her favorite teacher nun, the one person who knew her best. The one who spent extra time to coach her in debate, how to be more articulate, lose her accent. Her mental and emotional life raft, so to speak. She who saw the butterfly Nadia could become instead of just concentrating on her cocoon self others saw.

She with the porcelain like skin, bluish green eyes, body covered with the nun's all white habit and black head covering that swayed with the wind as she walked. Nadia always wondered what her hair looked like. Would she have what Jane Austen called "golden hair".

Nadia thought Sister will surely help her. After all, she remembers Sister Ingrid say she thought every problem has a solution.

Sister Ingrid listened intently. After much thinking she said she was sorry her parents were upset.

"Maybe the parents had plans for their daughter?"

"If they had, they never mentioned it." Nadia replied with regret. Or maybe she was not really listening. Unaware of her environment. Selfish with her time, too self absorbed.

"What should I do Sister?"

Sister Ingrid was silent, in deep thought. Then she said, with a twinkle in her eyes, "you don't know much about yourself yet. You could go to university to be a lawyer or a physician or an engineer."

"Wow, how is it that I never thought along those lines."

Sister really made her feel good that she'd think she was capable of doing any of those university studies.

"You were just being creative." Sister Ingrid said.

Or was she just not sensitive to her parents' state of mind? Unobservant of what they had been striving to accomplish. Immature? Selfish? Typical teenager?

Nadia knew numbers were not to her liking so engineering was out of the question. Her one use of addition and subtraction was to track her movements: ten minutes from her home to school, thirty minutes to her Aunt Bev's home, five minutes to church. Longer when walking with friends who slowed down, bodies contorted with the loudest laughs that made their stomachs cramp, or on high traffic days. Her mother wanted to be a lawyer, so maybe she can fulfill her mother's ambition. Being a physician was attractive though. There was no physician in her town. Just two doctors and dentists from out of town who would come and conduct clinics.

Learning about the workings of the human body would be quite an experience. She had observed what happens as people grew older, see their gait change, or lose the suppleness of their skin, wrinkles like ridges appearing on their faces, observe the deformities of their joints such that their shoes won't fit anymore. Change personalities with the season or with the moon cycle. White hairs if they haven't lost them, gums toothless. Lose their balance. She and her cousins would help Grandma Ida up and down the stairs. And Grandpa would sit shaking his hands while sitting in his rocking chair. And she had to repeat or talk loud while she practiced her Spanish lessons with him.

She heard how the locals interpreted such changes as part of some superstition, some food or drink mistakenly taken. Or some forbidden activity done. Or payment for some ancestor's actions.

Never mentioned it was just part of the aging process.

She once wrote an essay that was published in the high school paper titled "The World in a drop of Water" discussing the various organisms and other items when a drop of water was viewed under a microscope.

So maybe science was in her genetic makeup. At the time her parents were very proud. Had a typical celebration with mass and food. Her prize was a missal that she could use at church during mass!

She thought of how she could deliver this message to her parents. Although she felt some inadequacy towards these options, she proceeded armed with the nun's support. She told her surprised parents that she made up her mind.

"I am going to be a doctor. Not a Ph.D. but an M.D. A physician." Nadia declared, hearing something like confidence in her voice.

"How on earth could you come up with such a lofty goal overnight?" Aure and Tibo wondered.

They were concerned she was flighty. Had they been too harsh the previous evening? Had the winds and moon caused the tides to rise so high overnight, such that it washed away the past?

And created a new world overnight?

Over many lunches and dinners for the next several months, her parents invited their healthcare friends. Doctors, nurses, midwives. She realized later that the purpose was to prepare her for the hard, difficult life she was about to embark on although at the time she believed they were trying to scare, or discourage her from pursuing what they believed was a rebellious decision. Even though they had no evidence of this kind of behavior in the past.

Since her parents were educators they made sure she understood what her life would be once she started medical school. Their technique just made her resolve to go to medical school stronger.

Her parents discovered they had raised a strong minded girl. They advised her against it, she could see doubt in their eyes. But after several sleepless nights of her obstinate refusal to change her decision, her parents supported Nadia. There was no MCAT to take. One just had to provide transcripts of her high school record, fill up an application form. To her surprise and her mother's chagrin, she was accepted. So the long difficult journey to prove she had ambition was going to begin.

Like the winds of the sea are the ways of fate,
As we voyage along through life,
'Tis the set of the soul that decides its goal
And not the calm or the strife.

Ella Wheeler Wilcox

INTERISLAND TRANSPORTATION

"So those are the chocolate hills? What are they: They are about 1600 mainly limestone formations in almost symmetrical shapes, covered with green grass that turns brown in the summer hence the name."

Over 7,000 islands make up the Philippines. During her childhood, transportation between the many islands was by air or by passenger ships. For short vacations like Christmas, they used air transport between Manila and Bohol. This lasted one and a half hours. For three-month-long summer vacations they would take the three day boat ride. Her island home was located in the middle of the Philippines, in what is known as the Visayan islands. She did not just live in the large island of Bohol, but in an 18 km-long island connected to Bohol by two bridges. During her university years, twice a year she would take the three day cruise from Bohol to Manila and back. This was the routine for seven years. These ships would be full of young boisterous students. Lots of conversation, singing, reading, bonding with other students. Questions asked of their summer adventures such as:

"What summer adventure did one engage in? Really, you went to Badjang Falls, again?"

"Did one travel? We had relatives visit, so we took them to see the chocolate hills, you know how tedious that long drive is. Wish they could work on those roads."

"My cousin is an Engineer for the National Transportation Agency, and he said money had already been budgeted for road improvements for all of Bohol. Paper documents, show roads are already paved."

"Island hopping? We visited Siquijor island to attend their town fiesta."

"Any love encounters?" "You must be joking. There isn't anybody worth looking into!"

"Any new beauty secrets? Manang Taray said using lemons on your face lightens your complexion and is a good cleanser."

And of course some would flirt. She had a girl cousin who wrote for a magazine titled "True Confessions" and Nadia had access to some of these magazines. The imagination does not have to be extraordinarily stretched to come up with ideas as to the character of these stories. She shared these during the long boat rides and can still remember the resulting howls and giggles. And some would bring these American romantic novels, very explicit with their sexual overtones. More giggles.

We should be less naughty, after all we are in the open sea. We might be punished by evil spirits for our sins. Their Catholic consciences gave them pause.

Although she lived by the sea, she did not know how to swim. These boat rides were sometimes turbulent, the sea could sometimes show its fury with high waves that made the boat sway causing a lot of passengers seasickness. At times, all the blood rushed to her head, she'd feel woozy as though she were falling down a hill. However it must have been her youthful exuberance that allowed her to enjoy these trips without fear.

Or did she really just surrender her life to the Almighty?

There were no cabins in those ships then. Cots were lined side by side with a little space for one's luggages and for the passenger to be able to move around. It was a distinct possibility that one would be lying next to a stranger.

A lot of things could happen in a ship full of hormone-filled young men and women. Most of the girls were not interested, they were determined to complete college. The men, oh well? No harm could come to them regardless what they did. Raised in a place where their days were timed by the ringing of church bells for early morning mass, noon, and evening Angelus, nothing happened with her along those lines. Besides, she was tomboyish so she treated boys as friends. In fact she was more comfortable talking with the boys. She had no concept of beauty secrets, which was the subject of most girls conversations. She sometimes thought she was not meant to be a girl. Her parents raised her in the ways of wisdom and led her and her siblings in the right path.

Besides, she had a job to do. Prove she had ambition. There was no time to waste on silly dalliances. And her Catholic heart was fearful of actions that may come back to haunt her in the future. It is amazing how fear changes one's attitude.

For every joy that passes, something beautiful remains

Anonymous

COLLEGE

"That's Aure and Nadia after graduation ceremonies in the packed auditorium. Who is that guy behind you?"

Ferdinand Magellan discovered the Philippines in 1521. This started the beginning of Spanish influence, and later on colonization. Subsequent Spanish explorer Ruy Lopez de Villalobos named it Las Islas Filipinas in honor of King Phillip II of Spain. Spanish rule brought political unity and Roman Catholic missionaries converted inhabitants to Christianity.

They founded schools, a university, and hospitals. By the time she was a university student, the Dominicans ran the University of Santo Tomas.

The priests were tall, elegant, handsome, their tonsures well trimmed. Tonsures are no longer the norm now. They had a serious contemplative demeanor. They held a book, a rosary, a crucifix in the palm of their hand and on campus, everyone who met them kissed their hand, which they voluntarily extended. They walked all around the campus, like policemen.

The University of Santo Tomas (UST) was a private school, established in 1611; the College of Medicine was founded in 1871. The complete name is the Pontifical and Royal University of Santo Tomas, the Catholic University of the Philippines. It was visited by two Popes three times, Pope Paul VI in 1970 and Pope John Paul II in 1981 and 1995. Four Philippine presidents were graduates: Manuel L. Quezon, Sergio Osmena, Jose Laurel, and Diosdado Macapagal. The national hero, Jose Rizal underwent his schooling there too.

The university started female enrollees in 1927.

"Why can't I go to the University of the Philippines?" Nadia asked her mom. It was a public institution, hence not much of a financial drain to her parents, but they insisted UST is where she was going. They wanted an environment that would be like home. Indeed! Though it was coeducational, men and women did not mix during classes. Stairs and hallways were designated for women or men only. The genders could gather only in the auditorium for special lectures.

UST had a beautiful verdant campus surrounded by walls with gates in each. An arch stood at the main entrance. Trees full of leaves and well-tended shrubs enhanced the beauty of the campus. The cathedral with a tower was located by the west gate. The seminary school for advanced theological studies was behind the church. The talented young seminarians were enrolled there. Many different level buildings were spread across the campus.

She was admitted to the two-year premedical studies and eventually the four-year medical studies. This was followed by a one-year internship. During this phase they rotated to various specialty hospitals like the Orthopedic Hospital and the Maternity and Children's hospital. Most of her internship months were done at the University hospital.

Brother Rolando was an engineering student. Their building was located at the southeast corner of campus whereas the medical building was northeast. Once on campus, she saw him smoking.

No one smoked at home. Her father did not. His only vice was cockfighting, every Sunday, after mass, to her mother's ire. Full of anger at what he was doing, Nadia walked to her brother across campus to reprimand him when suddenly a priest appeared, would not believe this man she was talking with was her brother.

She was in trouble.

Her parents made sure she stayed at dormitories run by nuns, very strict, rigid. Times were regulated for study periods, meals, attendance at mass. She believed her obligation was to be at school, not to wake up at six o-clock in the morning to attend mass. Every morning the sisters would lift her mosquito net and ring a small bell close to her ears. She had a cousin priest, her mentor, who was at theology school at UST. He became her cheerleader, reassured her about her ordeals with the nuns. He counseled her to be patient. This too shall pass.

Happily, Nadia was able to persuade her mother to allow her to transfer to another dormitory the following year. The one across the campus was one run by a different religious order. At the new dorm, the nuns were more understanding of the students' schedules and did not insist on mass attendance. They only reported to her cousin priest that Nadia was a "heretic".

Although she stayed at these dormitories, a certain pattern emerged in her college life. Her lawyer uncle with his wife and three unmarried children lived about an hour away. He had a ranch split-level house with a wide open living room, a music room, library, office, dining room, kitchen, bathroom and three bedrooms on the marble first floor. A Japanese style bridge connected the living room to one bedroom. Adjacent to this was a grotto shaded by a mango tree. Under the bridge was a dry creek. Four additional large bedrooms were located on the second floor.

Wonderful Philippine antiques furnished the entire house, in addition to whatever fancy caught her uncle in his world travels. Crates would arrive following his trips. Windows were mostly glass with fancy iron rails. It was a two-acre walled compound with armed guards.

Two other buildings were within. His married sons lived in the compound. In one corner was a *nipa* hut, which became Nadia's favorite place. It was cool inside, and was located beneath an acacia tree.

The routine was: her older lady cousin would pick her up from the dormitories friday evenings, Nadia would stay with them for the weekend, then the same cousin would take her back to the dormitory on Sunday evenings. Just like the wild beasts in Africa, tired after long treks for food or fighting with other animals, who find a place of rest, a little corner with shade, Nadia's uncle and his family provided her such a place and time for relaxation. The entire weekend was for fun: attending social functions at their corporate offices, going to the movies, playing the piano, relaxing.

Her aunt was very generous, made Nadia feel like her own, a lifestyle that gave Nadia a glimpse into the life of the privileged. However it was her cousin *Ate* Norma who provided this service. Without *Ate* Norma's patience, Nadia would not have enjoyed that kind of life.

However this lifestyle did not allow her times to share with her classmates, to bond with them. Did not allow her to join organizations of students with common interests. The only friends she had were the roommates as well as other girls who lived in the dormitories. Most of them were young and silly, and they made her laugh. She read somewhere it is good to have friends who have nonsense in their veins. Because according to a French philosopher, Henri Bergson, laughter moisturizes the soul, a momentary anesthesia. Clearing the head follows. This routine allowed her to be ready for the next week's challenges.

The fifth year of medical school was called "internship" when they rotated through various specialty hospitals to hone the skills they learned from books in classes. Direct patient care was the new order.

One morning, there was a lot of commotion in the dormitory. Jumping out of her mosquito net and still groggy, out she went with the others to the hallway. Some girls were crying. Someone had killed the US President John F. Kennedy.

Her reality of the US President was what most of the young girls had: Jacqueline Kennedy. With the gorgeous, gracious elegance she easily carried, they wanted to look like her. Everybody tried, but the copycats were just that. This news made her reexamine who JFK really was.

He was one who was young, "cool", and exuded loads of hope and promise. He brought out the good in everyone. He did what the nuns and priests taught: to help others. To be brought down by a bullet during one's prime was easy for her to fear the danger out there, feel anger and anxiety. But the message she was hearing from his family was to continue to be kind and to reach out to others. That it was okay to dream. It was okay to care. It was okay to wonder. It was okay to share. These were difficult messages to understand. The other messages she got were that everybody had a responsibility to help make the world a better place.

Too difficult to imagine under these circumstances. And that day was imprinted in everyone's minds. People would know the answer to "where were you or what were you doing when JFK was assassinated?"

To graduate from medical school, one had to take the final exams called revalida. The candidate faces a tribunal of three professors. Up to this point she doesn't remember writing a thesis or debating seriously. And she was never a serious, studious student. She remembers these traumatic, anxiety filled days. She never prayed so much until these days. Everyone prays: to pass an exam, win the lottery, or for any material acquisition. She prayed not just to pass the exam, but to be granted wisdom and strength for that ordeal.

So many sleepless nights. She was cramming. After all, she never was a faithful student, her heart was not in her studies. Because she was a medical student just to prove she had ambition. Just studying enough to get by. Not a great idea.

When she faced her tribunal, to her surprise, the questions were about issues in which she was well versed. After a grueling hour, one of the members of the tribunal told her he was impressed, that he was going to do "something". The pleasure of his praise has stayed imprinted in her heart.

Great moments rarely come announced and here was one of them. The "something" was *meritisimus* in her diploma. Very meritorious. She was very grateful to him for his interest and praise and felt her heart dancing within her. Made her realize and regretful for wasting the years not concentrating on her studies. She knew she was most capable of more than what she had done throughout medical school.

This time her parents were happy. No annoying lecture but a celebration.

Taking and passing the medical board exams was next on the agenda.

Some people see things as they are and say "Why"
I dream of things that never were, and say, "why not?"

George Bernard Shaw

FIRST MEETING

"Does anyone still have the Thomasian? We could use it as a centerpiece for our reunion. Elevated over the lechon, and we need to surround it with gold and black tigers for the UST champion basketball team."

On the final return to Bohol, the end of the seventh year of premedical and medical school, when everything on her agenda had been accomplished, they set sail. There was no rush. No. Flying was not necessary.

Graduation ceremonies in the packed gymnasium with her parents and favorite aunt present, were memorable. There was a limit to the number of guests one could take along. She and her friends took final group portraits in their beautiful gowns, though hidden underneath their black togas, gold capes, and caps with gold tassels. The significance and enormity of the accomplishment overshadowed the inconvenience of the heat.

What is a little sweat in the usual places anyway? After all, they may never gather this way again, may never pass this way again, may never step in this beautiful campus again, never be tortured by the Dominicans.

Then the challenge of the medical board exams. What good is a piece of paper showing graduation if one does not get a license? Her circle of friends thought they should take the ECFMG exams also. Positive peer pressure, hello!

The Educational Council for Foreign Medical Graduates (ECFMG) was the bar they had to overcome if and when they wanted to go to the United States. For postgraduate studies. Not in her dream world at the time. But the planner she had become, *segurista,* she thought she was, why not cover all the bases while medical knowledge was still fresh in her brain.

Her whole family was with her on the ship. As usual it was full of students. Up till this point, typical her, she was leisurely thinking about nothing. Daydreaming. She realized she should think about the future agenda. She closed her eyes and imagined, listened to the wind and the seas' loud splashing waves.

There were many on her to-do list that could be checked off now. She was thrilled, now most everything was done. The ambition issue resolved, done. Her parents' finances would be more stable now. Being with her childhood friends was on the agenda, to do. Relaxing walks on the beaches, to do. Parties, yeah, to do. More hard work to do but the struggle to achieve what she had to do to prove ambition, checked, done. Her bloated ego told her she passed the board exams, but she did not verbalize that. It would be mean, she was too proud. There might be an evil spirit listening to her thoughts.

All she knew was that it would be great to be home again, be with her parents who she loved dearly and who loved her unconditionally. Being cared for by their maids who would make sure she had enough rest. They would not allow her to lift a finger to do household work. Not having to watch her allowance for laundry or food. Eat her favorite foods. Eat *puto* ni Cording or *pan ni* Pati. Her mouth was salivating as she was reminiscing when sister Sylvia tapped her on the shoulder disturbing her reverie. Bringing her back to reality. Sylvia whispered there were men looking in their direction while looking at a book.

"So what? It is none of my business." Nadia snarled, irritated by the distraction.

Men do weird things, who knows what book they were reading, after all she and her friends read some entertaining books and magazines too.

Who cares who they were looking at? After all, the boat was full of people.

Then Sylvia excitedly said one of the men was walking towards their direction. He proceeded to introduce himself to their mother, Aure, and engaged her in conversation. Turns out his parents were also educators just like Nadia's parents and Aure knew them. They had something in common to talk about. His name was Andy. That was all there was to it. He did not talk to her, not to her sister, nor her brothers. Just like that, then he left. What the…?

He had at least made Nadia notice him. In some distant future at another chance encounter he might start a conversation together. Now, there were at least four men together, why was he chosen to do the thing he did.

Was it a dare?
Did he volunteer?

He must at least have had a feeling of tension and nervousness. And she had an innate feeling of admiration for men who do not get intimidated by minor or insurmountable obstacles. For what would it hurt him to walk across the ship just to talk?

An indication of the strength of his mind and the essence of his personality.

The book they were looking at turned out to be their graduation yearbook, the Thomasian. They had also graduated from UST.

Notice her life pattern with yearbooks?

This yearbook showed photos with information about the graduate and since they both came from the same province, the men probably decided he should be the spokesperson. Come to think of it, there was a young seminarian assigned to her hometown of Panglao who was a friend of the young ladies at the time. Coincidence? Mr.-walk-across-the-ship was his brother. But George never mentioned he had a brother in medical school.

Nadia had been taking this boat ride twice a year for seven years, never meeting him. Destiny?

Arriving at the pier, they were met as usual by the whole clan. Her auntie Bev had a commercial passenger bus. Looked like the whole town was at the pier. So her life of leisure was about to begin.

Of course, there would be job interviews, but she did not have any resume to produce yet. That job search would come later.

Do the hard jobs first.
The easy jobs will take care of themselves.

Dale Carnegie

HOSPITAL LIFE

"See that trophy I am holding. I was the spiker for our champion volleyball team. That man was our coach, the chief of police, and that other man was the Chief of the Hospital. We had a lot of fun."

While waiting for the results of the medical board and the ECFMG exams, Nadia decided to work at a regional hospital hoping to be appointed to the medical staff should an opening ever happen. Other recent graduates were already volunteering and learning to apply what they had learned. These were some of the best times of her life. Though not on salary yet, she felt fulfilled. A good way to practice what she had studied. Learn from experienced staff members. And create a network of peers.

Taking care of the sick human body and mind was a tremendous but welcome challenge. After all, she had to go through seven grueling years of study to prove she had ambition. Now the rewards came in the form of a healthy baby delivered, a woman recovering from cholera, a man saved from many bullet wounds. Finding the collapsed blood vessel to start an intravenous fluid was a challenge initially, Nadia soon became an expert. There were still long nights "on call", but the stress of being judged by someone who decides whether one graduates or not was no longer an issue.

The art of medicine was what she had to practice. Book learning can be done by anyone. Developing the skill to really listen to the patient. Understanding their culture is followed by a capacity to come up with a list of diagnostic possibilities. This leads to better directed questions to prove or eliminate a diagnosis. She thought of this as solving a puzzle, playing mind games, sleuthing. Medicine, unlike surgery offered a greater scope to the imagination.

There were no fancy tests available in the hospital, so she had to rely on her diagnostic acuity. For the patients, doctors have their stethoscopes. With their brains, they listened, looked hard, literally sat and stood by their suffering patients, spent sleepless nights agonizing as they struggled against the enemy, Mr. Death. The icing on this cake was the respect earned and the camaraderie with fellow physicians, the dinners, bowling trips, picnics and many social functions she was now able to enjoy. No worries. The older and younger staff physicians were very kind and accommodating to the young graduates. And their irreverent youthful silliness added mirth to the hospital atmosphere.

She was late the first day of work. Not a good beginning. The hospital staff were on "rounds". "Rounds" were a way for all the staff members to be introduced to the interesting and/or difficult cases that came in, for discussion and further evaluation. A way to teach the young students and interns also of an interesting, unusual presentation of a disease.

With her high heels click click clacking down the tiled hallways, all eyes were on her as she joined. Some had their jaws wide open. One of the men, Alan, years later recalled this encounter to her son, Michael.

"She was dressed in her shapely whites. She was slim with a tiny waist. She stopped, then leaned against a post."

Nadia spent every weekend at the beauty salon for her hairdo, mani and pedi. Though she did not have any salary yet, she had access to small savings she had accumulated. The young had a different sort of priorities. And the services of the beauty salon were extremely inexpensive then.

Of course she must have looked gorgeous. They saw her actions as though she was modeling. Of course she was not aware this was how they perceived her. The poor men went crazy. She was absolutely unaware of the turbulence she was creating. One of those men was the man who talked to her mother on the ship, Andy. Of course it is a small world.

With the succeeding days, weeks, and months, everyone became familiar with each other. Habits, routines, nuances of their character. What makes people click, angry, what they like to eat, what they find annoying. It was not unusual that the older staff members start matchmaking the available single young men and women, dictatorial. A gamesmanship to distract from the ugliness and suffering one witnesses in the hospital surroundings. Jokes and subsequent laughter. Gave everyone hope that despite the surroundings they were in, outside in the world, children were playing in the parks, people were courting and falling in love, lovers were getting married, parents were busy working to provide for their families, and grandmothers were lovingly caring for their grandchildren.

Matchmaking occurs in any community.

The hospital was located in the city. Was a favorite hangout place for the bachelors to look and scout for prospects. There were many young student nurses, there were young nurses. There were young lady physicians and many young, eligible men physicians. Soon there were rumors about who liked who, who should be going with who, who was courting already.

So many matchmakers. Yente.

A rich bachelor engineer took a liking to Nadia. His best friend was one of the more successful lawyers in town. She heard the wireless network, but did not believe them until he came to visit her at her home on the weekends, accompanied by his lawyer friend. This usually meant a man was serious in his intentions.

Her mom would ask Nadia "are you home? So and so is here."

She pretended to be asleep. She believes her mom understood what this man meant to her. They would make up stories of where she was. Her auntie's house in such and such location. After all she had four aunts and they lived within a few kilometers of each other. And everyone knew everyone, so it was easy to get directions. It was one way Nadia could "disappear".

Some of the older lady physicians, would counsel her. They seemed to think not only her eyes but her heart needed to be opened, made aware of the various positive qualities of this gentleman. That she ought to consider, evaluate for her own good. On the evenings when they were on night call, sharing the one room off the emergency department, their advice, the stories they told, and the loud laughter that ensued, were the talk of the staff the following day.

But they could tell from Nadia's body language it was a NO.

They'd say "just close your eyes".

Though he was financially secure, came from a very good family, had a lot of personal assets, he was homely and so much older. Almost balding, teeth in poor repair, wearing old style eyeglasses. Posture, that of an old person. Not the lean, muscular youthful person that one gets attracted to.

Should she be rigid as an oak or be flexible like a bamboo? She might end up with no marriage and no career.

At this stage she was not looking for a husband, finally enjoying the companionships with professional ladies. Had two older physician roommates with whom they could girl talk into the wee hours of the morning. And one of them had two brothers, who were college graduates, single and available.

Because she was much younger, she had a few more years to think and choose, decide not to look toward the engineer and go for the untested man who was a mere pen pal or a dream world far away. Maybe she should decide for gentility and sensibility made flesh. Make her own decisions, for she was an adult. And if she made the wrong decision, she would be left with the chilly fear, no one else to blame, that results in weakened backs of unmarried girls lives of twenty three, an age considered old then. And in her old age with gray hairs and wrinkles, she would look back and see whether she had lived for herself only or accomplished any of the good she could have and owed her parents who gave her so much. Each gray hair and every line on her face would mean a wonderful character or instead be marks of shame.

The day-to-day jokes and teasing made her feel her stomach juices creating waves of panic. These nuisances were mere ant bites, not injustices hence the need for a sense of dignity.

Some cultures arrange for their children's marriages. This was not their culture. There were many available bachelors in her island. Professionals, gorgeous, tall. However they were all her relatives. Marriage between relatives was not the tradition. And parents and all relatives investigate the family or background of the suitor. Would he be a suitable prospective life partner. In fact her oldest uncle's admonition at the airport on her departure for the US was to let him know who was courting her so he could investigate.

Earlier during medical school, she had a suitor, Teddy. She thought he was dashing, tall, slim, a gentleman in every sense of the word. This was very important to a Catholic girl from a small island, important especially to her parents. That scene in The Godfather when Al Pacino is walking down the street with the girl he is courting was the life she had with him. Walking and talking was all they did. He courted her with his stories, of his friends, his life in the boarding house, the movies he had recently seen, of people from Bohol he had recently met, his classes, ever polite and respectful.

Her mother and his father were high school classmates. His father rose to high office in government and her mother although very intelligent, could not follow her dream to be a lawyer.

Because she was a girl! Resources had to be allocated to the boys first. Her wise mother taught first grade. She refused any promotion. Principal.

Supervisor. Superintendent. No, she insisted she would stay a first grade teacher. She believed her talents lay in molding the young minds.

And Aure did. Nadia heard of the successful careers of her students. Years later, many many years after she had left, during one of their missions, while entertaining American doctors, one woman, the high school principal, met and recognized Nadia as Aure's daughter. She told her they, who were Aure's students took great pride to be identified as such. It was a status symbol.

Cousin Aida asked her to be godparent to their daughter at her baptism, one of the three sacraments of initiation into the Catholic church. A godparent is one who agrees to help the parents raise the baby who is going to be baptized. She agreed, not knowing that Teddy was also asked and had already agreed. Suddenly one day when Teddy was visiting, she heard her mother comment on how godparents can not marry. She realized her mother sensed that she liked this man and was fearful. They could talk about anything. Funny, sensible, music, picnics, as well as serious issues. Nothing political or religious. Maybe they were soul mates.

During her medical school years he would wait for her outside the medical school building when classes end at night. To escort her to the dormitory just outside the campus gates. She doesn't remember the details of how this ended. She just knew she had to be focused. And he probably wanted more than just friendship.

Years later, as a physician at the regional hospital, they met again. By this time, the staff had already decided, that the man who talked to her mom on the ship should go a-courting her. Of course, he must have heard these rumors too. It was a small world. If he spread anything but the truth of their previous relationship, Nadia did not care what people heard. She knew the truth! And she believed he was a decent person who would not make up stories.

Over lunch, she and Teddy talked about this issue. She denied any relationship with Andy because it did not exist then.

Was it still his business to know?

Was he still interested in her?

Was he deciding on options he could make at the time?

She was sure he had girlfriends. After all, he was an attractive man with lots of assets probably with a lot of gorgeous girls at his command. She presumed. Men probably wanted closure.

And he probably sensed he could not compete. She does not like people who are insecure, people who do not fight for what they think they like.

Maybe he did not like her enough because she did not arouse in him memories of some past loves or a future loving relationship.

What makes someone love another after all? It can't be created by generosity or kindness or anything like those.

A short time later, the results of the medical board exams were published. She could still remember the excitement, heart beating fast and erratically, breathing labored, sweaty palms, reading the newspaper hiding in a room so no one would see her reaction, hoping to find her name.

There it was. She succeeded. She also passed the ECFMG exams. How tough was that?

Lucky? No, by the grace of the Almighty, she was given enough brain power to succeed.

Back home, under the shade of the star apple tree with the orchids behind her, and a warm bowl of *guinataan* for her *merienda*, she considered options on how to proceed with her life. She already proved she had ambition. Her parents counseled and insisted she stay in the island, open a clinic, after all she was the first and only doctor in town. And a woman too.

She decided she should stay, let her parents enjoy her success, their success.

There are many advantages growing up and living in a small town. The most important reason is that one felt safe. Everybody looked after one another, knew their neighbors and all townspeople. A stranger who walks into town would be recognized as an intruder. They never locked their doors or windows. So she decided to stay and start seeing patients, the obedient and thoughtful daughter she was. She understood her parents deserved this attitude. After all, they had spent for all her education. No loans of any kind.

Everyone she treated, spoke of how they took care of her as a baby, changed her diapers, fed her, cared for her. Watched her as a young girl as she played all over town or climbed fruit trees sitting on one of the branches eating the fruits like a little monkey. Now she's grown up. Everyone took ownership of her success. The message she thought she was hearing was that she owed them!

While also working at the hospital without pay.

Her young brother Rolando was already a captain in the merchant marine earning dollars while all these times, she was just an unpaid staff, waiting for government papers of appointment to the medical staff. Everyone knows the snail pace of the wheels of government. So she grumbled, pleaded, begged her parents to allow her to proceed to the USA. They saw she was miserable and understood she was not a financial success. More importantly, they understood she had an alternative, so they reluctantly gave her their blessings.

The chief of the hospital in fact asked her why she was not going to America. After all, not everyone could pass the ECFMG exams and why was she wasting this opportunity. Meanwhile, many US hospitals were soliciting for physicians, hence many opportunities were available.

One only need try to apply.

Although she had drifted into her profession by accident, she had become attached to it as fly lands on flypaper. Had completely adjusted to life as a physician. Developed her routines for her lifetime. She was also prayerful. Asked God for certain material things, for health, but she did not feel God was listening. However she understood that God's answer to her was not going to be as clear as his answer to Jonah, so she patiently waited. If she was meant to go to America, she would be accepted by one of the hospitals she applied to.

Believe in yourself and in your plan
Say not I cannot, but I can

Brian Holz

VIETNAM

"That's me with my mom, dad, brothers Berto and Rolando and sister Sylvia at the airport when I left for the USA", said Nadia. Maya had a smile on her face as she tried to place her mother's face over the body of the skinny person in the picture. "Three children did that to my current figure, you understand?"

The fighting in Vietnam had been going on for decades before the United States decided to get involved. The Vietnamese had suffered under the French colonialists, then Japanese imperial rule. In 1941, Ho Chih Minh returned to Vietnam and decided to unite his country, drive all foreign invaders away. He requested the US for help without success. The US decided to help the French defeat Ho instead. And the USSR decided to give assistance to Ho in this chess game. The French were decisively defeated at Dien Bien Pho, dashing US hopes of having a foothold in Southeast Asia. The Geneva Peace Accords were signed in 1954. Eventually Vietnam was divided into North and South with the United States supporting the South. United States ground troops in increasing numbers were sent to Vietnam after the Gulf of Tonkin Resolution, authorizing the US Government to escalate its Vietnam involvement, was signed. The US believed its strategy against the USSR was containment using the "domino theory". Once Vietnam fell to the North Vietnamese communists, communism would spread to the surrounding adjacent Asian countries just like dominos fall next to a falling tablet. The US expended every ounce of human and technological material to prevent this from occurring.

Nadia thought the US was recruiting foreign physicians to reenforce their healthcare professionals in Vietnam. She prayed and hoped she would not be sent to the war zone. In fact during her interview at the US Embassy to get an exchange student visa, she was given an option to become a US immigrant, reenforcing her suspicion.

No, thank you, she replied. Her plan was to return home to the Philippines after her five year training in the US.

To serve her people.

Once she found a matching hospital, she prepared.

She was beginning to like the prospect of this journey with its many open possibilities to explore and experience. Her parents did not place a guilt trip on her, like what other families usually do, so she had no feelings of anxiety or guilt. She knew her parents well enough at this point. She understood them and felt certain of their love. They were willing to let her go to the unknown trusting in an almighty being who they believed would continue to guide her. They truly believed they could trust that she had consumed almost all that they could provide. Like she had also graduated from their care and parental solicitude.

Like a bird, they allowed her to fly from their nurturing nest with the understanding she could return anytime she felt a need.

Becoming a parent later on, she would experience her own agony every time she saw her children at the airports as they left during their college years and beyond. But at the time she left her parents at the tarmac, she did not have such knowledge. She will always remember the texture of that day very clearly, the smells and sounds, the faces of relatives there to send her off. She meant to have these snapshots always clear in her mind, though she did not want to delay her departure

After all it marked the threshold of her new life.

Eagerly she was rejoicing "hurray, I am going to America", all smiles, hugging every relative who was there to send her off unaware that it must have been a heart wrenching event for her parents. There could have been a mist in their eyes or tears, unseen. Although they hesitantly gave their blessings for her journey, they tried hard not to show their sadness. They might have taken pride that they had raised a daughter with a sense of adventure.

The contract was for five years wherein they would not see each other. To the young, that was not a long time, especially for one who was going to an unknown place filled with the spirit of discovery. Years later, she came across a letter from her father-in-law to Andy wherein he articulated his sorrow and sadness, although there was no hint of bitterness.

Meanwhile Andy went to another province to work with a surgeon in his clinic. Clearly trying to find a way of proving himself. And he stayed on for a while because he had as yet no such proof. At this point Nadia heard rumors from the nurses that his father, uncles, cousins, and many relatives would drop by the hospital and inquire about her. They were already looking into her background, how she presented herself, looked, behaved. Most likely her relatives did the same. She did not hear any objections or advice. Andy had a brother who was in seminary to be a Catholic priest. His paternal uncle was a priest. His parents were educators, father was superintendent of schools.

In fact, Andy's father invited her to lunch one day. She accepted, no reason not to although she had felt butterflies in her stomach especially since her roommates teased and prompted her on what could possibly be asked.

They had a very nice one on one conversation. He was probably trying to discern her intelligence, her values, and her conversational skills. She did not feel any sense of dread, after all she was not seriously interested in a marriage job interview yet.

When Andy was away, it was then he started writing letters, that gradually developed into a mutual understanding with each other.

Finally realized he loved her?

Maybe it's true that absence makes the heart grow fonder. And she eventually felt the same. It was a long distance romance. It seems the distance could not keep true minds apart. Their awkward courtship was far more analytical than romantic. Anchored on levelheadedness. He had had his fill of puppy loves or more serious relationships by this time probably and felt he should check out Nadia. She believed he chose with his mind and soul rather than his heart alone. It was not enough that she thought he was a good man, everyone else believed it too. She had no delirious overwhelming wave of feelings of passion, but felt love that she was not fully able to express.

He was a faithful letter writer, written in simple words, so she knew he was not getting them from some guidebook for the lovelorn. After all, it is not just about passion. Love is about how you both choose to live your days. What you want to do together. Who you choose as your circle of friends, and what other plans you make. The love affair was more of an emotional and mental connection with shared spiritual values.

Obstacles are what you see when you take your eyes off your goal.

Anonymous

OFF TO THE USA

"Here we are tasting our first hamburger at Arby's".

There was a lot of turbulence as the Philippine Airlines plane she took, crossed over the Pacific Ocean though the sky was indescribably brilliant. She dug deep into her soul to find the courage to control the trembling that seized her. Nadia was unfazed. Her heart and mind were too full of the excitement and anticipation of her new life. She admired the scenery as the plane tunneled through the fluffy white clouds flying by with the sun rays breaking through, a kaleidoscope of colors, changing as the clouds passed through. She wondered if they would meet another plane en route. Like her inter-island travels by boat during her university years, they would come across other passenger boats going along or in the opposite direction as they admired the dolphins and whales doing their sea ballets.

Her concept of the United States of America was what she saw in the movies and magazines. Huge and tall buildings, clean tree-lined streets with white and yellow lines, traffic lights, fancy neon lights as though they are dropping off, going up, or moving along sideways. Cascading. Large marquees. Hollywood! Ladies and men wearing the latest fashion trends. Mansions with well manicured lawns and trimmed hedges. Trees with unnatural, unusual shapes. American people are truly different minded, they can even dictate the way trees grow, she thought.

The month was late June. Very pleasant weather but too cold for her tropical skin and bones. However with the two-day layover in Hong Kong she went shopping and invested in a black wool coat. One of the many recommendations given her. She was probably the only person wearing a wool coat in San Francisco at the time.

Her many months of preparation to leave for the USA was a period of optimistic enthusiasm. The days went fast, she stopped counting. They melted into each other like chocolate or butter in the heat. Aunt Trina was married to a Hawaiian and in fact lived in Honolulu prior to retiring back to the Philippines. She provided advice on the clothing materials needed for this journey.

But in retrospect what would a Hawaiian know about winter?

Her auntie Trina subsidized her with fifty dollars. Her financial contribution was to provide Nadia with necessities until she received her first paycheck. There was a job waiting for her already. While training, she was going to be compensated with a few dollars.

There were many hospitals to choose from. America was a blank slate on the map. She could just have thrown a dart, let it decide which state based on where it landed. However California was not an option. All the training hospitals were located on the east coast. There was no internet to Google for information. She completed an application to do a one-year internship, then another application for a 4-year residency in a particular specialty.

Which hospital to choose? Of equal importance was which city and which state to go to.

She knew about New York, but she did not want to live there. The map showed many good alternatives. She chose Pennsylvania. After all that's where Benjamin Franklin was from. A name familiar to her from the many nightly civics lessons at their dining table when she was a young girl. And the state was historic. Besides it was near New York and Washington DC, she thought!

The airplane descended on fabulous San Francisco. The airport was sparkling, with glass windows and walls. Shops with many current styles and thus tempting clothes, shoes, perfumes, bling. She could see this was a city by itself. She did not have to worry about her luggage. They were going directly to Pittsburgh, she was told. Although all her precious belongings were there, she wasn't concerned, just trusted they knew what they were doing. Innocence is bliss.

The city by the bay. The Golden Gate Bridge. The Bay Bridge. Wow, indeed it was what she had in mind. Hollywood. Tall buildings, some made of glass, rectangular, squares, and some with irregular angular tops. The streets were long, straight, were paved, like figures in geometry or trigonometry class and there were sidewalks for people to walk. Clean. Although the city itself had curved streets, one of the crookedest streets in the world is located there. So far so good. Had her first taste of American Chinese food.

After the initial layover, she boarded again, this time for Pennsylvania. The view on their descent was a far cry from Hollywood. There were vast expanses of green grass, forests, brown colored waterways, no tall buildings, but with red brick houses that were few and far between. She noticed smoke coming out from what she later learned were chimneys. So that is where Santa Claus comes in the Christmas carol, she thought.

There must be a mistake. This is not the place she dreamed she should be living in. It is always a huge disappointment when we feed ourselves with beautiful visions that do not become the reality. A new attitude was in order. Nadia allowed herself to think that expecting nothing makes the entire experience easier to accept. There was a smell to the river as well as a sulfurous odor emanating from the buildings with smoke, the steel mills. Unfortunately this was it.

So much for great expectations. However, she recognized this was just the beginning of exciting adventures and encounters which she could make happen and control the outcome. She was just on the threshold of discovering a new life. Determined to see with her spirit not just with her eyes. Filled with much hope, she asked a taxi driver to take her to the address she had. On and on she journeyed the same paved streets. Though the country was full of green trees along the route, the air seemed gloomy, cloudy, foggy. Or was it smokey?

The hospital was on a hilltop. Lovely views of the Pennsylvania countryside. One could see forever. Sunrises with the sun rays thru the flat clouds were a beauty to behold, creating various shapes and shadows on the ground. Sunsets with the orange to magenta skies were lovely. The yellow moon large and clear in the horizon.

Unfortunately there was a steel mill down the hill and smoke was polluting the air everyone breathed. She was still optimistic, after all this was just a one-year stint. The people were kind and helpful. Made her feel "at home". Very comfortable. No sense of being judged. Adopted her as one of their own children. Everything she did spread like wildfire. One example is an episode when she was learning to drive.

The men dreamed of owning a car and one by one they did. Her friend Noel bought a Ford Mustang. They were so happy for him and he drove them all over the countryside. Soon they taught her to drive. There were two girls but she was the more courageous so the first to take lessons. The car did not have power steering. She was trying to make a right turn to the incoming two-lane road, failed to have the strength to turn the wheel and landed in front of a car on the right lane. Luckily she knew how to push the brakes. This became the talk of the whole hospital the following day. She was like a favorite pet.

There were many physician trainees from all over the world. There was a doctor's lounge on the topmost floor, furnished with a kitchen, a television set, and a refrigerator. During breaks, this was the gathering place, not the watering hole, to share the day's experiences, and there were many. On Fridays, when their faith restricted them from eating meat, some would shop at the supermarket, some were designated to cook, and everyone else would watch the clock change to Saturday so they could eat the meat. It's truly incredible and what a torture withholding a particular food is even for just a few hours.

And to think of the many starving people worldwide.

She lived in the nurses' dormitory which was connected to the hospital through an underground tunnel. Her room was spacious, was pristine, was painted white. It had a bed, her own bathroom with a shower, and a desk. There was a window through which she could see trees like candle tapers, wide at the base, tapering towards the sky. The bark was dark, mosaic like, branches widely spreading at the base, but less expanding towards the top. The leaves looked like needles. Beautiful, like Christmas trees. She did not know what they were called. However there were other kinds of trees with wider flat leaves. She had to remember all these details inside her room and surroundings so she could write them to her mother. So they could talk across time and space.

Even in the USA, her life included a 24-hour housemother. Who would have thought it? Her parents would be thrilled to know. Because it was a training hospital as well as a school for nurses.

Off duty hours were spent in the dormitory in front of the television. She adopted opinions on politics, entertainment, sports, culture, from watching the rabbit ears. The many young nurses were eager teachers so her enlightenment of American culture came from them. Later on, PBS and Sixty Minutes were her favorites.

Years later living in Cleveland she enjoyed a television station with meaningful Japanese movies, captioned. And the PBS masterpiece theater was another favorite. She made sure all the housework was done so she could sit in front of the television to watch. She remembers Lily Langtry as a favorite, the beautiful Francisca Annis played her. This was the beginning of her addiction to masterpiece theater. America is truly wonderful, all these classics for free!

Sports. She understood basketball and boxing but why would men hit each other in the game called football. What are two lines? Penalties. Touchdown. She preferred basketball, volleyball, tennis, and soccer. Those were familiar team sports.

Freedom!

Opportunities to do whatever she liked to do.

To purchase any item.

To eat anything. No one dictates.

To move anywhere she wanted. Long weekend trips to New York, Boston, Washington with the other young single physicians. The men would take turns driving.

One of her first purchases was a stereo system. And she learned to purchase the 33 rpm vinyl records by mail, was able to acquire quite a selection. There was always music in her room. She loved Barbara Streisand, Herb Alpert and the Tijuana brass, Frank Sinatra, of course. Nat King Cole. Andy Williams. Perry Como. Pop music, Henry Mancini, Mantovani, and movie soundtracks. The Beatles and Elvis Presley of course. She felt great, able to purchase whatever she liked. An American. Imagined how Steve McQueen must have felt bouncing his ball off the walls in solitary confinement, as her stereo allowed the music to bounce off the four walls of her small room.

Just the beginning of her acquisition phase. Eventually she fell in love with lladro figurines. Even Maurice noticed this such that when he went to Spain for their school break, he purchased two one-foot-tall man and woman figures. China sets of five-piece place settings for eight included Lennox 'Autumn", "Aristocrat", "Holiday", Wedgewood "Cavendish", Villeroy and Boch "Xenia", 1975 Goebel "Le Rotisseur", Sasaki "colorstone matte black" and Butler's pantry supposedly for casual use, however she made other purchases for everyday use.

How crazy did she get?

And shoes! Every woman loves a shoe for a dress. Matchmaking, finding the right accessory for a dress. Just like Imelda. And books too. She did not have any financial obligations to anyone yet. No one to maintain financially so she indulged her whims. Although she would send gifts to her family in the Philippines.

There was a church down the hill where she visited daily. It was a Hungarian Catholic church. Apparently there was also a large Jewish community. One day one of the Jewish ladies visited the hospital and talked to the new interns. After hearing their stories, Nadia was requested to talk at one of their lunches. The Jewish lady was probably fascinated by her "ambition" issue.

There was not much adjustment her body needed to do the first few months, arriving at the end of June. Soon the trees turned a beautiful tapestry of colors, yellow, gold, red, orange, mustard, purple, brown, magenta. Awesome. Then they started falling. The streets were now covered with them, as they made rustling noises when she walked.

Oh, the falling leaves, the song she could play on the piano. So that's the reality. The view of the countryside from the hilltop revealed spectacular sunsets with the multicolored layers of the sun rays between layers of clouds. Now she could use her wool coat to ward off the autumn chill.

Then one day while looking out the hospital window she asked one of the nurses what those white cotton like materials in the air were.

SNOW!

Lovely white clouds in the atmosphere and on the ground. And on the trees, branches, and shrubs. Everything was now pure white, covered thick with snow, her breath frosting in front of her. She played like a child with her first snow experience. It was soft, and melted on contact, reminded her of *halu-halo*, a special dessert with a mix of tropical fruits, milk, topped with finely crushed ice, just like the snow, and the special ice cream flavored coconut, *mango, ube, langka*. She learned the rituals of winter creating a snowman with a carrot for its nose, stones for eyes, and a red shawl around his neck.

Of course when she first arrived in summer, she rode the roller coaster, so much fun for the young as if her intestines would come out of her belly skin. Made friends with some teenagers for she looked like a teenager, all eighty eight pounds, five foot three inches. With the arrival of winter, these same teens taught her ice skating. How much fun that was.

And skiing. That was too dangerous according to the chief of the hospital. They should not be too adventurous while working there.

Although her days were full of excitement with her new experiences, hospital work, conversations with the nurses and other coworkers, her material possessions, the nights were filled with sadness for the lack of the sense of "belonging". The nights were a new routine now. Missed her family, her cousins, her townspeople, all the familiar faces and traditions. Homesickness.

Especially on Christmas and Easter.

Although everyone was friendly, she felt different. However she did not have to justify who she was. Sometimes, she wished to disappear like a fish into the coral reefs and reminisce.

Through the eyes of children, we aren't judged by
the color of our skin but by the way we act and
conduct ourselves and the qualities within.

Anonymous

MARRIAGE

"She was my best friend, fed me while I was living alone in the hospital apartment the first year I moved to Cleveland. Her husband was a surgery resident. I would babysit their three children. Later, Maya, we asked her to be your godmother."

Everyone has a calling. We are students, daughters, sons, sisters, brothers, mothers, fathers, wives, husbands, grandmothers, grandfathers, religious, or single. All of these walks of life have corresponding problems and blessings. We learn or adapt to these pursuits hearing folklore, observing others, and living the state.

Nadia and Andy married in Cleveland during their residency training. She believes they were the first Filipino couple married by the bishop. He had to learn about Philippine traditions and rituals for the marriage ceremony. The veil, the cord, the candles, the coins, the sponsors, etc. Monsignor James was most kind, willingly patient, and cooperative as he was being educated on the significance of the various particulars of a Filipino wedding ceremony.

Symbols for unity include the veil which is placed over the head of the bride, wrapped around the groom and pinned to his shoulder away from the bride. The cord likewise is dropped over the bride and groom's heads and wrapped over their shoulders. The bride and groom each light one candle and with their two candles, they proceed to light one large candle. Symbolic of one light to shine the way for the two of them as they go through life together as one.

There is a small basket with silver or gold coins that the groom hands to the bride, as a symbol of his promise to provide for her and the family. Or if the coins are loose, he drops them into the bride's cupped hands, she making sure not a single coin drops. Various interpretations of how the groom does this process abound. Among them are: If he takes a long time to drop the coins, he is deemed a miser. If the bride drops a coin, she is not a good financial manager of the family's assets, she is careless.

Andy understood he had to purchase an engagement ring, living within his budget. She was not high maintenance so she did not expect a huge diamond. Besides, they were just on meager salaries. After all it is not about the size, but Andy learned about the 4 c's.

It was not a huge wedding party held at a hotel. Monsignor James joined. A few families from Pennsylvania, her adoptive parents so to speak, drove to Cleveland. So very heart warming. A few friends took off from their training in New Jersey, New York, Pennsylvania. And of course their doctor superiors shared in the celebration.

The young couple were now ready to start their joint American adventure. They decided before their marriage that they should complete their training. Since Andy's hospital provided them with apartments, she would do the commuting. Andy had a Chevrolet Malibu for which gas mileage cost about a dollar a week. Nadia used this to commute. One of the older physicians sold his dilapidated Rambler so Andy would have some sort of transport for short distances.

Living in an apartment, Nadia had to learn doing housework. There was a vacuum cleaner for the carpets. Washing machines and clothes dryers were in the basement. Which detergent to purchase? Rough plastic and steel wool sponges to rub the bathrooms and sinks. Oilcloth and which spray to use to dust furniture? Names like Murphy soap became familiar. They rearranged the furnished apartment that had early American style furniture and redecorated each room to be more pleasing to their tastes, discovering they had some creative juices. America provided so many choices. They received silverware, china, linens, cookware and other essentials as wedding gifts. She purchased a cookbook to follow cooking steps because now she had her own kitchen. Learned braising, steaming, grilling, marinating, baking, words she heard about but never had a chance to perform herself.

If I succeeded medical school, I should be able to do all of this, Nadia prodded herself. Watched PBS cooking shows. Somehow she and Andy managed, did not starve for her lack of cooking skills. Started inviting friends over for dinner to sample and critique her cooking. Her crab dish in coconut milk and ginger was a hit. She organized housework around her and Andy's schedule. Despite many strings on her bow, they managed. Since they came from the same island with its own traditions and dialect, they did not have to spend much time making adjustments living together, everything was built on unspoken assumptions.

However, memories of their honeymoon in Miami Beach must have generated certain routines creating a fertile environment in their marriage. With all the mansions, touristy spots they visited they somehow managed to find romance.

Ten months later their firstborn darling little baby girl arrived one early spring day. Despite the daily commute to work, resident workload stresses and anxiety, Nadia had a very uneventful pregnancy. A blessing. She did not ask for any special favors, nor did she take time off before delivery. Her workplace knew she delivered when she did not show up for work. In those days, maternity leave was only for one month. Paternity leave was an unknown entity. But she was allowed a five-day postpartum hospital stay.

The year was special. Neil Armstrong landed and walked on the moon. Pope Paul VI went to the Philippines and in Manila, Andy's brother George was ordained a priest in a celebration attended by millions of Catholics, and broadcast worldwide. That same morning life went on as usual while Andy and his friends went fishing.

Maya was born. One small step for the family, more steps to come.

Motherhood is a state that women enter into unprepared. There is no
school to go to prepare for it. The feminine genius starts from childbirth,
through infancy, the teen years. Nadia remembers her mother would
say, a mother is always a mother. One does not stop being a mother
just because the children are grown. People saw her, the same person as
before. However now she became a picture frame for her child. Nadia
did not mind this at all.

Soon, the mail delivered magazines and books with various opinions
and resources for new mothers.

How did they know she needed them? So informative. So she read them
all, making sure she remembered everything. It was easy to do since she
had no previous knowledge of any of this information. These common
sense messages were never taught in medical school.

Or was she sleeping when this was taught? She thought America was
really a wonderful country. So giving.

Having a baby is a life-changing experience. This precious human being,
just like an exquisite Lladro doll, needs delicate caring.

When to feed?

How often to feed?

What to do when they cry? She noted there were many kinds of cries,
just like there are many ringtones to choose for cell phones.

There was the decision which diaper to use. Disposable or cloth. How
to wash cloth diapers?

When do they sleep through the night? The day-to-day dilemmas were
many but she did not allow herself to be overwhelmed. She just did
what she had to do. Diapers, laundry, feeding, nap times, phone calls,
doctor's appointments, toys, social obligations.

What happens when they go to school? How would the other children treat them? How could they be protected from bullies?

She could feel their little hand crook her finger. So soft, yet as powerful as an electric current or an erupting volcano. As she folds their tiny clothes, she wonders how tall they'll grow. Like her two brothers who were basketball stars? Do other parents worry as much as she does? She understood she shouldn't worry about things beyond her control, nevertheless, the mind just pulls one into this lane, unfortunately. Will they be as good as...and of course there is the man in her life, who should not be ignored. One needs quiet times with the spouse.

Two boys followed Maya. Three children in five years. Boom, Boom, Boom!

With their own children, Nadia and Andy started their own family traditions. Family meals. Walks or bicycling in the parks, Andy leading, Nadia at the rear. Watching television or movies together. Planning family vacations, the children researching the destinations. Mass always for the holydays, and Sundays. Prayers every evening with the children once they could read, leading the rosary. Coloring eggs and participating in Easter egg hunts, dressed in fancy clothes. The Thanksgiving turkey and all the trimmings. Christmas took them to a farm to cut their first and last Christmas tree. The room where it was located ended up with many spiders. Artificial Christmas trees became the norm. Nadia discovered a base that rotated and had a Christmas carol recording as it rotated. Unfortunately after twenty years, it developed arthritis and had to be retired.

The Christmas tree ornaments were colorful irresistible temptations for the children. She placed an extendable hat rack around it otherwise, the balls would end up in Maya's mouth!

She heard of race relation issues as a problem in America. Heard of Martin Luther King, a pastor civil rights activist who led the non-violent successful fight against segregation. Even won the Nobel peace prize. His assassination was racially motivated.

How dare he voice his dream? Although she had not read or heard the whole "I have a dream" speech, she admired the man for articulating such a personal issue. For who does not have a "dream"?

Then Robert Kennedy, while a candidate for the presidency, who was a Catholic and had empathy for the poor, was shot after making a speech at a Los Angeles hotel. He was outspoken in his advocacy for African-Americans, for the poor. Was also openly speaking about the corrupt practices of the unions.

She also heard and read of the Japanese encampment during World War II, a topic of many novels. Now although the Vietnam war was done, anti-Vietnam activists were still loud. Nadia's family was Asian. This kind of climate was scary.

Who can anticipate what some politician would decide to do to promote his agenda?

She read the dailies. There was a page on the horoscope. Each new year Jeanne Dixon would write her predictions. One year she predicted that trouble would come from The East. She did not believe this meant the Philippines, for Filipinos were peace loving people, nor did it mean Japan for the Japanese Emperor Hirohito promised General McArthur that his country would no longer have a military department. How admirable. His action was real atonement. Any person can articulate their sorrow for the wrong they have done, but forgiveness is given to those who show remorse.

Of course there was China, a communist country. One of the communist mantras was expansionism. And North Korea. So yes, trouble might come from the East.

She had forgotten that there were other countries in the East. The Far East. The South East. The Middle East. True enough, there was trouble continuing to brew in the Middle East.

Life is the movie you see through your own unique eyes
It makes little difference what's happening out there.
It's how you take it that counts.

Denis Waitley

MOTHERHOOD

"Maya, that is you I am cradling during your baptismal party at the Brown Derby restaurant."

Nadia had another dilemma.

What is gained or lost if the mother works?

Some mothers choose to stand behind these child rearing dilemmas and decide to stay at home. It is a choice.

But the working mother does not leave this part of her life when she goes to work. She is still constantly distracted. The network news does not help when they highlight nanny abuses seen through hidden cameras. Of course one can get help with the non-essential details of living which nevertheless need to be accomplished.

However one can not delegate motherhood. There is no good substitute for a mother's loving arms, her cheerful familiar voice, the delicacy with which she carries her baby or changes the diapers, the caring hands that wash the baby's bottoms.

There is the daily dose of anxiety and guilt. And the responsibility to be cheerful and content.

This is what motherhood is.

It was not luck that she had found great caregivers for all her children. A lot of people prayed and their prayers were answered. She has a good friend who does not believe in luck or happenstance or coincidence, or good fortune, or chance. You can call it any name. Cindy calls it Divine Providence. And Nadia agrees. Coincidence is just God's way of remaining anonymous, she had read somewhere.

Is there ever a time when putting your needs ahead of your children's is acceptable?

She continued to work. At least, she should complete her training and maybe then she could decide to stay home. Fortunately, there were excellent mothers in the apartments provided during training. They chose to stay home with their children while their physician husbands continued their training. They were excellent, even better, more experienced mothers to her children.

Despite her age, and heavy work schedule she was able to have two more children. She was amazed at how easy her pregnancies went. No morning sickness, no swollen legs, no aches and pains. Despite the constant jokes and threats of the consequences of older women's pregnancies, nothing fazed her. She constantly trusted a Supreme Being who guided her life. To think of the many women who struggle through years of infertility testings and the endless waitings, and disappointments.

She was an anxiety ridden person and God blessed her with three easy pregnancies. Three pregnancies in five years! And she took this as a message that she had to continue the work she was doing, after all, she was also providing a service outside the home. Her three children had a huge dose of companionship, love, and care from their loving caregivers and their children. Nadia became the picture frame for her babies, for ice must be broken and what better way to do this than with babies.

Andy's training program included a rotation for the surgery residents to a hospital about an hour drive away from their home. He had to stay there for the whole week, come home for the weekends. Completely exhausted.

Life as a surgeon trainee or any physician for all intents and purposes was tough. Twenty four hours "on call" for all emergencies followed by the regular day shift takes a toll on the human body. And one had to be alert, always. Dealing with life and death situations all the time. However they were much younger then and were able to adjust. Andy would use his weekend days off resting and playing with the children. Other than the usual housework of cooking, laundry, and cleaning a two-bedroom apartment, there was no lawn or garden to maintain.

On one of those nights at the far away hospital, some students held an anti-war protest when the US extended the Vietnam war into Cambodia. This was in a small state university in Kent Ohio. Andy saw and treated some of the casualties and the sufferings of the many wounded students. It was agony hearing of these events, aware that the hospital was in the location of the riot and not knowing whether Andy was okay. Her heart was shrinking like a prune fearing the worst.

Experiencing an event like that creates unforgettable torturous memories. He relives those moments whenever there are crisis in the news. She was thankful for the bravery and activism of some young people, however as a young mother she prayed the young concentrate on what their parents spend their money on: their education.

Maurice would say, "you are wrong Mom. People go to college not to book learn but to see how life is lived, the way to live a full life, to be attuned to others. To observe government policies as it affects the people they serve."

"So those students who riot were learning the way to live life? Is that what colleges and universities teach? Free expression. Isn't it a waste of our financial resources? There must be other ways to protest peacefully."

Remembering her own college days, the only students who held rallies and riots were those at the University of the Philippines. This was the equivalent of the University of Berkeley. The reason why her parents insisted she do her studies at the Catholic university.

Part of life as a physician is the reality of danger lurking anywhere, anytime.

Even in church, emergencies can happen. A parishioner feeling faint. Is there a doctor in church?

Or in an airplane while leisurely trying to sleep, someone yells "Is there a doctor on board?"

On one of their surgical missions to impoverished countries years later, they realized that they themselves, were in danger too. Should an emergency occur, would the locals know what to do? They needed to take action to protect themselves and their family. Where to begin? Like Scarlett she said that is a problem she will face tomorrow, a subject for another day. Today is child rearing time above all.

Though physically taxing, they were enjoying themselves. The weekends were times to spend with the other trainees from all over the world, picnics, various socials. She did not know how to cook. The first purchase she made after she married was a cook book. She taught herself to cook various Visayan/Spanish dishes like pochero, paella, goto, arroz caldo, relleno chicken, lengua, pancit molo. And she experimented using various canned soups to flavor meats, a trick she learned from a very good cook/friend. That's how they learned how to cook: exchanging recipes.

She also watched Public Broadcasting Corporation (PBS) stations with their cooking programs: Julia Child, Jacques Pepin, Yan can cook. Her cookbooks told her measurements for all ingredients but these celebrities did not. Just a flick of the fingers or wrist. She also remembered their cook at home did not do any measuring. So she became a creative cook, using whatever ingredients she had and imagining what flavor she wanted the food to have. Years later Andy had a backyard garden therefore fresh herbs were available. They were the magic ingredients. Nieces loved her cilantro and avocado based salsa. Pizza using Boboli or Persian flat bread with or without tomato sauce with olives, sautéed kale with garlic, sliced mushrooms, sprinkled with mozzarella cheese. Buttered naan bread with feta cheese, cilantro, mint, green onions as appetizer, sometimes this was her lunch.

They had their first fondue at the home of a Chinese resident while sharing the week's experiences, the children playing. It was a wonderful experience, conversations meandering like paths in the jungles, childhood experiences in each one's country. Hence educational too. However fondue involves too much cutting, slicing, so labor intensive. They used soup broth instead of cheese as the French did.

She loved baklava that a Greek staff member brought to share with the residents. She learned how to prepare it with layers of phyllo dough, crushed nuts, and honey, then decided it was too much work and too rich in butter and honey. Although baklava is available commercially, nothing could satisfy her tastebuds the way Mary's baklava did. The first lovely taste always lasts.

However this idyllic life had to end. They had to move. The apartments they were staying in were just for those physicians in training.

They purchased a condominium. The condo was just two miles from Andy's hospital while she had to drive the fifteen miles to where she was offered a staff position after her residency and was appointed instructor at the local medical university. The surgeons would ask her opinions on their patients and addressed her as "dear". One of her co-staffers was upset on hearing this.

"Why do you allow them to call you dear?" asked a Greek Gastrointestinal specialist. This surprised Nadia.

"It is a term of endearment where I come from." Nadia replied.

Mary insisted it was condescending of them to use that word to a fellow physician.

"They must value my judgement and intellect otherwise why would they ask my opinion?" Her answer.

This was during the age of sensitivity regarding sexual harassment. Americans do go overboard sometimes.

They finally outgrew their two bedroom condo and with both of them working, they were able to purchase a home in the suburbs. It was a new subdivision added to an established group of homes. Although they had neighbors, her house was the only house at the corner on the new street. They wondered why they never received any mail. One weekend, she approached the postman. Her house was just about 50 steps from their backyard neighbor which would not cause exhaustion on the mailman who would be walking.

But that was the law. No mail delivered to houses on new streets yet.

Back in her hometown when they encountered a situation like she was in now, they would call the mayor. So she did, leaving a message. Thankfully the mayor returned her call. No one answered when he called home, so he called her at work. She explained her dilemma. Mail was delivered the following day. Soon, news spread like wildfire in the neighborhood.

"Who are those people living in that house, who talked to the mayor about her mail." People wondered. One by one they would meet them and Mr. Clark became a very good friend when one day he knocked at their door, wanting to meet the lady who had "spunk". He was in business with home appliances and soon, he would be bringing gifts, one of them, a portable metal rotisserie, is still working, and useful. They considered him their elder and he entertained their relatives when they visited from the Philippines.

Mr. Clark found her father-in-law's English entertaining.

Father was a school superintendent so he was very articulate, in fact, he was writing a book while he was with them for a year. He also wrote a cookbook for Nadia, which she took as being generous instead of an insult to her cooking inabilities. Many afternoons, he and Mr. Clark would spend their time discussing the intricacies of the English language, grammar, and sentence construction. Baseball, basketball, football were other topics of discussion.

Her father-in-law's "I think I'm sure" would cause Mr. Clark to double up in laughter.

A neighbor taught her baking: she learned how to make kuchen, a sweet yeast dough, and made various modifications from the basic dough. Then the children used a rolling pin to flatten the dough and fit it onto the cookie sheet. With her creative cooking habits, they experimented with various toppings. The basic topping was cottage cheese with egg, with or without cinnamon. Then followed the most awaited part. Various fruits were sliced, the favorite was sliced peaches. Sometimes she would use the basic dough to prepare her native *ensaymada*. The rolled flattened sheet was brushed with butter and a light dusting of sugar, then rolled to look like a rose. Children anxiously waited for the baking to complete.

All of them looked forward to Christmas when their Italian neighbor would bring them a tray full of sweets: cannoli, pandoro, pignolata, torta caprese. These would come with home made wine from their basement.

When their success drove them to the suburbs they lost the loving caregivers for the children. She became a stay at home mom for three years. What an experience. Outwardly, she was functioning well, exposing her children to the cultural, intellectual, spiritual, physical events that Cleveland, Ohio offered.

The internationally renowned Cleveland Metropolitan Museum of Art was where one could enjoy the huge collection of Egyptian and Asian arts for free. The unrestored Rodin's The Thinker was at the top of the main staircase. Going through all the art displayed allowed one to travel the world.

The children enjoyed the exhibits and workshops. Maya loved the ballet dancers, Michael enjoyed the various sculptures and modern art, and Maurice laughed at the naked chubby babies of Raphael. They had a huge dose of the master artists. The University Circle was their favorite hangout. The children could pay only so much attention to art at one time, hence the many repeat visits.

One time, the director of the museum had Michael in tow because Nadia was late picking him up after their workshop on the Egyptian exhibits, mummy and all. She still owns a copy of The European Vision of America published by the museum for the bicentennial celebration. It will have to find another home someday.

Next door was the Garden Center where they would sit and read books in the serene Asian garden, or enjoy the aromas of the many varieties of roses and herbs. There was a fountain in the front where the boys could splash themselves to cool the Cleveland summer heat. And on other days long hours were spent at the Natural Science Museum. They really enjoyed watching the skeletons of dinosaurs best. She took pride that the director had been credited with discovering "Lucy", as though through osmosis she was somehow a joint discoverer.

The Cleveland Opera at Severance Hall was conducted by George Szell, Pierre Boulez, then Loren Maazel and it was fun to get dressed for an evening at the opera. She spent so much time studying their librettos. They took the children to Cuyahoga Falls for their Blossom Music Festival where they would picnic on the grounds while enjoying ballet.

During their future travels, they would not want to miss a visit to the local museum to relish those portraits, sculptures, sceneries, all of which strike their hearts and set them blossoming like flowers in spring.

"What's the big deal about her smile." Comments as they examined the Mona Lisa at the Louvre. Nadia thought the painting would be larger than it was.

They laughed at the hilarity of the moulin rouge dancers, dresses, and hats.

And there must have been a strong wind for the irises and sunflowers to be swaying that much at the Rembrandt and Van Gogh museum.

What is great about those garden flowers?

Why are those naked men and women without arms? The children asked.

But psychologically, she was in turmoil. She pictured herself a leaf stuck on a twig on the side of a river as the stream flowed by. She envied the flowing waters on their way to the open sea. She was a disaster. Her children were her light in the wilderness of the darkness she was in.

The feminist voices were rattling her nerves. The feminists were touting their theory that women can be all they can be. How could that be when she was miserable doing her motherly duties. Unable to continue her medical career.

The feminists first worked on women's right to vote. Then they worked for women's legal and social equality which continues today. She thought they just believed that men and women are and should be identical, equal pay for equal work. Their voices were loud and made her even more bitter for giving up her career, albeit for a while.

But this kind of reasoning is inherently flawed. Equal pay for equal work is right. However science and common sense show the sexes are very different. Baby girls play with dolls and baby boys play with trucks, despite parents' friends giving pink and blue toys for each gender.

What is definitely true is that men and women have equal innate dignity.

Nadia's mother was a working woman, but she had a lot of help. Nannies for each of the children, a cook, a gardener, driver, laundress. Aure did not want her to stay in America and it did not help that when she would visit and see Nadia doing housework like ironing, she would ask "why do you insist on living in this country?"

When she prays, she asks God for wisdom, always. Like she mentioned before, her prayers were not to win the lottery, or to pass an exam, or to be able to purchase her favorite car, the corvette. Throughout her life, she believed, there was always divine guidance. Opportunities were strewn on her path as she walked this earth. She made the choices based on values from her childhood and her continuing spiritual journey. Whether she made the right choices are for her God and her children to judge.

A neighbor, Pam, an Englishwoman whose husband, also English, was an engineer, was her partner in fun. They had two boys, playmates to Nadia's children. Pam was a savior. Together, they played tennis, took sewing classes, learned needlepoint. The many framed specimens of handicrafts made, still decorating her home are memorabilia of that point in her life which she believed was the lowest.

So silly! Why would taking care of her children be considered that way. She needed growing up and thankfully she did.

Tennis, embroidery, sewing, needlepoint, bargello, walks in the park with the children provided some relief. They enjoyed shows at the Great Lakes Shakespeare Festival.

A funny thing happened. They watched "The Sound of Music" on stage, a good choice for the young children to experience. When the nun asked "Where is Maria", 3 year old Michael thought the nun was looking for Maya so he yelled "She is here" pointing to his sister.

Time off from work was very valuable. Exposing the children to various cultural events was time very well spent. The joy one gets from witnessing the fleeting phases of the children's physical, intellectual, psychological growth provided the most joy, easily missed when one is working. An enlightened woman is someone who knows her purpose and follows through to its fulfillment. She was glad she realized before it was too late that she did have a choice and she believed she made the right choice in life, a change in her attitude.

Whatever the future held for them, they planned college education for their children, the best university they could be admitted to and which they could afford. Like their parents they would provide the resources towards that goal. The children wouldn't have any debts to start their post college years. Their salary was just enough for their needs and they did not have any relatives to run to for financial help. So they followed common sense. Set aside a little amount of money every month for their education and for the "rainy day". She was not extravagant with her shopping, realizing she had a family to take care of. Her closet was filled only with the reassuring world of black and white. Color was added through accessories as in jewelry, a scarf, a pin, a hat.

They had a budget. The children were not overwhelmed with the latest toys or gadgets.

Books and games were in their lives. These were all affordable. Besides there was the library with their treasure trove of whatever topic interests oneself. She remembered her childhood spent with books and she was now living her dream. They may have thought they were deprived of toys if they compared themselves to their friends, but they learned living within their means.

They learned there is no easy or free credit card.

Whatever you can or dream you can, begin it. Boldness has genius, magic and power in it. Begin it now.

Johann Wolfgang Goethe

WORLD EXPLORATION

"Michael, you wanted a taste of Heineken beer in Amsterdam as we took the city tour by boat. See Maya with one of the jazz singers?"

Early in her marriage, she and Andy resolved that they would explore the United States with their children. And why not the world too. So they made week-long or month-long vacations to historic, cultural centers in the US starting when the youngest child was 2 years old and five other repeat visits along the eastern seaboard.

To Washington DC where the heart of US government was located. Joined groups to the White House. Awesome. Jacqueline Kennedy performed such a marvelous job with her redecoration. Nadia learned and particularly enjoyed the different personalities a room takes depending on the wall colors, paintings displayed, the window coverings, the moldings, the furnitures. They were so proud that America's home was this magnificent.

Outside by the iron railings, as usual, Maurice tried to scale the fence. Michael followed. No one bothered to criticize. Those were innocent times. Al Qaeda was an unknown entity then. She can still see them in their "love" tees. For her ease, safety, and convenience, she would dress the three children with the same design tees, to easily recognize them in the crowd. It was impossible to hang on tight to their hands.

How does one cage a bird who wants to fly? So they had free rein of the open spaces in the mall, historic museums, gardens wherever they went. The world was a much safer place then.

The Smithsonian is the world's largest collection of galleries and research complexes including 19 museums as well as the National Zoo. The children enjoyed the Air and Space museum best. Look at that "tiger" plane. "I want to sit inside that triangle", the Lunar module, Nadia believed it was. And their experience was reenforced when they also went to the NASA space center in Texas years later.

They were impressed with the Washington monument, the tallest stone structure in the world at the time and vastly taller than obelisks in Europe, Egypt, and Ethiopia. They were able to go up the obelisk then, a preview of many more mountains and monuments to climb. George Washington was the first president of the United States and led the revolution, defeating England. It is said that Washington learned an important lesson: the political nature of war was just as important as the military one.

Something Nadia remembered when she studied Air War College.

The Lincoln memorial is like a Greek doric temple with the seated sculpture of the sixteenth president in the center overlooking the reflecting pool. Passages from two of his most famous speeches, The Gettysburg address, and his Second Inaugural Address are inscribed along the walls. A lesson on the life of the 16th President was in order. He was a Republican from Illinois. Yet his mantra was to abolish slavery. She read somewhere that the oppressed once freed become the worst tyrant. This was the source of many discussions and controversies. Because of his success, some disgruntled people successfully assassinated him. Poor Mary, without much support from friends, she was institutionalized later.

The Jefferson memorial sits on the shore of the Tidal basin of the Potomac River directly south of the White House. It consists of a circular colonnade of Ionic columns with circular marble steps leading to it. A bronze statue of the third President of the United States and one of the American Founding fathers stands in the center facing the White house. On the wall are excerpts from the Declaration of Independence "We hold these truths to be self evident that all men are created equal, that they are endowed by their Creator with certain inalienable rights, among these are life, liberty, and the pursuit of happiness..."

So inspirational.

A lot of historical data could not be retained in just one visit, so they made many more return visits. Thomas Jefferson was a linguist, a great student of architecture and the home he built, called Monticello, was rebuilt based on ideas he acquired from Europe during his tenure as the first Secretary of State under President George Washington.

And all these historic sights for free. What an amazing country America is.

Visiting a zoo is always entertaining to any child. They had driven through the Ohio African safari with great delight as the wild animals roamed free. And many, many years later, Michael with his parents joined a memorable African safari starting from Moshi to Lake Manyara, Tarangire including the Olduvai Gorge in Tanzania where the Leakeys worked..... seeing the beautiful giraffes, zebras, antelopes, gazelles, various birds. The wildebeests, elephants, hippos, rhinos, hyenas, leopards and a group of lions resting after their meal.

The lions were the most difficult to see for their color blended well with the dry tall grasses. However, they believed the driver when he told them that there were five lions resting nearby, so they waited. Something they learned was to be patient. The animals have their own timetable. One of the lions sensed a warthog coming closer to their lair. The lion stood, slowly stalked the warthog who ran as fast as it could for dear life. The lion gave up. She must have been too tired or not hungry yet.

The safari driver wondered why Nadia kept asking which was a baobab tree.

"Don't worry, we'll see a lot of them soon."

And finally seeing the famous baobab trees she had read about was a delight. It was unimaginable that delicate beautiful white flowers could come from such a huge tree. So enamored was she of the flowers that had fallen to the ground, she did not notice she was walking close to an elephant. The guard whistled and motioned for her not to move. Whew! A close call.

Watched the migration of the animals across water to dry land. Amazing, the orderly manner as they follow each other moving forward. One would think there would be a stampede like the bull fight in Spain.

Humans have a lot to learn from the African wild.

She believed a visit to Washington DC would not be complete unless they pay respects to heroes in Arlington Cemetery. One summer they crossed the Potomac River and as they walked the cemetery, they met their friend Mr. and Mrs. C from Fair Oaks, California, with their son J who was a friend of Michael. Great minds think alike. Small world.

Well, during one of their visits to New York, while at St Patrick's cathedral, they also met Dr. and Mrs. R. After their quite long tête-à-tête, they walked back to their rental car to discover they had been vandalized. All of its contents stolen. Although nothing was visible to tempt burglars, for Nadia and Andy learned to keep items in the trunk. Apparently burglars identify rental cars and assume a tourist would have lots of souvenirs in the trunk.

They had driven in from Boston where Michael, an ardent Boston Sox baseball fan, had purchased many of his team's paraphernalia. He was the first to arrive at the rental car, opened the now empty trunk and to this day Nadia could still see his pale face, furrowed brow, and misty eyes. Burglary and mugging are par for the course in New York and they experienced heartaches. She believed this must have caused Michael many nightmares. They arrived in Philadelphia with nothing but the clothes they wore.

These trips were not just for the children to learn. She and Andy did not study American history in school. These were educational for them too.

They had walked the Freedom trail in Boston, the country's oldest park system, saw Fanueil Hall, the place where meetings and speeches by American patriots to involve and rally the people in their desire for independence from the British, now a marketplace. The aroma of the various eats woke their taste buds.

A visit to Paul Revere's house, the historic rider who informed Samuel Adams and John Hancock that the British were coming to arrest them, gave people a rare glimpse of his life at the time. They sat on the pews of the Old North Church which had the tallest steeple in Boston at the time. This steeple became the signaling place to communicate the approach of the enemy: "One if by land, and two, if by sea".

And many others. What a wonderful country this was. Since that time, America had grown to be the most powerful country in the world and no one had dared threaten this sleeping giant until the Japanese.

On one of their succeeding visits, they had to visit "Cheers" the bar made famous by the television series bearing its name. The John F Kennedy museum reminded Nadia of that morning several years ago when all the young girls in the dormitories cried at his assassination.

A trip to Boston would not be complete unless they visited Cape Cod where the pilgrims arriving off the Mayflower settled. The children enjoyed watching reenactments of how pilgrims lived.

Then they took the ferry to Martha's Vineyard and stayed a week. It was sometime in late winter and they were craving ice cream! They stayed at a time share in exchange for one they had on the waterfront in Lake Tahoe, a very desirable location hence easy to trade.

A visit to New York must include a ride on the subway, a show on Broadway, the Empire State building and the World Trade Center, the Metropolitan Museum of Art, a walk through the garment district, a ferry ride to Ellis Island and the Statue of liberty. All of this they did in one weeks' stay at a hotel across from Central Park.

They heard that New Yorkers were arrogant. The reality was just the opposite. Not knowing how to purchase tickets for the subway, they showed her which buttons to push and how to decide which number train to take. They had to take the bus and when it was time to get off, were completely embarrassed because they did not know they had to have exact change. Which they did not. Many stood up, hands in their pockets retrieving the dimes, and quarters to rescue them. They refused payment when Andy offered to reimburse them with their dollars. The children had a very hands-on experience of America. What a wonderful country they were living in.

Michael developed a love for architecture. His photos show his sense of composition, depth, perspective, contrasts. Later, he would counsel his mother with her own sense of photography.

No, you don't know composition, he told her. An irony considering the Great Wall experience.

Andy was the worst. He was the typical tourist with a movie camera hanging from his neck, a large bag to hold the tripod. And he would forget to turn off the movie camera from excitement at a particular scene. So his movie would show dizzying views of the concrete road, the tree branches, or people rushing through. A source of arguments.

They decided to drive through the country when they moved to California. From Cleveland Ohio, down Route 76 to Washington DC, then I-95 to Florida. Her mother wanted to visit President Carter's hometown in Plains Georgia so she could tell her students about it.

Nothing much happens in Plains Instead, they saw Billy Carter's gas station. Proceeding across the gulf coast they enjoyed the white beaches of Panama City, reminding her of home. Visited New Orleans and stayed in a hotel on Bourbon street. Her mother's exposure to this culture provoked her to make the sign of the cross and many Hail Marys with every door they passed by. There was a Fairytale Town they visited for the children to relax. Enjoyed the many fairy tales come to life.

Michael wanted to see the Superdome. Awesome. There was no game in town.

New Orleans food is fabulous. They loved the food and the many sounds of jazz musicians playing on the streets. One hears music coming from all the bars and restaurants as one walks the street. And there were street musicians too. The atmosphere moves one to sway to the various rhythms. Filipinos love to sing and dance, in fact, they love to make excuses to celebrate. A birthday, a new visitor in town, a wedding, a certain saint's day and so on.

The children wanted to visit the Houston Astrodome too. Texas is indeed a huge state. They believe it took them the whole day to cross the state. They were glad their Pontiac Safari did not suffer any problems in the hot July travel days. The fauna and flora were so different. Vast expanses of barren land and skeletons of oil drilling rigs both on land and in the gulf.

Nadia had her first taste of Mexican food in a small cafe in Wichita Falls when they arrived there one evening. It was the only dining place open. She believes she had chimichanga. It was so delicious. She had been searching for that taste since they arrived in California and haven't found it yet. Maybe the first taste is always special just like a first love, unforgettable. Andy and the children preferred good old American hamburgers and hot dogs. Not as adventurous as her.

Las Vegas with its blazing neon signs, cascading lights, huge marquee signs was disorienting. Andy was lucky. Alas, a mugger dampened their celebration. Her gold Bulova watch disappeared from her arm. Lady luck is fickle.

Finally they arrived in California, a land so rich in history and with many interesting places to visit too. The many missions, large museum complexes in San Francisco, the world renowned Golden Gate Bridge as well as the Bay Bridge which, decades later, would incur damage during an earthquake.

This quake caused a lot of stress for her family as Maya was a student at the University of Berkeley at the time. She lived in a high rise condominium near the Bay Bridge. Long hours of waiting, not hearing from her and not being able to reach her since the phone lines were not working. They shouldn't have been surprised. After all, they had moved to a state where the land shifts every once in a while unexpectedly.

What to do? Prayers, always a natural recourse.

Maya's thoughts: "I have to go home, see if I still have a home."

"Call my parents. Mom would be pacing the floor, kneeling in front of the altar at home, praying that I'd be safe."

"Would my land line still function? I do not have a cell phone." It wasn't a necessity yet. "Maybe this event will change their minds. Realize the importance of having access to each other at all times."

She related how scared she was, hid under a table in one of the University of Berkeley libraries, then proceeded to drive home. The city was very dark. Sky was dark. No stars. No moon. San Francisco city lights gone. Elation enveloped her as she saw the lights on in the 36 story condominium she was living in.

Whew! She grew a lot older from that experience and so did her parents' hearts.

In Los Angeles they visited the Griffith Park Observatory featured in the movie Rebel without a Cause, the famous Hollywood movie industry sites, the La Brea tar pits, rode through the Sunset Strip, took photographs of the stars on the Hollywood Walk of Fame, the Grauman's Chinese Theatre. They even went fishing to chase after grunions as they were washed ashore on Seal Beach. Saw how the Red Sea separates in the movie The Ten Commandments.

No, seeing the behind-the-scenes stunts did not diminish their appreciation of Hollywood movies.

Years later, they joined a group tour of musicians scheduled to perform at a Jazz festival in Montreux, Switzerland. They were basically groupies, the itinerary was expansive, hence very tempting. The children saw Germany, France and its cosmopolitan city Paris where they visited the Louvre and saw the famous Mona Lisa smile.

Twelve year old Michael was the guide maneuvering the subways in the underground Paris and they sought enough courage to climb the Eiffel tower.

Fourteen year old Maya did the talking for ordering meals, for she was well versed in Parisian French, however the waiter would say *"Arigato"* to the confused Maya. Japan was enjoying economic success at the time and Nadia explained most tourists come from Japan, hence they wrongly assumed they were Japanese.

In the Netherlands they were able to visit Madurodam, a miniaturized city, watched windmills, tasted their cheeses, and watched wooden shoes made.

They loved Switzerland with its beautiful green valleys and hills, watched the cows and listened to their cowbells, admired the Alps and saw the famous Matterhorn. In the north coast they walked on the boardwalk by a large casino.

Ten year old Maurice was the youngest in the group. He loved to doodle and the bus windows were display boards for his sketches. Everyone was being patient with him.

Later on, Maya would make her own hiking trips to the Alps and the Dolomites, the outback in Australia and Bali. Michael visited England and all over Europe when he and his friends were lucky to purchase World Cup soccer tickets. However, they who stayed home were able to watch more games then him.

But it is all about the ambience, the experience, and camaraderie of friends "being there" when some star made that famous goal that won the game.

He also made a safari to Africa. Wanted to climb Mt. Kilimanjaro but did not have enough time. His itinerary was cut short. He had found his future wife and was anxious to return home. Even Maria Luisa noticed how Michael was irritable throughout the whole trip.

Maurice preferred Spain with its soulful music and the bulls. Though among all the children he loved visiting the Philippines by himself. Did not speak Tagalog but was able to barter for souvenirs, as well as pedicab fare for a visit to see his grandfather and his uncles. Filipinos are patient, hospitable, and caring of the youth.

And many visits to Hawaii exposed them to the tropics without making the much longer trip home to the Philippines. Exposing anyone to travel expands their horizons and gives them a better understanding of human nature. She and Andy were satisfied they fulfilled another goal.

They purchased different souvenirs from all their world travels, displayed some of them in their curio cabinets. A landmark that might lead them someplace in time. Like bread crumbs, these would lead them back to where those memories began.

Hats and tees for Andy, which started conversations in the elevators or encountering people who had been to those places on the hat he was wearing. Rhodes, Venice, Croatia, Montenegro, Barcelona, Monte Carlo, Vienna, Luzern, Montreux, Paris, Amsterdam, Aruba, Panama Canal, Greece, Mt. Kilimanjaro, Cannes, Pompeii, Gibraltar, Portugal, Cartagena, Spain, Madrid, Rome, the Virgin Islands, Beijing, Shanghai…etc. Shot glasses and tees for Maurice and Michael, and jewelries from everywhere and fancy masks from Venice for Maya. Then for her, books of locations she visited, to read during leisure hours, relive the wonderful places in the world she was privileged to see. And brooches, pins, necklaces, pendants, anything with a butterfly. She had been enamored of butterflies. What they represent. Freedom, coming out of one's shell, joy, all representing her journey.

*Go placidly amid the noise and haste and remember
what peace there may be in silence*

Desiderata

CONFLICT

"Dad stopped on a side street so we could enjoy the rocky road we took and survived the drive to Hana. Mom thought she could just pick some mangos from the trees on the side of the road like she did in her hometown. Maya said No, you can not do that here!"

Nadia understood her responsibilities to her new family which included husband Andy, twelve-year-old Maya, ten-year-old Michael and eight-year-old Maurice. In addition, she had to assume leadership on the partition of their parents' estate. The latter was the more difficult task to handle. Her family gave her joy, laughter, and provided a distraction from the ordeals she had in dealing with her adult siblings. Each one had a different perspective of what was fair for everyone.

Human communication is not simple. It involves an initial concept by the sender. The message is then delivered by verbal or non-verbal means such as words, eye contact, body language. It is completed once the receiver of the message is able to translate or interpret what has been sent.

An alcoholic mind is no longer accepting or understanding of the usual tenets. Because Berto was one, their words with each other were just left in the air, ignored, waiting for the breeze to blow them away.

Communication is also suffused with culture and tradition. Nadia had been exposed to a different culture and hence her reality was no longer the basic simple realities of her childhood. It really was difficult to understand an adult man, the way Berto behaved. The old culture was that everyone took responsibility for one's action. The new culture she embraced allowed the entitlement mentality so it took her quite some time to enforce discipline on Berto. She made allowances for his behavior on the premise she did not know him. Maybe Rolando and Sylvia were wrong on their conclusions.

But Berto was not exposed to western culture. Not exposed to the secular mentality. Each individual for himself. No responsibility or obligations to siblings. Demand from siblings.

How did he become one?

It is easy to blame alcohol, however there must have been something else that happened to him. What? The subconscious causes some alteration to one's personality. She finally reached Rolando and Sylvia's conclusions.

«'Day, (short for Inday, a loving nickname for someone younger) since you, Rolando and Sylvia have successfully moved on with your lives, I decided to give Tibo's share of our inheritance to Berto." Aunt Trina told Nadia on one of her visits.

"I hope this is okay."

Her father had two living sisters and two living brothers. Every time Nadia visited the Philippines, she made a point of visiting them. Her aunt Trina would always have hot chocolate and native cakes to share on these visits. She always wanted to know about her growing family and they would keep each other updated on their health. During her last visit, Aunt Trina confided that she and her siblings had shared their inherited land. She hoped this was okay.

It was not okay. She should have informed all the siblings of the action, Nadia thought. However one cannot replace the genie into the bottle.

She did not allow herself to be annoyed. She did not want to cry over spilt milk. She closed her eyes and saw the whirlwind of awful thoughts running wild in her mind. But what bothered her most was what he did with that inheritance.

Sold it.

With Aunt Trina's assistance. Nadia was annoyed and disappointed with her aunt. And embarrassed too. She had respected her and she returned this close relationship she thought they had with what she thought was betrayal. There must have been something more to this. She thought. However Berto should have offered to sell the land to any of his brother and sisters if he needed funds, so the land remained in the family.

Eventually, Nadia was convinced that Berto could not be trusted. She realized patience with him was like teaching manners to lions. She agreed with Rolando and Sylvia to remove his powers to conduct business for their properties.

Meanwhile he had a growing family of three girls and two boys. One of the girls wanted to be an engineer. Nadia was requested to help send her niece to the engineering college of her choice. She agreed to pay for the college expenses. There was no precondition attached. Education was of utmost importance to Nadia and she was not going to skimp. Berto was happy.

Nadia set up a bank account for her niece and made arrangements with a banker friend for tuition payments to be paid directly to the school. Included in the arrangement was the student's monthly allowances. Everything was set up in place.

Just before school started, the ever demanding "entitled" man demanded Nadia also pay for the college tuition of his two other children. Shocked and finally experiencing what others have been saying, facing the reality of what she thought were just rumors, she said NO!

Somehow they managed. She finally realized now she could say "NO" without feeling guilty.

One spring day, years later, she visited with him to reminisce. He had amazing memory despite having had two strokes. He walked her down the family tree of Tibo. All the uncles and aunts. Tibo had two sisters and five brothers with many children hence many, many cousins. Berto was voluble, energetically telling her of his young life. He boarded with an aunt during one semester at the best local college. A school run by the Society of Divine Order (SVD Societas Verbi Divini) priests. Then he shuttled between several boarding houses.

Was he a difficult person who could not get along with others? Was he unable to adjust to the environment he was in? Unable to compromise?

Seems the beginning of self esteem problems. Easy to diagnose in retrospect. But why?

There was no way their parents could have been too strict with him driving him to excesses. Yes, they were disciplinarians, and she, the oldest was the guinea pig. All new parents learn when to let go and when to push as their child grows. There is a very fine line between comforting a frightened, unruly child, and smothering. A difficult recipe to cultivate. The latter children have mature, learned parents already. Is it possible their parents no longer enforced rules and wisdom with the third and fourth child?

Wonderfully physically endowed with extremely good looks, he was a star varsity basketball player. His muscles were well sculpted and he moved with a certain grace. Brother Rolando claimed Berto had many adoring fans. Plenty of very pretty girl cousins were his cheerleaders.

Probably, he developed a huge ego from all the attention he was getting. Having to carry his basketball team through many tournaments to win the coveted championship trophy could have been too difficult a burden for him. Too proud to accept this fact. A pretty cousin told Nadia years later, they themselves became popular at the college for their relationship to the star basketball player.

But she does not remember if he graduated. She knows Berto was much older than her and she had moved on to another school for further studies.

Another very good friend said he remembers Berto a star basketball player but thought it took forever for him to graduate, or does not remember if he did.

Was his basketball schedule interfering with his studies? Was he forced to drop out of classes because of the same schedule? Didn't anyone notice the difficulties he was having?

Aure and Tibo tried to teach the children in the ways of wisdom. Tibo was athletic and must have taught Berto the skills he was now showing, besides giving him the athletic gene.

Why was Berto unable to make decisions? Unable to make adjustments. Unable to move beyond whatever obstacles he was facing.

There were many sources of stories eventually, reliable or not, these were the facts she was able to gather.

He became a victim of his success. Belonged to the "in" crowd, using alcohol to celebrate or bolster their ego. Well known in the school as an alcohol user. Apparently he became verbally, mentally, and emotionally abusive to their parents. Tibo tried his best with discipline. Aure was more comforting, for she had no choice. Raising Nadia and brother Rolando without any stresses, life became very difficult for them. Regardless how much they reexamined Berto's behavior, they could not understand, hence were unable to find a solution.

How had they raised such an irrational son?

Nadia did not know if her parents were aware of Berto's alcohol abuse. By this time, Aure and Tibo did not have the support of their brothers and sisters too. Everyone had dispersed to other places with their children. Some had gone on to the next life. They had no choice but to surrender to his temper tantrums, to his every demand, an unreasonable person. He did not have any semblance to the loving son they knew they raised and remembered.

What did Berto see in his mirror?

Nadia saw every day of his young life etched on his face already as well as on his once gorgeous physique.

After lunch with friends during one of her visits home, Nadia met the owner of the restaurant. They were introduced by their hosts, proud and honored to have guests from America, who they believed were successful.

"I once had a basketball teammate from Panglao. He was our star. Do you know him?" Rolly asked.

This was the testimonial of Berto's basketball prowess. He really had the skills, once upon a time.

Most of his teammates are successful people, with their own businesses, engaged in politics in the upper echelons of government.

Berto, in the world he lives in his own mind probably thinks he is too. A man may become severely depraved and delusional with his mental habits and yet not be insane. She was thinking he already was. He was stubbornly entrenched in the path of the tragedy of failure. Although she thought it was cruel to think his brother was living a life of mediocrity, she could not help herself.

Was this a halloween trick or treat?
Give everyone thine ear, but few thy voice
Take each one's censure but reserve thy judgment

William Shakespeare

RULES

"The men are preparing a pig roast in the backyard pushing a long bamboo pole through its mouth along the length of its body after it has been killed. Maurice heard the pig scream earlier, felt sorry for the animal and vowed to be a vegetarian."

What is the weight of the rule of created law against the weight of family or town opinions and traditions?

Her parents kept their hardships and heartaches to themselves. No one wants to expose their dirty linens in public. Trying to save face. But Berto's excesses could not be hidden from the public anymore.

Trouble is, the whole community understood and sympathized with Berto. He was a lovable young man and did not engage in gangs or any violent behavior with others. Though they felt sorry for Aure and Tibo, in their minds every family has a "blacksheep", so why worry. After all, they had a successful doctor daughter, a son Captain in the merchant marine and a younger daughter chemical engineering student. To the townspeople's fanatically religious minds, God had already blessed them with so much.

"There is no perfect family. No need to be greedy and expect perfection from every member of the family." Was what they thought.

So what is a little turmoil with a second son.

Early on, while still in high school, the alcohol problem apparently started. A neighbor business family had a son, Berto's best friend. They spent evenings and weekends drinking what was available in the store. He was willingly initiated into the drug path. and definitely enjoyed the habit. Reason disappeared, spirituality, which was the core of their being, was easily discarded. About this time, she left for the USA. Within that year Tibo developed a stroke. Aure had no one else for emotional support but Berto and the household help. Oh, the help were very good, caring people.

Later, she learned Berto continued with his outbursts. No respect for his disabled father and grieving mother. No one was able to control his verbal, physical, and emotional outbursts. He was the only child left at home, yet did not make any effort to be of assistance. Aure had to get extra help for her bedridden husband. Tibo's stroke was a total surprise, shocking, as though an electric current shot through Nadia's body. Father was healthy as a horse. Lived a healthy lifestyle: the athletic director, teacher, home craft manager, rode his mountain bike, worked the gardens.

How frustrating it must have been for him to have an alert mind in a body he could no longer control. He lived for another five years.

When her father died Nadia was already two months on the way to delivering her first child. She and Andy were finishing their training, the last year of their visa status. Because it was an emergency the immigration services allowed her to travel. Andy could not take off from his training.

Her grief was overwhelming. There was no language for her loss. Here she was a physician, she could not take care of her disabled father, and now he was dead.

Her flight itinerary would take her to the island of Cebu. Though she had been through the piers during the ship layovers years ago in her university days, she had never been to this city. And she did not know anybody there to call for assistance.

"If you can travel to America, you can navigate this island." She told herself.

In her favor, she spoke the island dialect. Her first act was to look for a telephone book, to find a hotel, the criteria was how far from the airport.

The hotel was a five-story wood building, old. Thankfully there was an elevator. The lobby was just a cubby hole unlike the fancy hotel lobbies she was used to when she attended conferences in the USA and in Hongkong during her layover four years earlier. Creepy. It is just for one night, she managed to calm herself. Through the walls of her room, she could hear grunting and groaning. She was unable to sleep, counting the hours, minutes, and seconds for the sunrise to show itself.

Then she remembered one of her lady physician roommates when she was working at the hospital after graduation, married a businessman who lived in this island. Nadia found his name in the phone book. He owned a gasoline station. Used his last name. Cathy's voice at the end of the line was a Godsend. She was still her usual ebullient self.

"Why didn't you call earlier? You could have stayed with us. Where are you? We will pick you up. What time is your flight to Bohol?"

With her husband, Cathy picked up Nadia and went for breakfast.

Food was a good way to remember Cathy. Her family lived about 4 hours drive away from the hospital they were working at the time. Everyday they would send her food which she gladly shared. So they journeyed down memory lane, full of joys, fun, and nostalgia. She was no longer practicing Pediatrics. She was a full time mother and business manager to her husband's many gasoline stations. And her two brothers who they used to claim for themselves were married and had moved on to Mindanao.

Seeing her father's casket, she could not help but fall apart. The memories of her father's masculine build, vibrant personality, athletic prowess were just memories now. The Sundays when he would come home with his winning rooster from the cockfights and the resulting nagging from her mother, memories now. These were the movies now playing in her mind. She worried if she had been a dutiful daughter. She examined her life for possible episodes of anxiety she had given her father. Guilt. Remorse. Atonement.

The women nursed her well with their gentle hand massages.

"You have traveled far and you need to rest. That baby you have should not know your grief. Think only of the good times you had with your father. He loved you and was very proud of you."

After the nine day novena for the dead and the mini-fiesta, she prepared because soon, she had to leave her mother.

Alone, without the support of the three children who were now living separate lives with their own growing families far away, Aure became a mental and emotional slave to Berto, Nadia heard after the fact, when nothing could be done. Nadia was continuing her training, while raising her three children. Amazing how she was able to do all this. Having visited the USA, Nadia believed her mother Aure, understood the American way of living, no household help, no driver, no gardener, no Nardo, and like a typical caring mother, she did not bother Nadia with her family problems.

Besides unless it was an emergency, the immigration services would not allow her to disrupt her training, to travel overseas.

Whenever you are to do a thing
Though it can never be known but to yourself
Ask yourself how you would act were all the world looking at you
And act accordingly.

Thomas Jefferson

AURE'S DEATH

"The Christmas table is beautifully decorated with Lenox "holiday" plates, water and wine goblets, and a crown roast pork in the center. A friend who saw the picture years later, asked "do you set your table like that all the time?"

Aure died ten years later. Before she died, she would visit the USA every now and then to help Nadia and Andy in the care and raising of her grandchildren. She would take a one year leave of absence from her teaching duties. She enhanced her grandchildren's love for reading and music. They even learned to sing in Visayan, the local dialect, and on their visits to the Philippines, the children easily learned the dialect having been familiar with their sounds, able to make conversation with their cousins and many other relatives.

Although she initially had a student visa to come to the USA, the government needed physicians. They made it easy for the exchange students' visas to convert to permanent residents. And within a few years she and Andy were able to acquire US citizenship. She filed an application for her mother to become a US resident. Her petition was approved and plans were for Nadia's family to go home to the Philippines in the spring. Aure would join them on the return to the USA.

One Wednesday afternoon returning from work, she picked up their mail as usual. There was a letter from her mother. She waited to read it. Dinner had to be prepared for the family. Had already precut the meat to make beef bourguignon, which had become everyone's favorite. From Julia Child's recipe. Each of the children took care of the after-dinner clean-up.

Then Nadia sat down.

Excitedly she read. This letter was not the usual jolly news full of the town activities. Heart pounding, stomach aching, she realized what her mother was describing as an illness she was experiencing two months earlier. Sounded like she had a heart attack. After which she traveled by air, an hour away to Manila for a checkup then flew back home an hour flight away again.

There was a note below her mother's signature written by Sylvia.

Ate, I found this letter that Mom forgot to mail when she was here. But don't worry she will be back because Uncle Phil just died.

Sylvia lived in Manila.

Oh no, another trip. Her mother's poor damaged heart flying all those altitude changes so many times. This is not good, Nadia thought.

"Andy, Andy, we have to call home." She said.

They discussed the logistics. In the morning, Nadia would call her hospital, Andy would make arrangements with his office for the emergency trip they were going to take. Made arrangements for "on call" coverage. Called their travel agent that night for tickets for everyone, children included.

There was difficulty making the phone call to the Philippines. They could not locate where her mom was staying. But then the phone rang.

Cousin Connie. "Sorry to wake you up. Your mom is in the UST hospital."

Before they could even connect to the UST hospital in the Philippines, Connie called again.

"Your mom passed away."

So what good was her diagnostic ability when she could not help her mother?

Nadia flew via Clark Air Force Base to the Philippines. This time, she was met by relatives who were excited being allowed inside a US military installation. She could see her cousin walk just a little bit taller that day, escorting a USAF lieutenant colonel.

At the wake, all the relatives couldn't wait to tell their version of the past events.

Uncle Phil, Aure's youngest brother was a healthy person. He was the brother foretold by the traveling merchants, many years ago, that she would see die. It was an ongoing joke between the Uncle Phil and Aure. When they meet, he would tell her "don't you worry, I am healthy."

However he was murdered.

At his wake, *Ate* Annie was playing with tarot cards. She claimed she developed an eerie sensation looking at the cards. There was going to be another death in the family is what she saw.

How could this be? Everyone was getting annoyed with her. How mean she was, they thought, talking nonsense.

And ten days later, Aure died.

Deprived of sleep from the long trip across the Pacific ocean, she had difficulty digesting all these information. She had to pay respects to her recently widowed Aunt Bernie, who herself was grieving for the unnatural death of her husband.

Why the murder?

Her mother's casket had to be shipped to Bohol. All the relatives occupied almost all of the upper deck. In those days, there were still no cabins. The cots were laid out right next to each other.

All of them looked haggard, maybe even unkempt. One well dressed prima donna told one of the relatives they were occupying her cots waving off her supposed tickets. People from the island were intimidated by the "upper class" they thought she was, from her body language. Her dress style. Her makeup. Her shoes. Her handbag.

Meanwhile Nadia was quietly taking a nap while this was going on. And was awakened to move away.

Let sleeping tigers alone. Pretentious people are offensive to her. Nadia who was wearing crumpled black cotton dress faced the insolent well dressed woman and asked to see her ticket. She was as ignorant as ignorant is. The prima donna couldn't even read the numbers correctly. Prima donna coveted their cots and decided she could scare the group of haphazardly dressed people away.

Filipinos understand there is hierarchy in the society they live in like the soil of the earth that holds layers down forevermore. With education, they come up to the surface and just like every drop of the sea, waters flow freely through the deep gorges, some will glisten on the surface with the tallest wave.

Dear Lord, forgive me for being angry, for being insulting to this woman. For putting her in her place, she prayed. Despite her grief she should have maintained her dignity, she thought.

Oh well. Everyone on board witnessed the event and hopefully learned to stand up against oppression. They wondered and asked her relatives who Nadia was. They were surprised how she, the unkempt, haggard woman she was, was able to stand her ground. Outward looks, just like book covers do not guarantee a good story.

The whole town grieved with them. Some fishermen told her, they will miss her mom. Every dawn when they go to the sea, they could hear her mother pray. They believed her prayers gave them reassurance and confidence for the task ahead, going to sea in the dark.

Older people have difficulty sleeping, and they wake up early. Aure utilized her waking early hours praying, moving her lips, whispering. However in the silence of the town's atmosphere, her hushed prayers were carried by the wind, to the fishermen's ears on their way to the sea.

Berto, with his wife and 4 children had been living in the ancestral home with Aure. It had seven bedrooms, three kitchens and three bathrooms. The first kitchen and bathroom were outside the house, so called "dirty kitchen", the one used by the maids for daily cooking. The second kitchen was indoors, on the first floor, used when there was overflow cooking as on special occasions or holidays. The kitchen upstairs was for her mother's baking or for making preserves, was gas powered. The others were wood fired.

A family room on the second floor had book lined shelves and a cabinet where her mother kept her preserves. Behind the house of her youth was a pig house and a poultry house. They would wake up to the roosters cock-a-doodle-doo-ing and the pigs oink oinking. There was a small vegetable garden and a grove of bamboo trees. Everything was in place to feed the family. And fishermen would pass by her house on their way to the night market for her parents to get first pick of their catch. The market was in the business area close to their house and it was open every evening. So they ate fresh seafood every day.

Nadia, Rolando, and Sylvia, decided to allow Berto and his family to reside in the ancestral home conditioned on his maintaining the home, collecting the proceeds of their parents' assets, and paying taxes on all properties. After all, who would they allow to live in the big house.

A mature person would be grateful for this grace given to him. Like he had won the lottery! They gave him authority to sell some properties and to reap all the proceeds of their parents' properties to maintain him, his family, and the house.

Basically continuing the status quo. Berto's family had been living with Aure all the years prior to her death. These assets were what had paid education expenses in prestigious universities in Manila. Quite sizable. The siblings decided, this was the simplest route to take. Each one of them could just move on to their previous busy lives.

Several seasons later through their every 2-5 year visit home, they realized to much dismay, their kindness was accepted as entitlement. He sold properties, kept the money for his personal use, neglected their agreement. Coconut fruits would just fall off the trees, unharvested, rotted, hence no more income from them. The ancestral home with all the memories and dreams that developed and had been nurtured there, was slowly decaying, some partly the result of time, visible and invisible, but Nadia and the siblings believed were the result of neglect.

Their house was made of wood. Had mahogany hardwood floors. She could feel the age and warmth of the old floors as she walked. Outside walls were painted. The aquamarine paint had given much of its color to the intense sun, dried and peeling off. The aluminum tile roof had downspouts sticking out in all directions, a reminder of which directions the most recent winds were blowing. The poultry and pig houses were gone, wonder how long ago that happened. Cabinets that held books and photographs had been devastated by pesky termites.

A doctor cousin showed a renovated home years later on Facebook. The house was built apparently in 1964. It looked familiar but yet was wonderfully "new" looking. Nadia appreciatively asked whose house that was. Leo's house, his maternal house. He added "your house was the most beautiful house in town and you should do the same."

"Unfortunately, the person living there now is neglecting his job." Nadia replied.

The lovely well loved orchid collection gone. She wondered what happened to the farm she used to walk to or drive her bicycle to in her youth. Wonderful memories of labors of love by the farmers. She remembered the joys of service she was providing. What happened to that farm?

Berto does not deserve to continue living here, she thought. He, who has no sense of the importance of this gift he has been shared by the siblings. No hint of appreciation of the majesty this house once held. This home, built by the man for the woman he loved, the mother of his children, would soon fall apart.

Nadia could sense a migraine coming. Lets get some perspective here, after all, who else would she allow to live there.

How can she make him see through her eyes? Through Rolando and Sylvia's eyes.
How can she engage him in traditions that helped hold them together as the skeletons of their lives?

Maybe a new perspective. Tomorrow!

Her brother and sister complained about the loss of their properties. Being the oldest, she was supposed to be responsible for disbursement of the assets. When their mother died, she found among her possessions, the will of her mother's parents. She knew what land parcels Aure was to get. And Aure allotted her share for Nadia, the oldest of her children. She was to be the keeper of the ancestral heritage.

Her sister-in-law, Rolando's wife, who had lived with them for sometime remembered how Aure had assigned which parcels for each of the siblings. That was a good resource. Of course Aure and Tibo had also amassed lots of properties in their lifetime. Over many visits, the four siblings would sit down and try to work out the details of dividing their inheritance.

She knew her mother had jewels. All women have a collection. Especially Filipino women. In fact one day in church in California, she and her friends recognized a lady in front of them as a compatriot by the number of jewels she had!

Someone had gotten to them first. She only found a set of pearl earrings and ring, a set similar to what Aure had already given Nadia earlier. She took this to present to her daughter at the appropriate occasion.

Berto's wife told and showed her jewelries that Aure had given to her and to her children as if to give them back. Nadia reassured them whatever her mother shared with them was out of her love for them and belonged to them. Nadia was not going to demand them back. Whatever happened to her mother's jewels, she was not going to waste her energies on. Someone will mete some form of justice eventually.

She, Rolando, and Sylvia eventually decided on the proper course of action, thinking this was fair. They finally decided each would quit claim on the other's share so that they can proceed with titling their individual properties. Official documents were printed. The three siblings signed them believing Berto would do likewise. They parted to their own lives, leaving the documents with Berto to follow-up.

But to their dismay Berto refused to quit claim on their shares. What to do now?

If you can keep your head when all about you are losing theirs and blaming it on you, you'll be grown up, my child

Rudyard Kipling

THE MOTORCYCLE

"There's my girlfriends one glorious summer day after we had our nilamaw. The baby is the daughter of the rural health officer of the town. His wife was the nurse. The two young men are my cousins."

Earlier as part of his civil service job, Berto claimed his life would be easier and better, if he had private transportation. He needed and asked for a motorcycle. A bicycle would have been enough. He did not want to struggle. Did not want to walk. Lazy. When he asked, though Nadia was being judgmental, she felt as though her heartstrings were pulled. She perceived it was her mother requesting for help.

Because she wanted him to succeed she bought him one.

An enabler, Nadia had become one and learned in retrospect. He voluntarily promised his share of land they had in the capital city as a fair exchange. Problem was, she was still too trusting. And she believed him. No paperwork written, no contract made. Still her core belief was that everyone is inherently good. And she felt a responsibility to help him especially since he was her brother.

Maybe he would be successful at his job. Wouldn't that make everyone happy? After all they were raised on the premise, one had to help the downtrodden especially one's family.

As the years went by, his extended alcohol friends expanded. Many of them were overseas foreign workers. Their *pasalubong*, homecoming gifts to him, were always bottles of alcohol. Therefore the partying continued. Alcohol loosened their tongues and stimulated their minds to do some injustice.

Not just alcohol, he also smoked. As a consequence, Nadia could no longer stay in her ancestral home when her family visited. She had developed severe respiratory reactions to various allergens and irritants especially cigarette smoke, particularly stale smoke that clings to the smoker's clothes or pollutes the environment. Of course he was respectfully requested not to smoke.

Why is it that smokers believe it is an amendment right to smoke? Why don't they understand that everyone else is also entitled to breathe fresh, clean air?

The Philippine custom is such that children who visit stay with the family in their home. The ancestral home could easily accommodate Nadia's entire family. But this home was no longer the immaculate spotless home of her childhood. The townspeople started to gossip. They believed Nadia had changed, arrogant? Because she lived in America, she became too fancy to live in her old house.

Naturally Berto's children also believed this lie. Because it was reinforced by their father.

Who would not believe what their father says when it is different from some stranger's words? For Nadia was a stranger to them.

His temper became uncontrollable. Being a civil service employee means dancing with who was in power. Not Berto. He believed he was invincible.

Theirs was a very respected family in town. The town goons did not harass them. The politicians knew and protected them. They found a way to "retire" him eventually. One would think he'd rebalance his life. At this point he must have been numb already. No feeling of shame at what happened to him. He did not look for another job as far as she knows. His children were earning a decent livelihood, so they had funds to support him and indulge his whims. It was now up to the children to stop the progress of his disease or to continue to enable him.

Nadia had stopped giving him funds on their visits when she realized what he was spending them on. She counseled his children that they had control of their father's health. They could either continue to "enable" him and live with his outbursts or withhold supporting his habits.

His children decided to support his habits.

Ever watch someone during a withdrawal? How can one watch their father suffer after all. Because that is what they thought their father was undergoing. Besides, they were also fearful of those verbal and emotional, eventually physical outbursts. He mouths off unmentionables and does something violent. In fact during one of these outbursts, he went to Rolando's house and cut off the heads of Rolando's prize fighting cocks!

He developed two strokes and eventually had respiratory distress syndrome, possible heart attack. Hospitalized at HNU, the newest state of the art hospital. One would think at the moment one faces the possible end of life, one would reexamine his life. Make adjustments. Apologize for grievances made intentionally or otherwise.

He never did. Completely unrepentant.

He was incapable of reexamining his life. Unable to check for damages and accumulations that he had generated in his lifetime. He had made Rolando's life miserable.

As well as everyone else's.

Rolando's hobby was holding a cockfight in his arena on Sundays.

Cockfighting is a blood sport between two roosters called gamecocks, held in an arena, a cockpit. These are roosters especially bred for stamina and endurance. Ferdinand Magellan first witnessed cockfighting in 1521 when he went to the Philippines and this was documented by his chronicler Antonio Pigafetta.

The roosters fight to their death, though sometimes the game is halted when one is physically severely traumatized. People place wagers on which rooster would win. Well, Berto would enter the arena, interrupt the games and pocket the wagers, not paying the winner. Commotion would ensue and the crowd would counsel Rolando to leave. They would handle Berto. After so many years of this abuse, Rolando used means not to allow Berto in the arena.

An interesting tidbit Nadia wants to mention here. One weekend while she was preparing lunch at home in California, she heard a television program on cockfighting. She leaves the television on when she is alone, just so there is noise in the house. It seems the president of the Humane Society of America was revoking the license of the owner of an arena in Texas. The owner was a young man with small children. She recognized the voice, looked at the telly. The president of the Humane Society was one of her patients.

"Why couldn't you be lenient with the livelihood of that young family in Texas?" She asked him at his next office visit. "What kind of future would those children have with their father without a means for potential income to raise his family?"

"Well, before that man was born, a law against cockfighting in the USA was already in place." He answered.

Cockfighting is not illegal in the Philippines.

Rolando and his wife visited him at the hospital during one of his most recent hospitalizations for possible heart attack. One of Berto's daughters told her father to make peace with his brother. Berto did not budge. Maintained his anger and hostility.

When Nadia and Andy visited, she would bring him medicines, buy groceries, choose healthy alternatives. Bring him the most recent drugs, not even available in the Philippines at the time. Advised him on health issues. The importance of diet, exercise, blood sugar testing. Because diabetes was in their mother's genes. Their last discussion on this issue was one summer visit several years ago, with all his children present.

A meeting had been called.

Everyone chose their favorite easy chair, felt comfortable, prepared for a long discussion. Nadia noticed there were new curtains, and the Singer sewing machine her mother used, was located in one corner. She was happy to see it had lasted this long, was still useful. Evidence that someone was using it.

"I love the new curtains." Nadia commented. She thought one of the children must be knowledgeable in sewing and was making attempts to decorate the house. A positive change. And she articulated this happiness to everyone present.

The old grandfather clock had been replaced by a more contemporary wall clock. The seaman son probably bought it somewhere overseas.

Berto had been hospitalized during an earlier visit. She and Andy knew when they arrived and learned that Berto was in the hospital, that they would end up paying for this hospitalization. Andy insisted that people expected them to do so. He underwent prostate surgery. His children asked to borrow money for his hospitalization and surgery. Nadia paid his bills. When they offered to pay her back, with hers and Andy's consent, she recommended that they use the money to send their youngest brother to college.

At this meeting, Berto started talking about the expense of his medicines. He yelled at Nadia with fingers pointed that she did not help him during his surgery.

He was serious, she could read the rage that was inside him. She knew and understood this was not her brother talking but the devil himself.

His viciousness appalled her. Living with this kind of behavior daily would have taken a heavy toll on her health. She understood why Rolando would drive to Tagbilaran just to play tennis, his daily therapy.

She was still responsible for his expenses? After all, they had allowed him to live in the ancestral home rent free as well as access to all their parents assets, which were substantial enough to send all four children to private colleges and universities. The only stipulation was that he maintain the house and pay the taxes. Well, he did not.

Smells had seeped into the walls of their house like marinade. The cigarette smell was the worst. However going through her childhood home, she still found joy remembering the aroma of anise scented *torta,* the pineapples, freshly picked from a Dole plantation somewhere in Mindanao, her mother sliced and kept them in jars lined up in the cabinets. Bamboo cribs hanging from the ceiling in the room off the kitchen where her mother kept baked goods, high enough so critters could not access them since the refrigerator had other uses.

"But I paid all your bills." Nadia said. Embarrassed, because Andy was hearing these false accusations.

What was sad was that no one said anything to confirm that she did, not even the person she asked to bring the money. She had given the money to her sister-in-law, Rolando's wife, to take the money, pay his bills, in her effort for Berto to think Rolando was paying for his hospitalization so he would no longer create problems for Rolando. Make Berto feel a sense of gratitude towards his brother.

But he also said Rolando did not help him.

And more importantly, not even his children and wife who had come to the hotel where Nadia was staying. They had asked the guard to allow them to talk to her. They begged Nadia for money for their father's hospitalization. She did not tell her father, she did not tell her husband.

Or did he just not remember? Chose not to remember? Or was he in the beginning stages of alcoholic dementia?

Why didn't the children tell? Had they learned to keep silent when their father was having his temper tantrums?

Typical behavior of abused persons. She just raised up her hand in frustration. How does one reason with someone empty headed? How does one talk to a person who thinks he is entitled? How does one defend oneself when no one else would say the truth? How can one embolden the silenced?

When Rolando heard this, he barked at his wife for not speaking the truth. Now Nadia understood there was no one to depend on. She was so tempted to do her often repeated medical talk about prevention, or offer help, but she refrained. He has to ASK for help and this time, there has to be a document. Three of his five children who are college educated understand. Education is salvation. They may be able to reach their father. They are using whatever tactics they can on their father, most of which Nadia does not agree, but whatever works, everyone will accept.

With all its sham, drudgery and broken dreams, it is still a beautiful world

Desiderata

CONVERSATIONS

"After Sunday mass, Aure would invite Tibo's relatives to brunch at their home. Nadia loved those days when she saw her aunties, uncles, and Tibo's dad. They lived in one of the barrios. Here they are at the dining table."

Had a long conversation with two of Berto's children, Angelo and Barbara at her home one Saturday afternoon. She has done really well. A high school teacher. Married another high school teacher. Together, had purchased land where they built a three bedroom home. Nice and clean. He was in the backyard pruning the overgrown weeds with an electric saw. Nadia liked their home and told them so.

She could sense bitterness in Barbara's voice. She claimed people wondered why they had to purchase this land, when a large acreage was close by belonging to Aure. Instead of intellectualizing her father was the villain, she spread the gossip that her aunts and uncles were fighting over the land still.

Angelo was just listening. He was the younger sibling hence did not make any comments. He was already a working seaman, earning dollars. Barbara mentioned the land adjacent to their home was offered to them as priority buyers for sale and they could not afford. She could sense Barbara was requesting financing. If she was, there was no offer to mediate with her father, Berto. Berto's children are a success at following their father's techniques. No responsibility, just wanting to "take" without giving back.

Bottom line: Berto needs financial help for his medicines and funding to renovate the ancestral home he has been living in and neglecting for the past 35 years. Sounded like he wanted his siblings to fund him, still. After he had wantonly sold some of their properties for his enjoyment. But there is no offer to be cooperative. In fact his demand now is for Sylvia to share her parcel of land. Explained to them their father needs to practice humility. He is the person who needs help yet he attacks the siblings who can help. Told them of her discoveries: how it took him at least eight years to go through college. Their parents must have spent more for this long college stay. And what does he have to show for those years?

Their answer was very revealing. They said their father was not given the same opportunity offered Nadia, Rolando, and Sylvia. And they believed this falsehood. They who had lived in that home with Aure, their grandmother, who had raised them, funded their education, clothed them, fed them, sent them to school, would believe that Aure was unfair? They, who did not have to spend a penny for their upkeep because Aure took care of those? They are just like their father. Entitled.

However she grabbed this chance to state her case.

They who went to Manila suffered. They endured meals at the dormitories run by the nuns, had limited allowances to cover their laundry and school supplies. There was no entertainment budget. They had to live within their means. Whereas he had his every whim given. Told them about the motorcycle she bought him when he was a postal worker in exchange for his share of the lot in the city.

What did he do? Sold the lot and pocketed the proceeds. Berto was upset that another cousin was requested to conduct some business transactions instead of him. Well, Berto showed he could not be trusted.

However it doesn't matter what he does if he is willing to accept the consequences of his actions.

How would his life have been had he followed a different path?

Would he have understood happiness?

The only thing left for him was his drinking and emotional outbursts.

They will try.
To talk to him.
Said their father is willing to sign over Nadia's share of inherited lands but not Sylvia's. Nadia answered she did not have any control over Sylvia.
Told them about her experience with Sylvia.
Told about how she became a doctor, about how she agreed with their father, Berto, to send one of them to college, arranged with the bank to pay tuition directly to the school plus allowance. When it was time to register, what did their father do? He wanted Nadia to pay for two more of his children's schooling.

What an opportunist he is. She backed out, he was upset, but that is his nature. He expects to be given what he wants.

Nadia realized she was informing them of misdeeds by their father. However, nothing held her back. Her warm memories of olden days were what kept her going. He could have had a happy life. But now the new knowledge of this character with bad habits that was her brother was a dagger piercing her heart.

Was he really a loving father to them?
Didn't they not hear the trouble he was giving their uncle Rolando?
Shouldn't they have known?

In a small community, word spreads around at mercurial pace. Or did the townspeople learn to tune out, grow immune to Berto's stormy eruptions. Par for the course. However, Angelo and Barbara were educated people now.

Capable of discerning but unable to see clearly.

Teens, and young adults have a sense of what their parents are, compared to their friends.

Have they been completely brainwashed? Over twenty years of hearing the same story does that. How tragic that they were incapable of discernment. That the experience of life had not taught them of other possibilities.

An opportunity is just that. A door opened. A chance encounter. It takes initiative to follow through. Of course, Berto was given the same opportunity. Being educators themselves, Aure and Tibo believed all their children must be given a chance for a good education. They had dedicated their lives to fulfill this goal.

However Berto just wasted the parents' efforts and resources. Just like how his children were behaving now.

Angelo and Barbara had their mouths wide open. Is this really the first time they have heard such stories? Didn't education bring them insight? Why were they reluctant to accept the truth?

They must believe her, Nadia hoped. They were the key to the solution. What else must she do to convince them they had everything to gain or lose unless their father is enlightened. The cards had to be reshuffled. She thought of half a dozen more things to say, but they seemed futile at this point.

Nadia decided whether they believed her or not, she had no control. Of course the only truth they believed was what their father had been telling them all their lives which is: he was not given the same opportunity the other three siblings had. Why would their father not tell them what was really happening? No.

Oh how winter cold his nights must be. Hatching up theories to justify his life and how to cause pain to his siblings! His life was not dedicated to a greater goal. Wasn't that just a waste?

Does character develop over time?

Chance favors the prepared mind.

Louis Pasteur

PSYCHOLOGY

"This is at the crossroads of the business area in Panglao. Notice the large acacia tree in the corner. This is where people would engage in their daily coffeeklatz except they were drinking tuba."

Does character develop over time? Psychology claims personality vary with birth order. True?

Nadia was the oldest of four followed by a boy, another girl, and the youngest boy. Both parents were elementary school teachers. Aure was mom and Tibo was dad. She does not remember them talking do's and don'ts. In fact they believed silence was usually the answer to everything. And children were supposed to be present physically, not heard.

There were so many older boy and girl cousins. So she developed a keen sense of behavioral patterns, their rewards and consequences. She was not the perfect child but she learned to behave appropriately for certain situations. In retrospect, she understood her parents believed in the saying do as I do. Because there were many aunts and uncles, one could hear admonitions of all sorts from them. There was this particular aunt who would talk to her baby grandchild about an issue she wanted her daughter in law to hear.

Such was communication held.

Fr. Phillip, son of a neighbor businessman of her youth gave an impressive homily for the two Sunday masses she attended one spring vacation years later. Not the fire and brimstone sort she used to hear in her childhood. Not the thunderous ferocious sermons. She went to the sacristy after the mass and told him her appreciation of the homily. It is very seldom they hear someone give them such praise. She did not know him, nor did he know her, but he had heard of her.

In a small town, full of relatives, Nadia had become a legend. She was much older than him. He wanted to talk some more and promised to meet her at a fiesta celebration a few days later to enjoy a cup of hot chocolate.

She asked him to share his thoughts on how a person develops personality. He obliged. She knew she could trust his insights. After all, he counsels a lot of people. Both young and old, in and out of the confessional. In fact she thought mistakenly, that confessions must be a sad but interesting routine for them, listen to the same omissions and commissions. Because she thought the priest would become familiar with voices and know the person who is on the other side of the confessional box she had problems with confessions. This is how she felt.

Don't friends become annoying with the same stories of annoyances by another so-called friend? Get on with it. Move on. Ignore the story!

She was close to the priests so she would go to another parish to have her confession heard by a priest who did not know her. To prepare for confession, she would go thru the ten commandments and decide which she had transgressed. It was always the same. I was too proud, I became angry when my pride was hurt. I am very impatient. Imagine.

None of the thrilling offenses like stealing, murder, adultery. Father might think I am such a boring person. She believed confession is one station she had to endure. A source of conversations among friends.

One of those friends told her once that at his confessions, the priest told him, "Paul, your father would be upset with what you are doing."

Her instincts were right. Of course the confession is a secret contract, and the priest would never tell on the penitent, but how can one face the priest after telling him your worst behavior. However hearing so many people, the priest probably won't remember, she hoped.

Immature, but part of life's lessons. Learning to hold fast to one's belief and when to let go, that was the process to follow. *Bahala na! Que sera sera!* Let the drops fall where they may.

"No, confession is not boring." Father Phillip said.

"Because our job is to listen, remind the person of God's unending love and mercy. Give hope, sort of a cheerleader." He continued.

Yes, she knew this. At one time she used to think of the confessional as her psychotherapy session for free. Except it is held like a murmuring session at midnight when coming home from a night of partying.

And in her process of living, she forgot this message.

"If only people would take advantage of that sacrament, there would be less anxiety in their lives." He said.

"So Father Phillip, how does a person develop character? What molds a person's personality?" Fr Phillip was emphatic.

Home environment.
Parenting.
Nurture.

"But most important are PEERS." He said. This, from a man of the cloth. She knew about peer pressure, but his belief that it has the most impact was a revelation. Children, teens, young men, and women are with their peers more hours than with their parents. At school, at play, at work, this is the reality. Knowledge of this though is just a symbol of promise, not of triumph.

How to go about changing the environment?

Michael and Maurice's friends would stay home some weekends and sometimes watch television. She always watched with them. Once there was a program on PBS regarding the incidence of drug use among teens. Statistics on drug use: one out of ten use drugs. She stood up, counted the twelve boys and asked who among them was on drugs!

Years later, with the three of them adults, she had a conversation with Maya regarding a television program about teens.

"How did the three of you get it right Maya? I don't remember doing anything extraordinary, did I?" Nadia asked.

"Oh yes, you did. You sat down and watched television with us. And you mumbled many comments loud enough for us to hear."

Spending time with the children neutralized peer pressure in her family.

Pope John Paul II believed man has innate dignity. Able to discern right from wrong. She took her parenting job seriously. The transmitter of values. Trying to remove the chaff from the grain. She remembered as a teen trying to be helpful, she would shake a flat basket with rice after it had been pounded. Called winnowing. This was shaken so the wind blows away the chaff and the husked rice grains remain. This was the equivalent of her mumbling.

Additionally, God grants everyone grace. It empowers people to transform their hearts. It prompts them to live honorable lives. And there is proof of its presence in the lives of many people. The obvious one is Jesus. Mother Teresa. The famous scientist Albert Schweitzer who studied medicine, went to Africa so he could help the poor people there. So did Dr. David Livingston, a British physician, the only Westerner who first traveled across southern Africa. He publicized the evils of the African slave trade.

Are there current moral leaders?

And how about sexuality. Although an important aspect of the life of human beings, there was no sex education in school or anywhere else. The topic was taboo. There was catechism every day during summer. All about the Catholic doctrines. Good vs evil. They were saturated with everything that was good. And all that was evil.

"Where did sexuality fit in. Isn't it part of being human?"

This was left to the parents as in a casual conversation related to the reproductive system and personal hygiene. Puberty. She had to jump over lemongrass bush when she had her first menstrual cycle. To remove the smell of blood. Otherwise the knowledge was acquired from friends who were more sexually adventurous. There was no clarification of the physical, mental, and emotional aspects. All they knew were the extremely repeated warnings of the consequences of physical intimacy.

That phrase had not been properly described or discussed either. So there were no guidelines. Many of the ladies thus had different interpretations, meanings. All they knew were the differences between the male and female. The priests must have had several chuckles as he listened to their interpretations of mortal sins. Kissing on the cheeks, on the mouth, closed or open, french kissing. Necking, petting. reading books that sent tingles up their limbs, and flutters in their chests. Heady!

Years later with them married, they realized what they did in their youth was "Nothing".

Nadia learned more about teen angst reading Judy Blume books with Maya!

On one of their visits home to Panlgao, Andy took the children for a bus ride to Tagbilaran. The roads were not paved then. They called them "dancing streets." Some of the women in the back of the bus yelled at the driver to slow down.

"Slow down. Be careful. Our IUD's might fall off."

Though probably said in jest, it was reassuring the women of the island had heard of the item. Sex education had improved. Laughter ensued, plenty of them. Humor, not a victim of poverty in her town.

I will be unafraid. I will gather the courage to do what is right and take responsibility for my own actions.

Alcoholics Anonymous

SPIRITUALITY

"That old belltower is no longer used. It is leaning like the tower of Pisa, hence condemned, still has character. See the black spots. Those are where dusts were deposited by winds and birds who also brought seeds hence you see little green treelets sprouting."

Her parish church ceiling was painted like the Sistine Chapel. Not as grand. Various angels, sacraments, saints, heavenly visions. As a child she loved gazing at the ceiling while at church. It gave her hope and joy as well as many nightmares.

The sacrament of reconciliation shows a confessional with the priest in the center and one person on each side. The person who had finished his confession shows a happy angel by his side. The other person who has not confessed yet, shows the smiling devil with those wicked horns!

The sacrament of the Anointing of the sick is shown in two paintings. One shows the sick person in bed surrounded by the mourning family members. The priest's hands are raised, blessing him. The devil with his horns is under the foot end of the bed unhappy. The angel above is stretching her arms seeming to welcome the dying person.

The second painting shows the same scene except the devil is happy, the angel is crying, and the sick person is shown with his hands stretched palms out signifying that the dying person does not want the priest to perform the sacred rite.

How is that portrayal of what happens with sin?

Gave Nadia a lot of nightmares in her youth.

The artist was a local man who did not do any other painting as much as she could gather from the townspeople.

"How did *'Nong* Tasio come up with those ideas for the ceiling?" She imagined the movie The Agony and The Ecstacy with Michelangelo on many scaffoldings. Was her church able to provide such infrastructure for the painter way back then?

What he did for that ceiling must have been some sort of divine inspiration. The parish could not afford refinishing work on the ceiling as was done at the Vatican however centuries later, the painting is still fresh. Of course there were not too many tourists taking pictures with flashbulbs who visit her hometown church. And lighting candles as offering was not a practice therefore no smoke to cause havoc on the paintings.

Besides, there probably was no one to do justice to the work.

The church belltower was a fun place to climb up the stairs. Play hide and seek. Listen to the echoes. She and her friends enjoyed sitting on the lower steps when the bells ring. There was a variety of tones to the four bells as they were rung manually by the sacristan. The townspeople lived their lives by these church bells: six a.m. for the early morning mass, noon, and six p.m. for the angelus.

But the best place was at the top, where they could see the distant horizon. Most magnificent sunsets with orange, red, purple lines peeking through the gray clouds, the red orange sun half hidden by the sea in the distance and the light variegated white moon already up in the sky. Cool breezes coming in through the open windows, and in the distances the swaying leaves of the palm trees. It was a place to view the flat distant world.

The rhythmic sounds of the waves as they lap to the shore were soothing. And the flapping wings of the many seagulls added to the music.

The girls and young ladies looked forward to the merry month of May. Everyday, everyone picked the freshest and most beautiful flowers for the daily afternoon celebration to honor the Blessed Mother Mary in what is known as Flores de Mayo. A simple church celebration with prayers and songs. The young ladies hoped to be chosen to carry offerings to the altar. Similar to what her children performed as May Crowning at St. Patrick's school.

The three great essentials to achieve anything worthwhile are: Hard work, Stick-to-itiveness, and Common sense.

Thomas A. Edison

DECISIONS, DECISIONS

"Connie and I are wading in the shallow portion of the sea, I am whistling for the critter to peek out of its shell, sometimes successfully. Manong Ricky was a great photographer. Just look at the composition. The mangroves to our right side, the distant small boat with the white clouds against the bright blue sky on the other side. The water is calm."

Nadia continued to feel the burden of responsibility to her parents' estate. The primary issue was partitioning the lands. She remembers wondering whether it was worth the stress and anxiety involved to resolve the land partition issue. During these moments she thinks of Scarlett O'Hara waxing nostalgic about her father who said, "The only thing that lasts forever is land!" Tara was worth fighting for at whatever costs.

Was she as brave and determined as Scarlett?

The island of Panglao had become very valuable. The Scandinavians discovered it was scuba diving paradise, the natives were honest and respectful, and everything was inexpensive. Soon the politicians who had control realized the land's potential. Investors purchased acres from the locals who were just too eager to sell. Beach resorts sprung all along the coast.

She had lost the precious beaches she walked in her childhood to many investors who built resorts with fancy restaurants. Not a single inch of beach was available to the public except in designated areas only unlike the past where people and animals could roam freely. The clarity of the blue waters, the purity of the air, and the innocence of both land and people had been contaminated by pollution brought by foreigner cigars, the locals' desire to create lovely lawns and gardens using chemicals. And where there are nightly celebrations, ugliness comes. Human trafficking!

Rolando entertained her and Andy there one evening. The scene reminded her of the Caribbean, a journey not to her liking. Sure there were many stalls of fresh seafood, crabs, lobsters, mussels, clams, scallops, octopuses, different species of fish. Pick what you like and they will cook it however you prefer, all on beachfront properties. The air was pleasantly perfumed with the various spices used in cooking. To her surprise, town cooking had included herbs and spices unknown in her childhood. That was one advantage of the new foreign intrusion.

However, the loud music from competing bands, the sensual behavior of what she believed were instances of human trafficking involving the Filipinos, Chinese, and Caucasians (not the islanders) and foreigners were difficult to accept. However this seemed consensual.

An international airport was planned for so many years and had finally been funded. Unless those funds go into some politician's pockets the airport will not become a reality. The environmentalists fought hard to prevent it. The land is porous. The land area is only about twenty three square miles.

Would the island be able to handle the impact of jets landing?

Reenforced double thick, firm runways made of asphalt or concrete needed to be built. The present airport in Tagbilaran had a short runway. Tall buildings had been built despite laws preventing such. It was very easy to grease some politicians. So a gradual slow descent for safe landing was not possible, the source of so much controversy. This also required a speedy ascent for safe departure. Hence the need for another airport on flatland. Panglao was where there was so much undeveloped land. Commercial growth should be contained, and laws enforced, so they believed.

Sometimes Nadia asks herself "am I being a coward?" She had chosen to live her life in America where she could miss the day to day laughter. Hide and not experience the day to day conflicts that one encounters in families. She could pretend she did not have any problems. She had chosen a few friends who thought like her that intellectual adventure was more challenging and fulfilling than a social life. She was uncomfortable being in the company of people who had nothing to improve her mind. No pearl for the day for her to accumulate. Every new knowledge she gains, she calls her "pearl" for the day. Most of the time, these were people much older than she was. Therefore most of those friends, who she loved dearly because they had nurtured her intellectual and emotional life are gone. To other states, to the hereafter.

So now her reality is different. It is a lonely world. Not too late to cultivate new relationships and so she did. She made sure of celebrations for every simple event. Made sure every moment is not rushed through to something more important as she did in the past. Now everyday experiences were deeply embraced and adequately prepared for. Every detail slipped in between layers of her life like love notes hidden in books she loved.

But she believed the only relationship that really matters is with her God.

Is the right thing for her God to do justice in her relations with brothers and sister?
What is just for all of them?
Is enabling Berto the just thing to do?
Is it her business to continue educating him on the appropriate thing to do for peace?
Will his educated children talk their father through the proper route for all of them?

Compassion for the alcoholic is just but continuing to care for their wants and wishes is not the law.

Rolando and especially Sylvia continued to remind Nadia of their issues. During one of their family meetings, Berto insisted Sylvia had the largest share and he did not have any. All of his children sitting around the living room. They knew he had already sold his inheritance but for the sake of a peaceful resolution, Sylvia was willing to share her one large parcel of land, beachfront property, with Berto.

Nadia was shocked that Sylvia would agree to this. Hallelujah, peace at last! She felt a certain lightness in her heart.

Having been a religious and spiritual person with so many priests and nuns she count as friends, maybe Sylvia had a "conversion". Started thinking about the common good. She prayed and hoped this would be the new reality. They ended the meeting on a very positive note. They will definitely have peace, finally.

Not so fast. Too good to be true.

Nadia awakened to a phone call from Sylvia followed by a letter in the mail. She changed her mind.

Change happens without invitation. And most often it brings sorrow and anger with it. Apparently, she was unable to sleep that night. She had visions of their deceased mother telling her she made the wrong decision. An educated woman using night visions to promote her beliefs.

Do the dead really talk to their living children regarding decisions they have made or are making?
Do the dead parents really want to cause dissension in their children's lives?
Do the dead parents encourage selfishness?

Of course one can only surmise what Berto must have felt. This was going to just muddy the situation more.

But this was typical Sylvia. A pleaser on the surface. She was being manipulative. Who would talk and give her advice? Was that Nadia's job? They were all adults already. No one can teach an old dog new tricks!

Sylvia had been visiting Berto during her yearly visits to the island. And without any positive response from him. He must have already made his conclusions about her. Trust is something that is cultivated and earned. Trust is something reached after years of observation and discerned decisions. And an alcoholic mind is impressionable, very judgmental, and inflexible. This situation seemed utterly hopeless.

Meanwhile Berto's children started to have their own families. It was important that their land issues get resolved for their sakes. He had the most to gain and the most to lose, but like someone said "one cannot cure stupid". He was acting stupid.

The two brothers continued to have clashes despite the fact Berto was disabled at this point. So deep was his anger toward his siblings, he will carry this to his grave. It is clouding his reasoning, causing him not to see his children are suffering, their hearts filled with hatred for their aunts and uncle. Nadia finally sat down with them again.

She also wants to have a piece of her parent's estate. Unlike the salmon, she doesn't see herself and her family returning to live there. But it would be nice to build a little cottage for their retirement visits that would provide them privacy, instead of staying in hotels or staying in Rolando's little cottage in the back of his house.

For sentimental reasons, she would like to possess her allotted portion of her parent's assets so she can remind herself, she once had parents who walked this earth, parents who worked hard, parents who stimulated her intellectually, who loved her unconditionally, parents who had accumulated some assets to pass on to their heirs. Unless her share of the land is titled in her name, everybody's parcel could not be settled either.

All because of a piece of paper Berto refuses to sign.

Therefore land settlement might not happen. She convinced herself after going through all the stresses with Berto, she does not need a piece of land to have proof of the existence of her parents. She does not need this piece of land for her comfort. However does she still have responsibilities to her siblings, nieces and nephews?

Doing what was just had to be tempered with mercy and love. She had to be careful she doesn't burn her candle on both ends, otherwise she could get singed. It was abundantly clear she needed help. She felt so alone. The feeling as though the last train of the day had left.

At a Sunday homily, the deacon, who she usually doesn't want to listen to because he always talks about his travels unrelated to the readings. It becomes a nuisance, in her mind as though he is bragging about his travels. She developed this tendency to tune him out.

But this time he said he was going to talk about two things only: peace and joy. Exactly what she needed.

No one can make others achieve peace and joy.
She can't give peace and joy to her siblings, nieces and nephews.
Only they can make themselves attain peace and happiness.
Likewise, only she can achieve peace and joy for herself.

She has found the key to her peace and joy.

She decided that proof of her parents' existence is seen in her brothers and sister. In their children. In her grandchildren.

Proof of her parents exist in her who they had nurtured from childhood and on their visits to her home and on her every other 3 year visits home.

Proof of their existence are her grandchildren who they have never seen but who carry part of their DNA. She believes they were proud of her, were proud of her children, whom they saw as children during their visits and her parent's visits to the US, and would be proud and would love her grandchildren, their great grandchildren.

They are all contributing members of society, they have helped their community, they have traveled great distances to help the poor and starving, and she understands there are situations beyond her control. She should be content with what is possible and by the grace of God be thankful for what that is.

However she remembers something she read in the past written by Jacob Rus.

"When nothing seems to help I go and look at a stonecutter hammering away at his rock perhaps a hundred times without as much as a crack to show for his efforts. Yet at the hundred and first blow it will split in two. It was not that blow that did it but all that had gone before."

And Calvin Cooledge has been quoted "Nothing in the world can take the place of persistence. Talent, genius, education will not. But persistence and determination will prevail."

Nadia sits contemplating that which she has to overcome. One can not always fix everything. Life is not like a book. There are no instructions to put the pieces together like Lego toys. Hopefully, she will be blessed with the grace of courage and patience to wait for that final push.

Mountains fall and seas divide before the ones who, in their stride
take a hard road, day by day, sweeping life's obstacles away.

Brian C. Holz

HOME VISITS

"Every 2-3 years, the children would excitedly go shopping and packing for an overseas trip. When do we leave. I need bathing suits. Where are my books to take?"

Nadia and Andy had been taking their three children to their home town of Panglao and Corella Bohol almost every two to three years since the youngest was three years old. So they would know and understand Philippine culture. To know the older generation and bond with the younger ones. Experience life as she experienced it.

They were warned there would be no television or movies. But there would be many journeys of exploration and discovery of open spaces, the seas, the sandy beaches. Watch the waves, listen to the wind as it moves the coconut branches, blow the dry seaweeds to float in the air. Picnics with families and friends. Going to market for fresh vegetables and seafood. Racing with the roosters, and chickens, and observing pigs.

The growing delight of picking up newly hatched eggs from the poultry to bring to the kitchen for breakfast cooked however their choice was. While watching a pig prepared for roasting, Maurice thought this was brutal. Decided he was going to be a vegetarian.

Making toys made from banana and coconut leaves, tree branches and twigs, aroused their creative senses. Running around bathing during a rain and allowing the heavy flow from the downspouts under the gutters. Oh the simple joys of her childhood, her children were now living it.

And lots of books to read. The many books of her childhood that hatched those dreams. Aunt Bev asked why Nadia would point to the individual words as she read for the children.

For goodness sakes, she was a teacher! And Nadia had to explain this to her. However she must have done something right though for she later had a doctor son and a nurse daughter.

Listening to the rhythms and beats of Philippine music with which they had been familiar from the many records Nadia played for them in their childhood.

"Mother's life was not so bad after all." They must have thought. In fact, Maurice loved living in the Philippines.

From their lenses of US hospitals and their medical practices, they witnessed the disintegrating quality of not only medical care, but the languishing ebb of skilled surgical care. The hospital buildings were in varying stages of decay, crumbling walls with graffiti, ceilings with cracks, peeling paint. Equipments were outdated. No electrocautery machines, hence every bleeder had to be sutured. Suction machines were old and without much power. Oxygen tanks were few. Ventilators were rare and the various hospitals borrowed from each other. Emergency skills were lacking (CPR/Cardio Pulmonary Resuscitation) or none that they could see.

They had firsthand experience. An uncle who wanted to be with them in the island during their visit developed coughing and chest discomfort. The so-called best private hospital and specialists could not help him. The family decided to airlift him to Manila.

There was no furnished ambulance. They had to use their connections with the local public hospital hierarchy to borrow emergency equipment to take on the plane. And the plane, that was the airlift, did not have any emergency provisions. Andy had to ask the airline personnel to rearrange the seats to provide a makeshift bed. And request the pilot to fly at a lower altitude.

Andy had not planned to accompany the flight to Manila, however there was no one else to care for her uncle during the flight. And the Manila traffic prevented prompt arrival to the hospital despite the phone conversations of their arrival and dispatch.

"Has she forgotten the reason she went to the USA? To further her medical training and go back home to help her countrymen." Nadia reminded herself.

This thought kept gnawing at her conscience. Andy had exactly the same reasons for his journey to the USA. And felt the pangs of guilt too. One day, that return trip home will come.

Tomorrow!

During one of those visits to sunny Philippines in the midst of an Ohio blizzard, the children realized there is sunshine out there in San Francisco and in other parts of the world. Shortly after their return from that month long happy enjoyable vacation in the tropical paradise, seven year old Maya started asking questions. "Why do we live in snowy land? We don't have family here." She reasoned.

So many days, they could not go out to play because of snowstorms, so many days she could not play with her best friend outdoors, ride their bicycles. Besides, for Andy, night calls were becoming difficult with six to eight feet of snow covering their driveway. He realized he would not live long enough to see their children grow if he had to constantly shovel the driveway during the evenings he was on night call. Blackouts were common and there was always news of people dying from cold exposure in winter or heat exhaustion in summer.

Life in cold Cleveland continued. Days ran changelessly from autumn to winter. Not too many people seen on the streets. The crocuses signaled spring. Soon their viburnum tomentosum blossomed, children came outside to play after their long hibernation. Everyone had grown taller!

She and Andy did not forget Maya's comments. It was haunting them through many sleepless nights and hectic days. They were still young. They had just started their private practices. They could try to restart somewhere. Maybe.

They finally reached a decision. They tried to search for opportunities to move to California. If they had to move, it was only to sunny California.

One of Andy's friends had a flourishing surgical practice in Sacramento. Actually, Stan was his chief resident. Andy liked and respected him and the feeling was mutual.

"Why don't you visit, check out the place." So they did.

Who wouldn't love Sacramento? It had a small town feel then. They couldn't see downtown, it was hidden by the many large grand old trees. And they couldn't see the Crocker Museum. Oh no, where will the children go for cultural exploits? Being the capital of California, there had to be some very interesting places to visit. There was no internet yet. So she will do that research in the library, tomorrow.

Of course San Francisco was just an hour drive away. They would not be missing the art worlds with the San Francisco circle of museums. And the many theaters, and the beautiful bay, and the Golden Gate Bridge.

"Why is it called Golden, Mom?"

And they wouldn't miss the snow.

Less than an hour drive away was snowy Lake Tahoe with its restaurants, ski resorts, casinos, and shows headlined by famous Hollywood celebrities. There was no appeal for casinos, however they had friends who were gamblers. In fact, one of her coworker physicians would arrive several mornings claiming he had lost his paycheck to the casinos over the weekend. And he had ten children to put through school. Of course his wife was also a physician so they managed.

Amazing how being in the snow by the lake was not colder than the Cleveland snowy weather.

Why was that? Was the heat generated by their excited hearts and minds changing the climate such that the north wind did not give them chills?

So how do they move to California?

The USA Military services were recruiting physicians. Many postcards and newsletters came in the mail, easily thrown into the trash bin. But this time she finally sat down to read them. Discussed with Andy that evening an option that just opened for them. Army, Marines, Navy, Coast Guard, Air Force? It really did not matter which service they applied to since they will be assigned to a hospital setting.

They also determined their life was already a success, and maybe giving back to the USA by serving in the military would be the right thing to do. After all, without the acceptance by the USA of their applications for training so many years ago, they would not have attained the residency training and eventual American Board Certifications in their specialties.

One mentor during her residency training, who was foreign born, advised her, she should pass her specialty board exams to be able to compete in the USA. We will be judged by the number of letters after our names!

So Nadia and Andy made sure they could add those letters.

It is a funny thing about life;
If you refuse to accept anything but the
best, you very often get it.

Somerset Maugham

MOVING ON

"Those are the movers who packed all of our belongings for the trip to California. We did not have much possessions then, however there was a very sentimental bench I bought when the baseball stadium was refurbished. Sadly we had to give it away."

So, early in their careers, Nadia and Andy decided to join the military services for an assignment in California. They determined the Air Force would be a good fit if they were accepted. Three air force bases in California where they had vacancies were offered. They visited at their own expense. Aure was visiting with them in Cleveland at the time, so they could afford the luxury of leaving the children with someone loving and trustworthy to inspect potential workplaces.

Three air force base hospitals in California were offered. Would they be able to accommodate them?

Unfortunately for her, their need was for a general surgeon only. Her husband Andy was. No opening for her. The locales were in the desert. One of their most important requirements was that good schools were available for the children. Not available in the desert. They prayed over what decision to make.

The decision: they will go home to Cleveland and reexamine their options.

Meanwhile, prior to leaving Cleveland, they had already arranged to visit a friend assigned to a military base hospital in Sacramento. She was Nadia's senior resident in Internal Medicine at the Montefiore Hospital, one of the University of Pittsburgh hospitals. Noemi introduced Nadia and Andy to the Chief of the Base Hospital.

Colonel Zenk was very pleasant and a good conversationalist. Made everyone feel very comfortable. Besides, they no longer felt any pressure of a job interview, hence Nadia and Andy were relaxed. The colonel had a gift which allowed him to gather information without appearing like he was conducting an inquisition. Then, voila, he had an opening for her. Offered Nadia a job. And they had the wisdom to walk through this door that opened.

The course of their lives had changed in that one moment. The colonel probably did not realize what he had done.

Amazing grace! Great news does not come announced. Just when they decided this trip would not bear fruit, she was given ambrosia.

She was recruited, was advised to go to the local recruiting office. Happily they decided to accept the position. The scenario they had envisioned was going to pass. While Nadia worked for the Air Force, Andy would try to start his own private practice. Now, they could safely move to California while she had a job.

Andy had a surgery practice in Cleveland, however the spring and summer allergies Nadia developed were worsening and they reasoned, while they were still young, it was worth taking the risk to start a practice all over again.

Her ragweed allergy started one summer during a trip to a park in Sandusky, Ohio. She went through ten boxes of tissues during the ride home, with constant sneezing and continuous watery nasal drip. She noticed her symptoms disappeared with the first snow. She dreaded

August 15, the onset of her season. And she must have been the only person in Cleveland praying for the snow to arrive, the end of her allergy season.

Her military career started with the movers arriving at their home. One of them asked what her husband did for a living. They knew she was the military person. When she answered he was in private practice, he winced and remarked, "Lucky guy!"

That was her introduction to the Rank has its privileges mentality. They only heard the word "private". They believed her husband was a "private" in the Air Force.

She had a very rewarding military career. Working with disciplined young men and women was awesome. She was Chief of Laboratory Services. It was a twenty-five bed hospital with three surgeons, three obstetrician gynecologists, four ophthalmologists, one dermatologist. They provided surgical specimens to her, her daily workload. Additionally, the Hospital command decided she should open a Cytology section. Two wonderful new cytotechnologists were brought in to assist in the process. A year later, another physician joined.

Professional Military Education was a requirement. One was Air War College. She must take and pass. After years of refusing the sessions, she finally enrolled in the one year course. A step that could not be bypassed for promotion to a higher rank, this time, Colonel. A course needed so the military person would understand War, its strategy, tactics, use of Intelligence both human and technological. How to conduct war using air power.

She was reluctant for she did not understand war. She did not go to watch war movies at the theater. At home, with the family watching television, when it is about guns and fighting, she walks out of the room. Nadia did not think she had the mental stamina to endure such studies. But after much persuasion and with the support of Andy she studied and graduated Air War College. She was the only female in a group of fifteen.

Every word she read from the many books in the curriculum, she absorbed spongelike. Her parents would have been proud at her promotion soon after graduating the course. Finally pinning her eagle. Nadia visualized them happy with her progress recalling that one evening so many years ago, when they thought their daughter was a lost soul.

She retired after twenty five years of service.

So she has soared, her journey still continuing with many more mountains to climb and clear blue skies in the horizon to see.

The children had no idea what her uniform meant. All they knew was that at the gate, the guards would salute as their car entered regardless who was driving, to Michael's amusement.

One day, she had a lunch date with them. However she had to go to one of the clinics to pick up a report first. With the three children behind her, she entered the room. To their amazement, everyone in the room stood when she entered. Back at the car, she heard them whisper to each other.

"Wow, did you see that. Everyone stands when mom enters." To them she was just mom.

Do not follow where the path may lead
Go instead where there is no path and leave a trail

NEW BEGINNINGS

"The photo is of a yellow Volkswagon parked in the hospital apartments' parking spots showing Nadia with baby Maya in her stroller. She remembers one of the hospital photographers commented on what a speedster the driver of a yellow bug was and to his surprise it was her."

Andy's first car was a Chevy Malibu, then they bought a Buick Skylark. Her favorite was the yellow volkswagon, automatic of course. That little beetle saved her many a winter storm clinging to the road while other fancy battle axes were stuck and could not maneuver the thick icy snow.

For long drives, they had a Chevy van. Safety seat belts were not the law then. They would play various games as Andy drove. Count the green cars, the red cars, the trucks. Check the license plates. Which states are they from? The children learned the state logos and nicknames. How many miles to…so they read the road signs.

And best of all, Andy had built a stand for a portable television set, right between the driver and the front passenger seat. It had a cord they could attach to a power source. Thus they were able to watch television as they drove. To this day, the children brag about how their parents were ahead of their times!

Then there was the Pontiac Safari they drove from Cleveland, south to Florida, along the southern coast towards California. It was awesome, it did not experience any hiccough driving the five of them and her mother through the blistering Texas heat and the Mojave death desert.

Yes, the Cleveland winters successfully drove them away to sunny California. The one month long trek took them to all the interesting, historical places along the way.

Andy found a home in Fair Oaks. A five-bedroom, four-bathroom split level. There was a huge finished game room with a pool table over the two-car garage. A vast expanse of land with mature oak trees and a flowing creek in the backyard completed the package. Enormous blackberry bushes to the westside of the backyard provided them buckets of berries to eat and share.

Abundant fresh tropical fruits were available in California to flavor homemade ice cream. They had the old crank type using large chunks of ice and rock salt. The resulting ice cream with fresh fruits were ambrosial. Not the recent push button types. The old wooden ice cream maker is still in their garage. More casual conversations ensued while anxiously waiting for the ice cream to "cook". Some of these treasured pieces are difficult to part. So many great memories of their childhood.

Those stately oak trees, the free flowing creek, and spaces to play war games or camp out, provided relaxing entertainment, and were utilized well. Parties including roasting a pig in a makeshift roasting oven resulted in good neighborly fun over bottles of beer. Tiny gold nuggets in the creek would twinkle in the moonlight. The children really believed they were panning for gold in their backyard. New Year's ritual was for the children and their dad to shoot cans over the posts that they had made by the creek.

Gardening means digging deep into the rich soil that was Fair Oaks. Everything grew well there. One did not need to have green thumbs. In their large backyard, they would plant vegetables, varieties of flowers, especially bulbs. When her father-in-law visited years after his retirement he made several rows of vegetable plots. It kept his energy level high, gave him something to look towards to everyday. He could still ride his bike in their cul de sac hilly neighborhood.

An excellent role model for the growing children: work hard for food, live well, exercise. One day as they were digging to plant tulips, four year old Maurice asked how much deeper before they reach hell!

Grandpa just shook his head with a wide grin thinking, this kid is smart! Able to connect the Catholic belief of heaven above and hell below.

Arriving in Fair Oaks in late August, it was too late for Maya and Michael to register and be accepted at the parish school. Just like their parents, Nadia and Andy wanted a Catholic education for their children. The Catholic schools were preparatory schools for college. They were not preparatory schools for the boys to be priests or for the girls to become nuns. The only alternative was the public elementary school that was just a walking distance from home.

The children attended CCD at the parish church after school hours to learn about the Catholic doctrines. Sister Elizabeth must have recognized a behavior and attitude her children possessed that made her think they had been in the Catholic school system. She wondered why they were not. Talked to her and Andy. They explained their difficulty during registration having just moved in from Ohio, no residency in the parish, hence no identification. She decided these children should have priority for enrollment the next school year. Meanwhile five-year-old Maurice went to a Christian school for kindergarten.

Maya and Michael enjoyed their year at the public school. Made new friends. Participated in many extracurricular activities. Maya excelled in gymnastics and Nadia thought her daughter had great potential. Her teachers and friends encouraged her. At this time she was playing the piano and everyone enjoyed her interpretation of the Star Wars theme.

The first year was a success. No adjustment problem. Were able to assimilate well into their Fair Oaks community. A year of exploration of their new surroundings. There was a quaint little corner in old town, where children gathered in the park. The local businesses were children friendly. The local barber was very inquisitive. Small town inquisitive, getting to know his neighbors. Maurice and Michael would share these encounters with her eliciting warm memories of her island home neighborhood. Fair Oaks was an ideal place for them after all, family friendly.

July came giving them more time to explore their new surroundings including Lake Tahoe. They enjoyed climbing the mountains, wading, and fishing in the lake. We should come back here to ski, they thought. Then August arrived with its ferocious hot nights. Soon, September with its autumn chill came and dressed in their plaid uniforms, they proceeded to St. Patrick's school. Maya in fourth grade, Michael in second grade, Maurice joined them for first grade the same year. Although new to the school, Maya had been exposed to the Catholic school year environment her first grade at St. Bernadette School in Rocky River Ohio, so she was familiar with the routines. It was like coming home for her.

Maurice and his boisterous classmates were the toast of the school. His classmates were mostly the youngest in their families. Very lively class according to the teachers.

Although irrational, people tend to compare abilities between siblings. Nadia remembers her sister's annoyance when compared to her, the older sister. She believes this was happening with Maurice, being compared to older sister Maya and older brother Michael. It is a reality and amazing how siblings raised by the same parents in the same household develop different personality traits.

Teachers recognized Maya's talents. The principal tutored her after school in advanced math and English. A new student, who excels, and maybe because she was of a different ethnicity attracts attention.

One day as Nadia was walking in through the garage door from work, Maya asked what a "dive bomber" was. Some school kids had called her that. And another name they called her was "Dexter".

Heart aching, she placed her handbag on the dining table, stripped off her uniform, hugged Maya and sat down by the fireplace. She did not think she had to deal with race issues in California. There were so many Asians wherever they went unlike Pittsburgh and Cleveland. With a heavy heart Nadia had to start a long discussion regarding race relations with her. She had thought and believed that in America this was no longer an issue, that people had gone beyond what Martin Luther King stood for. And to think, St Patrick was a Catholic school. Are they the most prejudiced group on earth?

However this discussion was necessary for education.

"Some people do not know and understand that there are places other than America." She started. Well, Michael had classmates who had not even been to San Francisco, a one and a half hour drive away. She brought out their globe. A review lesson in geography is what followed. Showed her the continents, the oceans, and the seas. "There are people who come from those different places in the world. Your mom and Dad come from Asia."

She continued a discussion about differences of culture and others including politics. "Some countries want to expand their lands for their people which results in war. Just imagine how you would feel if your friend would grab one of your favorite toys. Of course you don't start a war, but you would feel anger, and that is a natural human reaction. And you would try to reason with that friend."

"Friends don't do that," Maya replied.

"Wars are violent behavior between various states or countries. World War II was a war that was going on in Europe. The United States of America was not involved until Japan made a surprise attack on Pearl Harbor in Hawaii which was US territory."

She kept her eye watching Maya's face figuring if all these were registering.

"Yes, mom, I am following you."

"They used Japanese fighters, bombers, and torpedo planes in many waves damaging US Navy battleships. It was a devastating blow to America. Many Americans were killed, many were wounded. There had been many unannounced military actions by Japan and this was the worst because it was carried on while negotiations were going on in Washington with the Japanese."

"Thus, there was a resulting natural disdain for the Japanese."

"Those children who called you that name thought you were Japanese. It showed their lack of knowledge of where people come from."

"Why is that?"

Children learn what they hear at home from their parents or friends. Intolerance or bigotry is a learned behavior which starts from childhood. Some parents are unaware of how they behave and talk. Conversations among adults are conducted without consideration that impressionable children are within listening distance.

Children who talk nonsense about her or to her are basically ignorant of what they are saying and she should learn to ignore them. The world is populated by some people like them. Fortunately, there are many more kind and understanding people. Thus she should learn to be proud of what she is and continue to pursue her excellent educational habits.

Maya was very perceptive.

As a four year old, she had a very good friend Sandra, whose mother was an artist. Father was a physician and the parents were from the Middle East. They would play every weekend, she would come home with various artsy crafts they made. One Saturday, Maya was mournfully sitting in the kitchen while Nadia was cooking.

Suddenly Maya asked. "Which nursing home do you want to live in, mom?"

Oh my. What could she be thinking now?

Hugging Maya, she asked what was making her sad. Simple. She and Sandra could not play. Talk about the extended family in the Philippines where the young learn living with older people, is also a Middle Eastern tradition. Turns out, Sandra's grandparents were visiting. They lived now in a nursing home. Sandra had to stay home to be with them, after all they just visit occasionally. Naturally Maya believed, as her mom and Dad grew older, she would have to place them in a nursing home. A promise of things to come!

Still cuddling her, they walked to the couch in the family room. They layered many multicolored plush pillows for a comfortable position to discuss life's difficult phases.

"When that time comes, which is a long, long time from now, you will take care of us." Nadia said. "You do not have to send your parents away."

She did not know if she would see joy or fear in Maya's eyes but then she smiled as though light had broken out at dawn.

The deeper discussions will be done at a later time when the natural course, rhythm, and order can easily be understood.

Where is God now that she needs Him. His answers come at his own schedule. She wanted His answer now!

At one of Nadia's confessions, she expressed her "loss of faith" in God already. For her son was no longer a practicing Catholic for the last twenty years. The priest reminded Nadia of St. Monica who had prayed for her son St. Augustine. It took thirty years for the great doctor of the church St Augustine to find his way back!

When it was time to discuss puberty and all that is involved with the female organs, Maya asked whether Trisha, a childless neighbor in Cleveland ever had her reproductive cycles. Good thing she did not have to discuss men yet. Otherwise it would have been difficult to explain what was wrong with Henry, Trisha's husband. Oh how complicated it is to be a mother.

All I really need to know about how to live and what to do and how to be, I learned in kindergarten.

Robert Fulghum

SECOND GENERATION

"Remember this photo of a perfect, soft sponge birthday cake the shape of Fenway Park, complete with the green monster wall. The Louisville slugger bat was signed by Carl Yaztrzemski. And a glove. Michael's birthday celebration with his buddies, wide grins on their faces."

A neighbor with two boys, was kind enough to babysit the children after school. Her house was conveniently located across their home at the center of the cul de sac. Earlier and on some weekends Sesame street with Oscar, Elmo, Ernie, and Bert, as well as Singing in the Rain, and West Side Story were babysitters. Andy loved The Count best. He would hilariously imitate counting to the children's amusement.

All the kids in the neighborhood played in the streets and into Nadia's driveway. The traffic consisted only of residents moving in and out for errands and to and from work.

Maybe an occasional solicitor would drive by, however almost all drivers knew the children. It was safe.

Games varied with what the sport season was. Hockey was their favorite. With their roller skates, they handily maneuvered the curves of the sidewalk, their bodies would hit rock embankments, dive into the front lawns and hedges, all in good fun. And the neighbors did not mind these intrusions into their yards. The many yells and screams at a goal made did not bother them.

In fact as Maurice started playing the drums, Nadia was anxious at how the noise would impact the neighborhood. After six months, the neighbors commented, "It is sounding like music now".

Thankfully, there was no broken bone, or is it just her memory failing her. She remembers there were many scratches. Just band aids, no emergency room visits needed. How joyous it was to hear their laughter, cheers, and the sounds of balls being hit or a hockey puck careening off the cement.

Oh, the number of broken window glasses. What is a broken glass compared to the happiness of the group of children? They apologized. And that was enough. For they are kids for only a short while. Be patient mother, she would talk to herself.

They would play war games in the backyard. There was a greenbelt with a creek and although they wanted to purchase part of the property, the county could not allow it but informed them they could do whatever improvements they wished to their property. Behind the house and beyond the oaks and the creek was a hill and open space. No neighbor to be bothered.

"I caught the most balls."

"I picked the most gold".

"I chased the most squirrels".

"I tagged you the most".

Joyous pronouncements of the days' adventures as they drank lemonade and ate cookies at the dining table.

They decided to create a pier. Andy dug deep for pillars, tied ropes between them. Next came a curved bridge made of wood, over the creek, elevated enough to allow the water to flow. An inflatable raft with the children on it made for wholesome soothing fun summer relaxation. Andy would set up a tent for slumber parties in the yard or upstairs in the game room.

Years later, the boys would volunteer to have their school outing and meditation in their backyard while their dad prepared hot dogs and hamburgers.

Some more weekends were for more work. By the sweat of his brow, Andy showed the children how to create a brick patio floor. Beneath their feet were layers of bricks in a herringbone pattern, they had completed in one weekend. Naturally they had purchased the bricks from a garden center eight kilometers away, followed by everyone hauling the four by eights from the van to the side gated entrance to the backyard.

The brickwork patio led to the freeform swimming pool with a spa. Another Japanese style bridge connected a redwood deck from the house to another larger redwood deck among the oaks. The atmosphere was parklike. Architectural landscape designs had been researched and this is what Nadia had come up with for their huge backyard to everyone's enjoyment. She and Andy were able to create their nest with much love and concern for the children's entertainment.

A huge area in the backyard had blackberry bushes. Scary to think that snakes could be hiding there. One of the neighbors would knock on everyone's door checking out prospective weekend projects that he would schedule. Hence another backyard project by the neighborhood work crew was started. It was getting rid of something potentially dangerous in order to keep what was more pleasurable. The place became wonderful like a warm bath. There were still more blackberry bushes to pick fruits far out the other side of the creek. When the berries started to ripen, there was no need to hang a scarecrow. The children playing in the back were the living scarecrows.

Green olives littered the backyard gravel path from five mature olive trees. Nadia looked into how to cure olives without success.

Tomorrow!

Living in the wild involved living with wild animals. Though they are entitled their space in the land they inhabited first, humans had to be protected from them. There were beavers. The would come out from the creek at night and destroy the fruit trees. The neighbors called animal rescue and they came with huge cages to take them somewhere else.

If you have built castles in the air, your work need not be lost;
That is where they should be.
Now put foundations under them.

Henry David Thoreau

A NEW PHASE

"Maurice, you climbed one of the sculptures at the San Francisco Museum circles, reminding me of my childhood climbing trees and eating the fruits up there with my cousin."

As adults, Nadia asked their opinions or advice. Maya would simply roll her eyes. Nadia assumes Maya thinks "here we go again".

Didn't we discuss this already? It is a pity we can not choose which memories we can keep.

As a student at the UC Berkeley, she once said that her mom did not understand "stress". Oh yeah? How about flying to this huge country, the US of A at twenty two years old with fifty dollars in her pocket. She did not know when she would get her first paycheck. That was stressful.

Although she spoke very good English, she was not used to hearing Americans speak. Would they understand her? Or would she understand them? That was stressful.

She did not know anyone. That was stressful.

She lived in the nurse's dormitory by herself, in her own room. That was stressful. She had been used to dormitories with roommates. Even when working at the hospital back home, she shared a room with two other lady physicians.

She believes Maya was in a phase in life when one thinks she knows everything. Everybody else is not as smart as her. Youthful fantasy that was, another rite of passage. However she was valedictorian when she graduated from elementary school and again from high school. Captain of the debate team, senior class president, and editor of the school paper. At Berkeley, although an academic scholar, she was just a small fish in the big, big pond. Everyone was also class valedictorian. So, Nadia understood the stress Maya was under.

Weren't we all at one time all-knowing? The young were always so sure they knew all the answers. Her children were no exception. Nadia realized she had to be elastic.

Michael, the special child. Labor pains started two weeks early not unlike her first pregnancy. She had just driven home from work. The pains were rhythmic, predictable. Skipped her dinner, tidied up the rooms, packed a few necessities and as soon as Andy came, they walked across to the hospital. The boy who ran five towers at the Great Wall, he, who wanted to play baseball, breathed his first at five minutes after midnight February 29. First baby born in Cleveland that leap year.

What are the chances of that happening?

He was a gentleman. Michael would listen, think for a few minutes then say: whatever you think mom.

Not what she was hoping to hear. Like a volcano lying dormant for years, he had his eruption in China. She should have known he would not open up for discussion, unless he thinks like his sister. Mom is dumb. Mom does not listen. However Nadia felt his hesitancy endearing.

She's been listening.

Make her understand.

Say it in simple English. Not in a twisted round about way.

Sarcasm is what the younger generation use. She feels like she is put on a guilt trip. Damn if she does, damn if she doesn't. Like the song says: Know when to hold 'em, know when to let go.

Just be patient mom, she would tell herself. After all you raised them to be independent. You never helped them with homework. You were unaware of what they were doing at school. Just trusted that the nuns and other teachers knew what they were doing.

What to do? Dear Lord, grant me wisdom. This is what she always asks when she prays. She doubts her parents thought about what was on her mind until that memorable evening. Were they surprised?

Now she's the mother agonizing over every single encounter with her children. This should not be difficult. Nevertheless it is.

Does this happen because of culture clash? But Nadia raised them according to her culture tempered by what she learned that was good in America. Besides, they were exposed to many different cultures, their peers, these same young adults having clashes with their parents too.

"You sound like a Jewish mom!"

Or "you act like an Italian mom!"

Comments she heard from them over the years. So her traits were universal traits of mothers after all.

She remembers Maya telling her that it is okay if she does not do the calling. Her friends especially boys understood.

There were so many things Maya could not do because her parents were Filipinos. Knowing there were certain limits is conducive to behavior modification. Otherwise chaos or anarchy rules. It was educational for her and her friends to know tradition and values which they learned to respect. However this is how hearts are broken. By love and allegiance gone awry.

On the other end of the paradigm, Maurice would debate her on every issue. Actually she enjoyed their exchanges, although there were many times when this could be annoying. Nadia felt Maurice had anger in his heart. She hoped she could wake up a happy memory in him to heal his heart. He evoked in her the nasty feeling of important things left undone or forgotten and her visits with him left a deadly coldness from the middle of her chest, as though the molecules in the universe realigned.

Is it inevitable that the present contains so much of the living past that was intact, damaged or distorted? Nadia worried so much for how Maurice's future would be. Would he marry? What of his children? Would he guide them with the values Nadia had instilled in him, issues she was raised on, she hoped would be passed on to the next generation.

She prayed and hoped Maurice would not be like her brother Berto. He reminded Nadia of some of Berto's character traits. Their discussions gave her an insight into his life, the same ballet of omissions and submissions. Another promise of things to come, whatever that would be, she hoped and prayed it would turn well by God's grace.

Maya and Michael would call home on either fridays or sundays when they were away to college. Maurice once made a comment on hearing these conversations.

"*Ate* (older sister) and *Kuya* (older brother) are dumb. I will not report to you when I go to college." Maurice proclaimed one evening.

Nadia explained to him, they are not calling home to report. Just making sure mom and dad are okay. When he leaves for college, there won't be anyone with mom and dad. So he should make every effort to call to make sure they, his parents were okay.

When Maurice was at UCLA, he would call just like his siblings. When Nadia answered his phone calls, he would say: "So you're okay. Bye."

Living life like an engineer or an accountant, with a certainty like a computer or a robot can't be more pleasant and joyful than simply letting go and hoping for a lovely surprise. She had to be flexible. And Andy was. When the children were all away to college, Andy joined various service organizations.

Lions Clubs International. After all, this was about service. Their free times were dedicated to working with Lions on their weekend projects. And she was a partner in service helping too.

Some days out of loneliness or boredom, she gets a sudden urge for the comfort food of her childhood. Sweet rice cooked in coconut milk and ginger was one of them. When Andy comes home, he would know what's been cooking. He'd kiss her on the cheeks, and breathe in the soothing aroma of the ginger that marinated her skin, clothes, and permeated the air.

Memories of days gone by would bring rivulets of tears years later. She maintains their rooms clean and dusted. Fresh linens are in the beds all the time hoping they would pop up anytime for a visit. She even kept their memorabilia in place. And they have plenty. She dare not sort through them. Friends tell her she should put them in storage. How can she continue to live in this house where every nook and cranny reminded her of them who had gone to college. And did not return except for occasional visits. She should be comforted they are making successful and productive lives on their own.

Being independent. Wasn't that Nadia's goal for her children?

Will they come back to this cowtown they used to live in now? Her heart was hopeful for those visits.

The people who get on in this world are the people who get up and look for circumstances they want, and if they can't find them, make them.

George Bernard Shaw

FRIENDS

"Michael, you and Maurice are looking for shells among the rocks while Dad is fishing. Maya is not in the picture, what was she doing? This was at the Tahoe Waterfront condo where we spent our Thanksgiving holidays and opened the skiing season at Heavenly Resort."

Embee was the mother of Michael's classmate. She was very friendly and articulate. Just moved into Nadia's neighborhood. During children's soccer and basketball tournaments, they would sit together and discuss children's issues, not just behave as loud cheerleaders. She taught English, however at this time she was working for the California legislature.

Nadia did not realize that there could be job openings in government for whatever one's specialty is. The state employs English teachers to write their newsletters and pamphlets, she learned.

She just assumed one had to be involved in politics to work there. Just the kind of nonsensical person her children thought she was. She actually doesn't blame them. Being an immigrant to this country, she had no clue. Sure she could speak, and write, but the customs, the slang, the nuances of the dialect and the culture were beyond her. And Nadia thought she had successfully assimilated!

One day they had lunch at the capitol building after they viewed the various exhibits. Embee was really educating her on the workings of the government. The many cogs on the wheel that make government work. Nadia appreciated her friendship. Her husband was a lawyer and was such a bulwark of knowledge for her, a rich source of legal expertise.

No, you can not go to the dances!

"Why don't you allow Maya to go to the dances? The dances are a way for the genders to socialize." Embee asked.

She was caught unaware, unsure how to answer. She closed her eyes, trying to remember the many nights she and her cousins would discuss the "dances" in her hometown.

But that was so very long ago in another country, maybe it is different here, she thought.

Their daughters go to the Catholic school for girls. Their sons go to the Catholic school for boys. There were two boys' Catholic schools, and two' girls Catholic schools. Four single-gender schools. Each school provided the venue for the dances, one weekend a month, hence there were four dances a month held every Saturday.

She explained what she thought was her Philippine custom which she believed was not appropriate for her daughter yet.

"NO, you are wrong there. That's not how it works."

"The nuns and priests as well as the school administrators believe they can provide a pleasant, safe environment for the boys and girls to meet. The students gather together, talk, show off their new clothes, new shoes, new bling, whatever young people want to display." Embee explained.

Not what Nadia was thinking.

"These dances are chaperoned. It is what is called social networking."

Nadia had a very limited interpretation of dance. Did not understand that it is not only erotic. It is a form of human expression as done in ballet, gymnastics, synchronized swimming, and others.

"Oh really, is that all there is to it?"

Pleasantly assured, she thanked Embee for the information and promised she would talk to Andy. Together, they will discuss the situation with Maya.

Andy was appreciative of the explanation. Satisfied, she talked to her daughter. They discussed what she and her friend Embee had discussed. When Nadia said No initially, Maya did not argue. She believes Maya was also scared of what would be happening at the dances.

Sometime earlier Maya was taking ballet classes. So dancing was not foreign to her. At home she and Andy just like typical Filipinos would dance. Andy taught Maya some dance steps primarily for the waltz or the two step. She knew dancing involved a boy and girl holding each other. Nadia remembers her first dance experience, how uncomfortable she felt even though she knew the boy she was dancing with. Or because she knew the boy she was dancing with!

Dancing is about timing. The partners moving as one to the rhythm of the music. Then of course there was disco dancing when anyway your body moves is dancing.

Peer pressure?

They agreed she was going to try going to dance at her school then expand to another school as her comfort level increased. Eventually she decided on doing two dances a month. Yeah!

I do the best I know how
The very best I can and I mean to keep on doing it to the end.

Abraham Lincoln

SHARING

"Sometimes you would just play tennis in the public park close to home, just the four of you while Mom would prepare dinner."

Shirley was an excellent tennis player. So was her husband Hermie. They belonged to the same country club Nadia and Andy belonged to. Their children knew each other as they played with their racquets and balls in the courts. She liked the fact she could discuss children's issues with friends like them.

Coming from a different childhood background, Nadia wanted to bridge the culture gap. She was a sponge absorbing every drip of knowledge she could get from any of the parents. She knew of immigrant families where the children clashed with the parents. She decided that would never happen here in her family. She was going to educate herself, make herself adjust to the different culture of teens in America. When other family's children refused to attend family gatherings to be with their friends instead, that was shocking to her. Growing up, she treasured these family gatherings, listening to what the elders would talk about. It was learning about living well.

She knew she could trust Shirley's instincts. They spent hours at the tennis courts playing singles or doubles with their husbands. And would spend tennis vacations together. Many winter ski vacations they would spend evenings by the fireplace discussing children issues. She realized, they had the same values, well, almost.

"I have this dilemma." Nadia started, while they were preparing dinner. Hermie and Andy were still with the children playing in the snow. They could hear them roaring with laughter, probably as someone's snowball hit the mark, they imagined.

"OMG, is it about"… another friend whose husband was suffering from the roving eye syndrome. Shirley can be overly melodramatic sometimes.

"Maya has been requested by her boy friend's parents to visit with them in their home. My initial thought was "NO! You can not go visit your boy friend's family in Minnesota."

"But am I thinking the worst of the situation?"
"Am I sending a message that I don't trust my daughter?"
"I know the boy. He seems like a good person and his parents wrote to us promising to take care of our daughter."

There, she poured out everything that had been bothering her so many nights. Nadia's chest felt a little lighter with the release.

A girl just doesn't go stay in her boyfriend's house. That is a situation ripe with anxiety. This was the Philippine custom of old, the tradition Nadia was raised in. Maybe times have changed there too!

Shirley was of the opinion that it was a good idea for Maˆya to go for the visit. The best reason would be that it would give her an opportunity to watch how that family treated each other.

That did not enter Nadia's mind at all. Thankful for the different and new perspective she resolved to rethink this issue.

"Additionally," Shirley continued, "Maya will get to know her friend better, get to understand his parents and his sister, bond with them.

If this ends up in marriage, she will not be going to strangers." Good reason, Nadia thought to herself.

However she was not convinced this was a good idea. And Andy was of the same opinion. Later on she wondered and recalled someone say hearts are broken by love and allegiance gone awry.

Would her daughter's life have ended differently had she acquiesced? She and her husband revisit this decision many times over. And they still come to the same conclusion. No regret for the path they followed several winters ago. Not that they did not trust their daughter. The reasoning goes this way. There is so much stress put on the young especially to the young women. Her daughter said this to her once. Peer pressure is present twenty four/seven.

Maya had never shown any hint of a rebellious nature anytime. She had always done her class studies well, her artistic pursuits practiced passionately, her sports experiences performed to the best of her abilities. There was no reason for Nadia and Andy to worry.

However, why expose their daughter to a stressful situation? In a place far away from home. Be the bad guy and just say NO, like Nancy Reagan said in her anti drug campaign. Another affirmation of "tough love".

Make no little plans
They have no magic to stir anyone's blood
And probably themselves will not be realized.

Daniel Burnham

MICHAEL

"Nadia is sorting clothes. Tears streaming down her cheeks. Tees with high school logos, tennis tournaments, swimming tournaments. There's the lettermen jackets from high school that she had their names embroidered. Michael's jacket was stolen from his locker."

She could leave the three children at the country club during summer. It was like a summer camp for the children members. Nine-year-old Maya, seven-year-old Michael, five-year-old Maurice. They played tennis and the tennis pro would take them to summer tournaments. They were all very good beginners, especially Michael. Because he had long limbs. Able to stretch far for a good return. And he had speed. And he served aces. Nadia thought he would make an excellent tennis player.

However Nadia noticed there was no spirit in his playing. No intensity. No fire like Bjorn Borg or James McEnroe.

One day, Michael asked if he could play baseball. Little league it was called.

"NO, only bums play baseball." Nadia replied.

She knew baseball even from childhood. This is what she knew. It is a bat and ball game, played by two opposing teams. The defending team on the field tries to prevent the hitting team from scoring a run, while the hitting team tries to score a hit or a home run by running counterclockwise on the baseball diamond. Baseball is called the United States "pastime" or "national game".

Living in Pittsburgh earlier, she and Andy had enjoyed watching the Pittsburgh Pirates play. Those were the days of Roberto Clemente and Bill Mazerowski. And the Steelers' years of Terry Bradshaw's accurate arms and the graceful receiver Lynn Swan.

They had lived, in fact the three children were born in Cleveland, Ohio. They watched the Cleveland Indians play baseball at the municipal stadium. They also watched the Cleveland Browns play football in the same stadium during bone cold winters. She could not imagine any of her sons playing that brutal game called football. She'd think of the injuries to any part of the body of her son. It was just absolutely insane to do that for a living, she imagined. She did not know otherwise.

Similarly, she could not see her son playing what she thought was boring baseball. Nothing much happens until someone hits a strike or hit a home run. She did not understand the details of the pitchers caressing the ball as they throw to the catcher. The good teams usually go overtime. Neck strains as one follows the ball fly into the air, everyone holding their breath hoping it is a home run. Or if it is the opponent batting, hoping it is a foul ball or caught by the outfielder. Seeing players spit into the ground, and/or chew tobacco gave her a negative impression of baseball players. Nothing else to do but eat popcorn and drink soda. Although the special hot dogs with red peppers and onions at Fenway park were super delicious! Memorable indeed.

What a waste of her son's tennis skills.

She did not understand.

Michael went to his room which he shared with Maurice. Located in the corner front of the house, at the far end of the hallway. There were traffic signs on the walls. Red signs that read

WARNING: STOP LOOK LISTEN BEFORE CROSSING THE LINE;
20 MPH; and
SPEED LIMIT 65 MPH

Those signs were on the walls when they bought the home. The two boys liked them and did not want them removed. They chose that room for themselves.

Michael pondered on his next course of action concentrating on those signs. How to make mom understand?

Later on she realized he preferred the team atmosphere, is a better team player than an individual player, as in tennis. Bonding with the coach and other teens, sharing experiences. Being part of a group with complementary skills, being interdependent. Creating synergy with their individual skills towards success. Like bees in the beehive, sharing common experiences, carrying the load together to achieve the goal and share the victory. And most importantly, listening to the roar of the crowd!

Was she wrong in her assessment! Actually baseball could also be interpreted as an individual sport.

Between the pitcher and the hitter.
Between the hitter and the fielder.
Between the pitcher and the catcher.
Between the pitcher and the coach.
A game of strategy, nerves, and will.

They continued playing games in the cul de sac in front of their home. As well as their tennis tournaments. Many days they would come home with a trophy. And lots of stories about the volley that got away, or the many aces they claimed they made. The routines of their daily lives proceeded.

Michael interrupted Nadia's nap with a hug, carrying the sports section of the Sacramento Bee.

"Mom, what do you think of Stanford?" He asked.

Still a bit disoriented, it took her sometime to see the headline of the Sacramento Bee that Michael was placing right in front of her face. The Sports section he placed in front of her still unfocused eyes.

"New NCAA baseball champions, Stanford!" The headline.

"Is Stanford a good school, Mom?"

Well, in her mind Stanford students stand out for their academic excellence and intellectual vitality who were chosen to represent economic, and racial diversity. Now she learned their sports program was also competitive.

"No, they are not bums."

Michael has always been a good researcher. Looks like he had been reading the sports section of the Sacramento Bee all these times. He made his case for baseball, she was convinced she was wrong in her opinion. It was easy to persuade Nadia as long as the request was reasonable. Case closed. They registered him for little league baseball, subsequently to big league.

He had a very auspicious beginning to his baseball career. The year he joined, they were local and district champions. He plays with his head. And because he was tall, long limbs and all as well as speedy, his reach was incredible. Not too many balls escaped him. The coach, trying to figure where to place Michael, moved him to play short stop, first base, second base, and finally once, he was substitute pitcher. He won that game. The impressed coach used Michael as his starter pitcher. They ended the year undefeated.

He showed his heart was in baseball.

There was very good camaraderie among the parents.
Some were more boisterous than others.
Their son should be allowed to play the whole time.
Why is my son in the outfield?
He should be in first base.

Difficult to be a coach, must have a lot of patience and be very diplomatic. Andy became the unofficial team physician. And the fun, and recap of the game details were discussed at the customary pizza party afterwards especially during a winning season.

Graduated cum laude from high school.

Where to go next? They had spent a two-week summer trip during his junior year on the east coast checking schools, the campus, the student demographics, their dormitories. During the three days they were in Boston, they spent every evening at Fenway Park. He had timed their visit on the days the Red Sox were in town. And when they were not in town on subsequent visits, they attended their minor league play at Pawtucket stadium in Rhode Island. They were the only foreigners. Everyone was friendly and respectful. They loved that experience. In a small stadium, one hears every hit and miss of the swing. Baseball is really his game.

Had always loved Boston and favored attending Boston University. He was accepted. However when he received the acceptance letter, he went through a tough time making the decision. Weighing the impact of the presence of Fenway Park across the street from the school, he told Nadia he might not be able to concentrate on his studies if he studied there.

Well, at the same time, he was given an academic scholarship to the University of San Diego, also a Catholic institution. Should he live in snow land or in sunny California? He probably remembered the Cleveland winters too. So the decision was made easy.

There were dormitories on campus which was a beautiful community located on a hilltop. Easy walking distance to the school buildings, however Nadia and Michael agreed a bicycle would be nice, to shop at the nearby shopping mall. So they went shopping.

Once enrolled, he went to check out the baseball team. To his surprise he was allowed to walk in, join the baseball team. Wisely, he decided not to play baseball for the same reason he did not attend Boston University. And possibly lose his academic scholarship. Besides, the San Diego Padres was not his team.

Graduated in four years cum laude again with a job waiting for him. She and Andy share tearful moments reminiscing how blessed they have been.

San Diego is a good place for biomedical sciences job hunting and he had no difficulty finding a job. However housing was very expensive. With rents for his apartment skyrocketing every year, they decided to purchase a home which he has maintained very well.

Postgraduate evenings and weekends, he played whatever sport was in season. He must have been good, since he would be chosen to play in tournaments. Nadia would occasionally nag him about his addiction to men's team sports.

"Where would you find a girl to court and marry if you are with men in the sports field all the time?"

She believed he was not interested in the feminine gender in high school either. He did not attend the junior and the senior prom. Though Nadia begged him to go for her sake! Part of the passages of youth in America, she believed.

Was she wrong. On one of her visits, she saw girls walk onto the field. It was an eye opener. Like the movie "If you build them, they will come", one by one the ladies came into the field.

At one of their discussions he told her the criteria for the girl he will marry: tall, sports minded, and intelligent though not necessarily in that order, her memory may have failed her. He took his time choosing. He had many female classmate friends. They were protective of him, like Nadia's family back home who check into the background of potential suitors, so did Michael's girl friends.

Now a father, he still plays baseball and had just won the Triple Crown. His wife is tall, athletic, and she believes intelligent too.

Their sports exposure was not limited. While they still continued joining tennis tournaments in their childhood, they also joined the American River Swimming team. Practice sessions were scheduled by age. Driving to American River College, about five miles away from home four times every night was a new routine for Nadia. Very hectic, no time to rest, however, children are only young once. Give them all the opportunities for sports options to pursue. Maya tried her best, Maurice loved to swim and his best was the breaststroke. Won many trophies. For he started young. She could tell Michael did not enjoy swimming. This lasted 3 seasons.

To thine own self be true and it must follow as the night the day
Thou canst not then be false to anyone.

William Shakespeare

MAURICE

"Nadia is up on the rooftop helping lay shingles on a home remodeling to make the house handicap accessible."

Maurice was the most energetic of the children, believed he knew everything there is to learn, Mr. Know-It-All.

Walking from his bedroom across the hallways to wake his parents up in the morning was a daily routine. He'd walk in the hallway in the darkness to enter the open door to his parents' room, then crawl under the covers. Talk of the dreams he had. Asked questions of the shadows he was seeing through his window, which he thought were real. Never still, moving over and under the pillows as he talked, eyes wide open, the faces he saw delivered with much energy. His nanny told him not to wake his parents. But Nadia was raised to be close to the family, so she did not mind. Her husband did not mind either. Hence the practice continued. Because he wondered why his genitalia would stick up in the morning.

Evenings, they would pray the rosary together. Each child would take turns leading the prayers. He did his share of leading. They hoped to provide their children with an environment that was loving, prayerful, and an awareness that there is a supreme being loving everyone, who they could call on for the grace to face life's joys and difficulties.

Raising three children while nurturing a career was a challenge. She was on autopilot. Remembered and understood that "God did not promise days without pain, laughter without sorrow, sun without rain, but He did promise strength for the day, comfort for the tears, and light for the night".

His classmates were the toast of the school. Creative, adventurous, carefree. She believed Maurice needed some structure in his life, better than they were providing for him. He talked about the fun he would have at the public high school he and his friends were planning to attend.

Also talked about being a pilot. A top gun pilot. A pilot who lands on an aircraft carrier. Such lofty goals he had.

She enrolled him in the Civil Air Patrol program. Exposed him to the disciplined life in the military. Made sure he understood what was involved so he will be successful should he pursue his dream to be a top gun pilot. They had weekend drills which involved marching, wearing a uniform, following orders, organization, and as he excelled, he became team leader. Whereas, he did not make his bed at home, he learned to tuck the corners of his bed covers, huge improvement. After three years of this experience, Nadia no longer heard him speak of his top gun goals.

Public school accepted children within their school area. Maurice and most of his classmates at St Patrick's School planned to attend the public high school, Arden High School. During Michael's preadmission interview, the Jesuit principal asked her why she wanted her son to attend the Catholic institution, Jesuit in particular. Without batting an eyelash, she replied, her son would be at school longer than he would be at home and she wanted those times to be equal or better than what she provided at home.

This is what she wanted Maurice to have: a loving, caring place where discipline, responsibilities, and consequences were taught. Because he had a questioning intellect, skeptical sometimes, but not seditious. On some of these discussions, Nadia encouraged him to take theology classes and join the religious orders. He would make an excellent model for the young with his articulate discussions on the why's, how's, what's, and where's in spirituality. With his music, he could have been the pied piper of the youth!

No, you are not going to public school. You are going to Jesuit, otherwise I will buy you a one way ticket to Timbuktoo and pick you up when you graduate in four years.

Maurice offered no objection. He understood, since his brother had gone to the same school and his sister went to the Catholic girls school, that he should do the same.

Unlike Nadia's brother Berto, who wasted the opportunities he was given, she was so happy Maurice enjoyed Jesuit High School. He was creative with his music and the arts, a good writer, very articulate. Was in advanced English and the humanities courses. Joined several music clubs. He was the drummer in the concert band, sports band, and symphonic band. And he managed to be part of the football team. She thinks he was also part of the debate team. There is a trophy in his bedroom a testament to his verbal prowess.

Very social. Unlike his brother, he attended both his junior and senior proms and was asked to escort some girls to their junior and senior proms too. He had quite a few girlfriends. Nadia liked one particular girl for her manners and character.

"Hello, Mrs…, this is Sage, may I talk to Maurice please." Others would just say "May I talk to Maurice".

He did very well academically and was accepted to the University of California at Los Angeles, graduating in four years.

And later on pursued and graduated a masters course in public health administration.

She remembers an incident he told her regarding one of the classes he was taking. at UCLA. About Women's issues. After the professor asked the students to share their experiences with the female gender, she told Maurice how wonderful that he had good role models of the feminists: with a physician mother, a sister lawyer, engineer, and physician aunts.

"I don't think my mother, my sister, or my aunts were thinking of the feminist movement. They did what they thought was the good thing to do for themselves!" Maurice replied.

How perceptive. How did he get that notion?

Nadia guided him to publish a local newspaper. Be the boss. She new Mr. Know-It-All would be critical of any future boss. So he became Mr. Publisher. Very eloquent with his editorials. Was a success with his paper. However, newspapers are dependent on the advertisers. He needed a marketing manager. Was not a financial success but he did not mind. After all, he was doing something he loved to do: Reporting the news, educating the readers. People took advantage of his youth. Would advertise, but withhold payment.

They will pay. Tomorrow, like Scarlet.

May the road rise to meet you
May the wind be always at your back

Irish blessing

MAYA

"Fr Ric would always bless Maya after church saying "May your life be full of trials!"

Maya went on to do postgraduate studies. She thought Maya wanted to be in the medical field. To their surprise, she had taken the LSAT (Law School Admission Test) and went on to graduate her J.D. degree. Many of her friends went into law school. Fr. Phillip was right about peers. While studying her law studies, she worked as an intern at a twenty-one lawyer firm amassing a lot of experience so that when she graduated, she was offered a job and she had no difficulty finding other venues.

Several opportunities came her way. The senior law partner of their firm set up his own practice for a special clientele and took Maya along with him. She was happy with her job, their office was on the topmost floor of the tallest building in Sacramento with a three-hundred-sixty-degree view of the city. However shortly thereafter, she was offered a clerkship for the Chief Justice of the Supreme Court in Saipan.

Let's talk about Nadia's husband Andy. He is the most humble, hard-working man she knew. Does his job well rather than just slowly working on it until the clock strikes "go home". Wanted to help others. Would go out on a limb to help someone. His joy came from the satisfaction that at the end of the day, he knew he did his best and made someone's life more satisfying. Well respected by fellow workers in fact his first year in America, he was honored with the "Karawan Award for Best Intern" besting twelve other physicians. Moreover he was not humorless. At any gathering, Andy's jokes were enjoyed by very captive audiences.

Not a good businessman though.

Service is what medicine used to be about. His medical office saw patients regardless of insurance type. He accepted emergency room calls, and usually many of those patients did not have insurance coverage. His employees enjoyed the office atmosphere of a caring, compassionate physician.

But one had to be realistic. There is office overhead. Their accountant wondered with the many patients they saw, why there was not much income to go around.

How does one refuse caring for a sick body? Some of those patients did have insurance cards. However, it takes at least a month before an insurance rejection of coverage is received. Eventually, the office approach to patient visits had to be changed. The accountant insisted, it was a business and had to be run as one.

The only thing that doesn't change is change. And it comes unexpectedly. Medicine changed. American medicine became a business. Technology and electronic medical record (EMR) keeping became the norm. He had already used EMR before it became the norm. Nadia made sure they had updated their office with EMR. But Andy became unhappy. Still, his core belief was about helping others and loyalty to those who have helped him along the way. This core value he taught their children.

So when Maya told him about the job offer, he told Maya she should just decline. He reasoned that since she had been handpicked by her new boss from the large firm where she was working at the time, she should show "loyalty" to her new employer.

Maya was given a moral dilemma. The issues of good vs evil, right vs wrong, were no longer as clear as black vs white. There were many shades of gray in the real world.

Nadia intervened for Maya.

"Andy, there is no such thing as loyalty to employers anymore. Why should the employee show loyalty when employers are concerned with their own bottom lines only? One has to plan for family, for education, plan to survive."

It is a different world order now, a different moral culture. Times are tough. This did not mean one had to change one's internal moral compass. The traditional concept of working for the same firm until retirement was no longer the norm. Yes, maybe only an occasional employer still practiced this tradition. Maya should discuss these issues with her boss. Be truthful with her beliefs, consider options available to make adjustments.

"If I was you, I would accept that offer.
I was given that opportunity in my youth.
I took it.
It is a wonderful opportunity given to you." Said her boss.

With a lighter conscience, Maya told her father the news that night. Of course another celebration followed.

She thought she was living in paradise the three years she lived in Saipan. Maya loved living in the island, wished her parents lived there, so that wherever in the world she worked, she could always visit.

The Commonwealth of the Northern Marianas Islands (CNMI) consist of a chain of fifteen islands in the western Pacific, the largest of which is Saipan. She felt at home because the fauna and flora reminded her of Panglao. The eastern shore is made of sandy beaches. The west has rugged cliffs and a limestone formation believed at some time to be a volcano. North of this is Banzai cliff, a ridge of hills.

In 1944 during WW II, the Americans landed on the beaches. The islands were a well protected stronghold of the Japanese since they represented the last barrier for the Americans to attain a foothold in Japan. The Enola Gay, a Boeing B-29 Superfortress bomber, carrying the atom bomb that would decimate Hiroshima, left from Tinian, a neighboring island. The remaining Japanese known for their tradition of not "losing face" jumped off the Banzai cliff in mass suicide.

So much history she was compiling. The "dive bomber" story in her youth was making more sense.

The Supreme Court of the Commonwealth of the Northern Mariana Islands is the highest court of that US possession. It is situated in Saipan. Maya enjoyed observing and learning how the lawyers made their presentations at court, or argue their cases. She also loved the camaraderie of working with fellow young lawyers from all over the United States, networking with them. She gathered more experience clerking for Saipan's Chief Justice and must have made an impact on him.

Years later when the Chief Justice was invited to be commencement speaker at a California law school, Maya was his guest. She had left him a good impression.

All life is an experiment
The more experiments you make, the better

Ralph Waldo Emerson

SUMMERTIME

"What does it mean you can appear at the Supreme Court of the United States?" Maya sent a photo of her with other men and women with Justice Anthony Kennedy at the steps of the Supreme Court Building after they had been sworn in."

The Ninth Circuit Court of Appeals is located in San Francisco California. It covers the western United States and Hawaii. Soon Maya learned this Court was interviewing for 3 vacancies. Of the numerous applicants, she was selected.

Her parents, filled with so much pride and joy, wanted to celebrate their daughter's success, but could not. How do Filipinos celebrate? However she was still in Saipan and her parents' schedule did not allow them to travel at the time. Instead, they prepared for a surprise welcome home party on her return.

Did she come home with a heavy heart leaving her so-called paradise? Was she just acting when she enjoyed celebrating with her Berkeley and local friends?

Several years later, she mentioned a lot of her coworkers at court, besides being smart and graduates of prestigious law schools, also had political connections or had relatives with judges in their families. Nadia's family was neither political nor had lawyers or judges in the family tree in the USA.

One time Nadia heard her comment: "They (the Ninth Circuit) must have been needy at the time I applied, they had to accept me."

"No, Maya, you were accepted because you were one of the best." Nadia assured her.

She remembers during the college application process while still in high school, Maya asked which ethnic box she should check. Those were the days of affirmative action. Nadia and Andy believe in meritocracy, were raised on the values: working to one's own best abilities to achieve the imagined or desired goal.

"No, you are an American and you'll be accepted because you are very good and deserving, not because of a quota!"

It was a huge step for her from the sheltered home life to a large university. Nadia did not see her ready to fly, perched on the edge of a chair with legs uncrossed as though waiting for the start gun to sound. Instead Maria of the Sound of Music singing "I have confidence" was playing daily in her room during the college application period.

What will this day be like? I wonder.
What will my future be? I wonder.
It could be so exciting to be out in the world, to be free
My heart should be wildly rejoicing
Oh, what's the matter with me?

I've always longed for adventure
To do the things I've never dared
And here I'm facing adventure
Then why am I so scared?

Oh, I must stop these doubts, all these worries
If I don't know I'll just turn back

> I must dream of the things I am seeking
> I am seeking the courage I lack
>
> The courage to serve them with reliance
> Face my mistakes without defiance
> Show them I'm worthy
> And while I show them
> I'll show me

Maya was very accomplished and well rounded. A musician too. Played the guitar, was the guitarist at her elementary school masses as well as school programs. Played the violin and she won a violin competition at a local college, despite the fact she was jet lagged having just returned from a long plane flight from across the USA. And of course she was an accomplished piano player. Was also a tennis player good enough to be on the high school varsity team which was the local high school champion.

Eventually, Maya moved on to private practice and was recruited to be chief of the division of a medical malpractice law firm, with multiple offices all over the United States. She chose Washington, D. C. for her headquarters. Nadia and Andy very often request information on the cases she is working on, however she never shares.

"You may know these people, and this is confidential information". She would say.

Her parents took pride hoping they could be useful to her as a resource regarding the medical aspect, yet Maya never requested. Just like in the earlier days as children, Nadia had told them, they had to do their own "homework", Maya remembered that lesson well. Oh well...her parents' concern was really just to see how "malpractice" is perceived by consumers. Still trying to continue to learn.

To know even one life has breathed easier because you have lived....
This is to have succeeded.

Ralph Waldo Emerson

SERVICE

"Of the four operating rooms, only two were allotted for the missioners. This patient was an add-on. One surgeon insisted she be included that day. A breast cancer patient. Nadia shone a flashlight so the surgeon could remove some armpit lymph node in addition to removing the bulk of the rock hard small cancer. All done in the recovery room."

When the three children were away to college, Nadia and Andy became empty nesters. Now they had time to plan return visits to their homeland to help the poor. Finally fulfill the objectives they had made those many years ago when they came to the USA.

There was an energetic young man in their youth who upon graduation from law school gathered the young men graduates to create a "youth corp". His goal was to have their voices heard in the governance of the province, as well as to inspire the young men and women.

Andy was recruited to be the medical director of the group.

The energetic young coordinator became a successful politician starting at the local level then governor of the province, later congressman, speaker of the House. Some of the group members progressed on in their careers as well, becoming provincial engineers, prosecutors, defense attorneys, some went into the priesthood.

Point is these men had goals. They succeeded in their pursuits. Group journeys with shared ideals and values usually meet success. They motivate, inspire, as well as provide mental and social support after all.

Early on, Nadia told her children, one needs to know and choose their destination otherwise their ship will just drift with the wind and land on some unknown shores.

Because they had noticed the inadequate state of not only medical care, but also the availability of skilled surgeons, they understood what they had to do to achieve the goals of their youth. Furthermore the hospital buildings were decaying.

There was nothing they could do for the building. This was a federal government hospital, and funding was a responsibility of the politicians. Over and above all of this, the hospital equipments were also deteriorating. These they could help with. They had already discovered earlier the lack of emergency skills in their home province. They decided on starting their own surgical missions. They heard and joined the first *Balikbayan* (returning to the town) Bohol surgical mission. That experience created an awareness of the process to follow. They organized their own teams with four goals.

"Let's recruit American surgeons so we can provide free surgeries to the indigents.
Let's bring books and lecturers to improve and introduce the local surgeons to modern techniques.
Let's not forget to network with local physicians, let them understand the work we will be doing. Not meaning to intrude on their businesses. And let's try to research where we can secure hospital equipments to update theirs.
Let's figure means to raise funds to ship these supplies and equipments."

So very ethereal goals! Were these reasonable? To their minds, nothing was impossible, so they researched.

They discovered that US hospitals phase out equipments every five years. And Americans are altruistic. Through their network of local physicians in California, news spread of their work overseas. Hospitals and laboratories donated their surpluses.

Hence they were able to ship four forty-foot containers to the Philippines in seven years. Alcon donated lenses for their cataract surgeries. Andy's earlier network during his "youth corps" days was of tremendous help in assisting to clear their containers of hospital equipments through the bureaucracy of the Philippine Bureau of Customs.

They were helping the locals improve their skills by allowing them to assist at surgeries. They brought and donated surgery books starting a hospital library. Though equipments were still antiquated, their shipments were adequate replacements. Maintaining those equipments was an issue that needed to be resolved locally.

When her uncle developed pulmonary problems during one of their missions, the emergency medical system was glaringly deficient. The family had to hire an air transport from Manila. They discussed "emergencies" with local contacts. The Bohol hospitals needed more updated equipments to handle and transport major emergencies to the next island with better facilities. Some items discussed were: a helicopter transport and superspeed ferry.

Implementation was next on the agenda.

Nadia also thought what would happen if some sort of emergency should befall the missionaries?

"Would the local doctors know ways to handle emergencies?"

Aha, CardioPulmonary Resuscitation (CPR). That is something Nadia can tackle. She studied, learned, and became a certified CPR instructor. She needed supplies to perform this task well and was able to obtain donations of adult ResusciAnnies, child, and infant mannequins.

Health Care delivery in her province consisted of a federal hospital in the capital city, smaller district hospitals, and rural health clinics in every town which was headed by a local physician, nurses, and various assistants. She started at the local level by conducting CPR sessions for the local municipal health officers (Rural Health Officers). Forty RHO showed up.

She started her CPR sessions:

"In the United States of America, when we encounter an emergency, we call 911."

"What do you do here?"

Answer: „We pray."

One of their concerns was the prevalence of infectious respiratory diseases therefore they dreaded mouth to mouth resuscitation which was part of the ABC's at the time. They wanted the mouth guard she had. Fortunately she had Ambu bags to distribute to all of them, as well as for all the ambulances.

A defibrillator was also donated.

Their missions take almost two years to coordinate with various Philippine government agencies and hospital venues including the Celestino Gallares Memorial Hospital in Bohol, Quezon Memorial Hospital in Lucena Quezon, and Ilocos Regional Training Center in San Fernando La Union.

Surgeries performed included thyroid goiters, cataracts, tumors of the uterus, ovaries, soft tissue tumors, breast cancers, colon cancers, cleft lip/palate, salivary gland tumors and inguinal hernias.

They also donated graded and cleaned used eyeglasses, about twenty thousand. Through Andy's Lions Clubs International connections.

After they retired they also joined three other missions organized by their classmates.

Word of their missions spread.

They accepted an invitation to go to Tanzania, in East Africa. Without surgeon contacts they could not perform surgeries, the main purpose of their missions. But they could not deny the request for their help. So they researched what the needs were.

Fresh water
AIDS treatment
Malaria treatment

Their church community assisted in raising funds to purchase a well drilling rig that was shipped to Dar es Salaam. A contact had already surveyed where the best water tables were located. The locals helped dig wells and work is continuing. Nadia remembered a novel she read about a lady world war survivor who used her legacy to drill wells in Alice Springs sometime in the past. Now Nadia understood that feeling of satisfaction.

Malaria is preventable with the use of mosquito nets. The mosquitoes bite at night and the blood they suck which carries the parasite will be deposited to another person they bite. However the government did not have funds and the five-dollar mosquito net expense was needed for food rather than for malaria prevention. In one of the clinics they witnessed an infant with an acute malaria attack. Nearby was a new building construction that was going to be a maternity clinic.

The next project came into existence: Mosquito Nets. Every baby born in that clinic will have a mosquito net. And they contributed enough funds for that clinic to last at least five years.

During some of these missions, her children would join, however the joy of medical service did not inspire them to follow their parents footsteps.

Meanwhile medical and surgical care in their province in the Philippines improved tremendously. Local surgeons were now able to perform the major surgeries they had witnessed and assisted during the missions. And they were able to mentor the younger surgeons.

However the need continues to this day. The needs of the indigents never end.

When we do the best we can, we never know what miracle is wrought in our life, or in the life of another

Helen Keller

HOME AGAIN

"Dad and I decided to go down the steps instead of using the gondola. The aroma was that of donkey droppings. The view was spectacular."

Greece is historic. It is at the crossroads of Asia, Africa, and Europe. The education one gets from witnessing is so much better than textbook learning. Nadia and Andy were able to amass more information, not just on healthcare in Greece, but also historic Greece. It is amazing and they are thankful that some people are interested in learning and preserving the past glories of humankind. Their ingenuity with massive construction projects without help from modern machinery was easy to see beyond belief. They saw the ruins, they experienced the marvelous sound at an outdoor gymnasium.

That experience was inspirational.

Home again, Nadia was relaxing while reading in their backyard, when she noticed bermuda grass insinuating itself in their beautiful lawn. Their yard was professionally maintained, however the lawn had bermuda grass creeping and causing havoc. She imagined her husband crawling, digging those cancerous roots. The inevitable back, shoulder and knee aches followed.

Andy was passionate about their yard. Dressed in rags, wide brim hat, and dark glasses, one could not recognize him. Some people would stop by their house while he was working. They would tell him they loved the yard he was maintaining, then ask if he could "do" their lawn also. There were many hilarious stories to these encounters.

Of course they had used gardeners but, no one could pass his approval. Besides it was therapy for him. He really enjoyed 'nature". In fact he had been trying to get Nadia to play golf. She refused because she was of the opinion that the ball should go where she wants it to go. She did not want to go chasing after it. His answer would always be "but it is one way you get to enjoy the trees, the flowers, and listen to the bird chorale".

Her concentration was distracted by a sound coming from around the cherry trees. The branches were shaking. A bird had flown away. She went to investigate. The bird had eaten all but four fruits. The birds had been feasting during their absence. Jet lagged and too busy with unpacking, Nadia and Andy forgot to check the fruit trees.

What to do for their backyard?

She remembered the deep blue Aegean sea that was so calm and relaxing. How about a swimming pool? They had enjoyed a Geremiah built pool in their previous house where there were many oak trees. It had a freeform shape with large boulders as highlights. Rose bushes, tree roses, a grotto on the east end with a waterfall, and a spa on the west end made a spectacular appearance.

The children enjoyed the pool with their friends. Marco Polo. Shark. The joyful musical yells and screams of the children heard all over the cul de sac. When all of them left for college and afterwards, their friends also left to pursue their own dreams. Andy would swim only to skim the leaves of the many oak trees. They decided that when should they move in the future, there won't be a swimming pool.

But what else can be done for this backyard?

There was no oak tree where they lived now so no need to worry about those perennially deciduous leaves. Aha, a lap pool. Water exercises are good for the joints and lungs. She had developed breathing issues already due to her allergies.

The pool man asked questions and painted on the grass how the finished pool would look.

Ugly. A rectangle. The yard could only hold half a lap pool, the way it had originally been designed. It would be four feet deep throughout its length, thirty five by twelve feet.

"But I would like the kids, when they come home, to have a diving area too."
"I don't want a diving board."
"I would like a stage." She was thinking ahead to holding backyard parties.
"And a waterfall."
"And I want it low maintenance so no rocks or beautiful freeform shape. However I don't want a straight long border. I want a shallow" … and she proceeded to show with her arms an extension to one side towards the house.

Some of the many requirements she provided to the surprised pool man, who answered: "Aha, you want a wading area close to the house."

"For your grandchildren?" he asked.

No answer.

"How many do you have?" He asked again.

"None."

"Oh, if you build them they will come!" The pool man said.

The following month, digging started and the lovely simple pool was completed in six weeks.

A week or two after they started digging, Maurice and his wife announced they were having a baby. Yeah, they are going to be grandparents.

Coincidence?

This was seven years ago. There is a cast iron bench with a trellis in the stage area, a sign hanging from it with her grandson's name. The paint has not been damaged by sun and rain through all these years.

Love never fails

1st *Corinthians* 13:8

GRANDMOTHERHOOD

"A very good friend suggested we do a fashion show during the baby shower. Many ladies obliged. Here are the models Candi, Mandy, Lulu, Sandy, and Mercy, while the ladies in the audience are enjoying mojitos."

Nadia married late in her life, hence she was an older grandmother. Her children followed the same pattern. They did not marry until years after college. After they had settled and established their lives.

The son of her son was born one spring day. She heard of his arrival after over 24 hours of waiting and a sleepless night. Of course he was so gorgeous. His aunt claimed he was a camera whore, already posing for pictures.

She wanted to be of help to her son and his wife in the care of their son. Sort of paying her dues for not being available to her children all those times, so many years ago.

It is understandable that new and first time parents prefer child rearing their way. On her weekly visits, she might have been a nuisance to them, but she just did it on intuition: what did she wish for when she was in their shoes so many years ago. Trying to remember what she felt was an

290

important need, unfulfilled, that she could provide now. That's what she did. Grocery? Toys? Clothing?

The age of high technology had improved so much. Her children's moves were documented only with polaroid and simple cameras. And super eight movies. That she would show to them on holidays. For them to remember. That they had good times. Trying to survive in this new world is difficult and can be depressing. There is a need to reawaken good memories.

This baby boy has all his moves documented by so many videos and photos, how technology has evolved. Of course the product turns out only as good as the photographer. Nevertheless, a picture is worth more than a thousand words. These same remembrances are what occupy Nadia and Andy reviewing them in the wee hours of the evening when they don't see him.

Having retired for quite some time, coordinating and planning play things for Paoyo became a pleasant hobby. And plans on how to challenge him intellectually. They did not baby talk.

Twinkle twinkle little stars show him moving his fingers to the music.

Who has seen the wind made his eyes grow wide in anticipation of the breeze as well as the trembling of the leaves.

High five's when he did something right became a habit. He was an inquisitive toddler.

To be successful is to achieve an objective,
But to be a success is always to have yet another
objective in mind after you've achieved the last one.

Anonymous

POGI

"There's the fisherman at the Berkeley marina pier. Paoyo asked if the fishes were biting. You're better off going to market, he said."

Her life changed dramatically. The daily routines that define a lifetime were ignored. Time became elastic. She arranged their schedules around visits to see their future.

Andy felt he was a complete man. His lineage was assured. Still the traditionalist. Most of their conversations were about the physical, psychological, intellectual development and progress of Paoyo. And how they can help shape it. The change in her heart was dramatic.

She believes all grandparents brag about their grandchildren more than about their children, if that is ever possible. She had listened patiently to her friends discuss their grandchildren's accomplishments, as though it would never end. As though they were raising another Albert Einstein, or another Marie Curie.

So now it was her time under the sun to do the same. Every encounter with him was so joyous, entertaining, and they felt so blessed as they saw the strength of his mind and the essence of his personality emerge.

Waves of several emotions swept Andy and herself during these visits. They hadn't seen him acting like a child in a fit of passion. So calm, but not robotic. They indulged him with a passionate love for learning. The alphabets, vowels, consonants, books. Because reading is the first step to learning. Opens up a whole new world of adventure. Pre-nap times in the afternoons were spent on making sounds. Eyes aglow with joy.

When he could talk, she and Andy taught him the alphabet, vowels, and consonants, the way they learned to speak English back in the Philippines. Concentrated on the sounds of the various combinations of consonants and vowels a, e, i, o u. And they would spend their afternoons reading with emphasis on the syllables. Ba, Be, Bi, Bo, Bu, Da, De, Di, Do, Du and so on.

One afternoon, Paoyo said "da, da, da, Darth. Va, va, va Vader. Darth Vader! With a smile as wide as the ocean and as beautiful as a fully opened fragrant double delight rose.

Evidence of the influence of the environment he had been exposed to. And people say television or movies, or commercials do not have any impact on child development! Why would corporations pay huge dollars to produce commercials otherwise?

Soon, he would talk so fast she could not understand him, his mind was so crowded with millions of ideas, his heart too hopeful to stop, and his mouth too slow to articulate yet.

Maurice shared with Paoyo his own childhood book. "Where the Sidewalk Ends" by Shel Silverstein. Nadia would read him some poems prior to his afternoon naps. One of his favorites was "BandAids" because besides learning his body parts, he could not imagine putting bandaids over his eyes.

However one morning he said: Nana, va, va, va vagina!

She had to impose severe self discipline to suppress laughter. Okay, that is normal anatomy. Just another body part. No need to make the word unwholesome. She did not think he meant to be naughty. Just one of those issues toddlers ask about and was given the correct answer.

His parents must have done something right, after all Nadia always believed that characters of persons are molded and inspired by what their parents have done.

The grandparents should just fill in the gaps. Besides, she and Andy had been interested in the life of his mind, filling his mind with great ideas for his own good and to prepare him for a good future. He's had his abundant fill of love to promote the health of his soul from his aunt Maya, Uncle Michael, Aunt Shelly.

They would drive around in an SUV. She would point out to Paoyo the many traffic signs, the shapes, the numbers, the arrows. He was fascinated by the many cars "flying" up there. From his vantage point he could see the vehicles move up there in the many freeway interchanges in the San Francisco area.

Here are examples of his critical thinking skills.

While waiting for their food at a Chinese restaurant, two-year-old Paoyo watched the goldfishes in an aquarium, a ubiquitous display in any Asian restaurant. This aquarium was at his eye level. His curiosity fulfilled, he went back to his seat.

But then he saw another aquarium above the cabinets. He stared at it. There were two huge dark fishes. He got off his seat and went near this aquarium. Then he went back to the goldfish aquarium and looked back at the larger aquarium above the cabinet. Satisfied with his discovery, he went back to his seat, and made this pronouncement "that," pointing to the goldfish aquarium "is the baby fish and that one," the aquarium with the huge fish "is the Daddy fish!"

They have a condominium in the San Francisco Bay Area where they stay when they visit him. One day, when he was three-and-a-half years old he asked "What is the difference between a building and a condominium?" She explained.

He questioned: "So a building is like where my Dad works?" Amazing, how he is able to grasp these concepts and apply to reality.

Walking along the Berkeley marina one beautiful sunny cool day he asked: "Is it better to walk in the sun or in the shade?"

Nadia explained. "On a beautiful day like today, I prefer walking in the sunshine because I need the sunshine to help my bones." She tried to make it simple.

A few days later, he was walking with his grandfather, Andy. Paoyo calls him Papa. Her husband preferred to walk under the shade of the trees. Paoyo asked him the same question. Papa said he preferred to walk in the shade. He did not want to feel the heat of the sun.

Paoyo corrected him. "No Papa, you should walk in the sunshine because it is good for your bones."

Such critical thinking skills he has developed at such age is a tremendous blessing, a gift they have been given to enjoy. As though he is also doing his own research. Like the song says, "Amazing Grace, how sweet the sound…."

Paoyo has some of her parents' genetic make-up. He is proof that Nadia's parents existed.

Since her retirement, Nadia had been searching for something with meaning. Nights were filled with anxiety, like there was a telephonic ringing constantly humming in her mind. As though the movie does not stop. Searching for something that would capture her heart and imagination. Something warm and fuzzy like a warm bath. She was just an accidental physician after all, but she was determined to find "it".

Ask, and it shall be given to you
Seek, and ye shall find
Knock, and it shall be opened unto you.

Mathew 7:7

NANA

"They were privileged to bring the offerings to the altar one Sunday morning mass. Sandy and Nadia in front with the wine and host, Michael and Andy behind. The priest asked how Sandy was related to Nadia and how is she as a mother-in-law? "The best." How could Sandy come up with an answer like that in a second?

Michael's daughter was born early September morning in beautiful San Diego California. She and Andy visited Harriet when she was 1 week old. With her long fingers, long arms, and long legs, she is her parents' daughter.

Sandy is 5'10 and Michael is 6'2". Additionally, her brothers had the tall gene too. They don't see her as often as they did Paoyo, but the Internet has resolved that issue. She has grown into a tall sweet little princess with huge round eyes, the color still changing. She has curly blonde hair like her mother and Nadia swears she has her thick angled eyebrows which had caused her distress growing up. Harriet carries her eyebrows better than Nadia did, though.

Andy really felt more than complete.

How grace has filled them with a grandson, and now the icing on their cake, a beautiful granddaughter.

Blessings poured out to them throughout their life's journeys, too numerous to count like the stars in the skies.

Life has been wonderful. Full of light and sunshine. They go on bended knees as often as their aging bones allow. Contentment is what brings happiness. Yet they believe they are still a continuing work in progress.

EPILOGUE

Maya

"What did you do with your legal problems before I was a lawyer?" Maya asked after one of her mother's many legal consultations.

"That's why I was happy to pay for your law schooling." Nadia replied.

She had lived in a high rise condominium that her parents purchased for her to live in when she went to the University of California Berkeley. On her graduation, Nadia and Andy thought of selling the unit. Maya had the wisdom to convince them to refrain from that decision.

"Location, location, location are the three important issues in real estate." She said. Maya does not live there anymore, she has her own.

Earlier in her teens, she had given Nadia a mother's day card that stated she was not going to contribute any grandchild. Instead she has been a very loving aunt to Paoyo and Harriet.

Michael

Claims he did not remember any of Nadia's comments about baseball! He only remembers his regrets not being allowed to play team sports! He therefore was negatively impacted by his mom's first response to his request.

Nadia and Andy remembers that he had a very good team sport experience. He was pitcher of his undefeated little league baseball team.

How can one forget that? What he remembers was that Nadia insisted on his playing tennis! Which he did not pursue because she gave in to his baseball wishes.

Memory is like wine cork, once it is removed from the bottle it expands and changes. In his old age, retired, with his daughter away, living on her own, he will have plenty of time to remember and relive his childhood. Then that will be his time to reexamine and celebrate their lives.

Maurice

He was celebratory when Nadia told him she was writing a book.

"About what?"

She recited the first four lines.

"I like it. It sounds like poetry."

He is the writer. Was a publisher and editor of a local newspaper earlier. And is a wonderful father to Paoyo. What more can one ask?

I want to thank my husband and my children for the inspiration to write this book. Made up of experiences from observations of my youth in my home in the Philippines, adult life in the United States, and my travels around the world. Any similarities to actual people or situations are just incidental.

Special thanks to my daughter, Victoria, who spent countless hours copy editing, content editing, and formatting so this book could be published.

This book is dedicated to my parents who raised me up on their shoulders to be a someone!

REFERENCES

1. Global estimates and Trends. International Trends for Migration 2008
2. Global Migration: A world ever more on the move New York Times
3. International Migration Reports 2006. United Nations, Department of Economic and Social Affairs, Population Division
4. The Great Wall of China...Encyclopedia Britannica
5. The Great Wall: a cultural history. Cambridge, Mass: Harvard University Press.
6. Terra Cotta Warriors.... National Geographic
7. City of Tagbilaran www.Tagbilaran.com
8. History and Culture - Washington Monument National Park Service
9. Washington Monument: Tribute in Stone National Park Service
10. Hufbauer, Benjamin. Presidential Temples: How memorials and libraries shape public memory
11. Thomas, Christopher A. The Lincoln Memorial and American Life
12. Heather Ewing, The Lost World of James Smithson: Science, Revolution, and the Birth of the Smithsonian
13. El Filibusterismo, Jose Rizal
14. Noli Mi Tangere, Jose Rizal
15. The Philippine Review

Edwards Brothers Malloy
Thorofare, NJ USA
May 13, 2015